THE KEEPING

THE SA TSKIR BROTHERS CHRONICLES
BOOK 2

DANIELLE KAHEAKU

THE KEEPING

A SCI-FI ALIEN ROMANCE

Book Two of the Sa Tskir Brothers Chronicles

Copyright © 2014 by Danielle Kaheaku as Erin Durante
Copyright © 2019 by Danielle Kaheaku

All rights reserved.

No part of this book may be reproduced, scanned, or distributed in any printed or electronic form without permission. Please support the authors and do not participate in the piracy of copyrighted materials.

This is a work of fiction. All characters, names, and events in this book are fictitious. Any resemblance to persons living or dead is purely coincidental.

Paperback ISBN 978-0-9994495-4-7

THE KEEPING

THE SA TSKIR BROTHERS CHRONICLES
BOOK 2

DANIELLE KAHEAKU

ONE

"Don't use the elevators!"

A race for the stairs through the darkness left several people nearly trampled, and many screamed and scratched as they fought to keep their footing on their way down to the lower levels of the hotel.

Carly turned back and grabbed her dark-haired friend's shoulder, pushing her opposite the crowd.

"Let's take the stairs at the other end of the hall," she whispered in Samantha's ear. "So, we can get down in one piece."

Samantha nodded back, and together they wove their way against the current of fleeing patrons toward the west hall. Soon they broke free and felt their way along the walls until they were around the corner.

Carly looked around, her eyes trying to adjust and find meaning to any of the faint shapes before them.

Move, move, we have to move...

Samantha clicked on the tablet she still clutched in

her hands and turned on the screen. The glowing backlight acted as a small circle of illumination, a small comfort now. Carly let Samantha lead the way, stumbling over a body—

A body?

No, not a body, a man and a woman moaning and thrusting, frantically copulating right there on the floor.

This isn't right. There's been an earthquake. Why would you have sex at a time like this?

The man looked up at her, smiling with glowing cat eyes. Carly stepped over them, only to stumble against another. Then another.

"Samantha?"

Samantha's outline had faded. Carly looked around wildly. A green haze was growing denser, more potent. She stumbled forward again, hands out, feeling for a wall, a door, a person. Something.

"Samantha!" she cried. "Where are you?"

"Carly?"

"Please don't leave me!"

The haze shifted, and Samantha stood a few feet away.

"Come on," Samantha said, holding out her hand. Her face was unnaturally calm. "Come on, Carly."

Carly could not move.

Heavy hands landed on her shoulders, and hot breath brushed against her lips as muscular arms wrapped around her body and pressed her back against the wall. Carly screamed as the uniformed man leaned forward, pulling at her pants with his free hand and leaning in for a kiss. The cat eyes glowed as he chuckled and bared long fangs that oozed honey from their razor tips.

Carly turned and screamed, "Samantha!"

Samantha shook her head and smiled sadly, her eyes glowing amber, and then turned and ran.

Carly lashed out at her attacker, clawing across his face. She broke free and got two feet away, but the green haze grew worse, blinding her, and then came a painful jolt as a lightning bolt struck between her shoulders. Her nervous system revolted, freezing, short-circuiting, and she felt blackness seeping over her eyes as massive claws reached for her neck.

Samantha, why did you leave me?

"HELP!"

Carly jerked away from the arms around her, stretching frantically for a weapon; anything to use against the clawed hands twisted around her shirt. The arms and heavy blanket fell away, and Carly tumbled out of bed, landing hard on her side against the wooden floor. She coughed, the wind knocked out of lungs and lay panting as the blood rushed in her ears.

"Carly?"

She heard a hushed call behind her.

"Carly!"

Carly suddenly became aware of a chill in the room that dried the cold sweat dripping down her arms and face with the blanket gone. The bed creaked as the weight shifted from the edge of the mattress to join her on the floor. Warm, powerful arms gathered her up and pulled her against a solid warm wall of muscle.

Carly choked back a sob, bowing her head in the darkness.

She felt one of the arms reach out toward the bed stand. The light pressed against Carly's eyelids as the lamp switch clicked on.

Carly wanted to twist around in the man's arms and properly embrace him, to hold him tight and squash out the remaining shadows of the nightmare.

But that would require looking at Krissik's face—a mirror of the faces that had tried to take her away and only reminded her of the nightmares' truth.

Krissik kissed the top of her head, his breath warm against her chilled skin. "I am sorry," he said in his broken and accented English. "I am here. You safe now."

Safe now. Carly squeezed her eyes shut. *Am I really?*

She tuned out Krissik's softly whispered endearments, focusing on his steady heartbeat as she pressed her ear against his firm chest. She breathed in the scent of sleep and kitten, her fingers mechanically playing against the soft patch of white fur that grew down the center of his chest.

Breathe, Carly. Just breathe.

Slowly, her heartbeat steadied, and her breathing evened. At least it seemed the nightmares were fading more quickly as the days from the encounter passed. Maybe soon, Carly hoped she would be able to segue entirely into another dream.

"You know," Carly whispered, once she trusted her voice, "the psychiatrist at the hospital offered me sleeping pills before I left."

"You no want them?" Krissik gently ran his hands up and down Carly's arms, keeping her focused.

"No...the dreams kept coming. When I took the pills, I just couldn't wake up." She shuddered. "I was trapped in them."

The hospital. God, what a joke that had been. Carly knew the truth: that the major gas leak at her and Samantha's hotel in Las Vegas was simply a cover-up for a government-assisted alien abduction of child-bearing-aged women. The images of that terrifying night, of running through hallways and people falling left and right at the clawed hands of their attackers, haunted her every sleeping moment. Golden eyes stared back at her every time she tried to close her eyes.

Yet, while her best friend Samantha had been hauled off to the stars and kept prisoner on an alien planet, Carly's abduction had been botched. Instead, Carly was left behind on Earth with a significant concussion and vibrant flashes of horrific memories that seemed permanently burned into her skull.

Carly supposed she ought to be happy that she had gotten off lightly.

And she might have been at ease—if one of her attackers were not now holding her tightly in his arms.

Carly leaned away.

Krissik released Carly without a fight; a small, defeated sigh the only sign of his disappointment in the situation.

Carly stood and hurried out into the dark hallway while Krissik stayed kneeling on the floor. Harmless. Waiting.

Carly crossed the quiet hallway, locked herself in the bathroom, and switched on the light.

She did not look any worse for wear. Her blonde curls stood on end, and she still seemed pale and drawn, but she splashed cold water on her face and saw her color beginning to improve. She braced her hands against the counter and stood, head hanging over the sink, just letting the sound of running water wash over her. She thought about turning on the shower and standing underneath the spray to rid herself of the last traces of the nightmare and any remaining scent of Krissik. Though the chance of waking her best friend Samantha and the alien Rikist held her rooted in place, not wanting to wake them and face any inquisition about another of her sleepless nights.

No. The less of this I admit, the easier it will be to recover.

Two weeks ago, she'd come to Samantha's place looking to reunite with her best friend after the worst girl's trip to Vegas in history. When she'd arrived, she'd practically attacked Krissik, jumping him before he'd crossed the bedroom threshold. For the first few days, they'd only left the room long enough to eat and shower.

Then, three days ago, Krissik's little vial of mind-blowing climaxing liquid became nearly drained, and the honey-colored stars dimmed as they cut back on the dosage.

Then Carly remembered who—or rather *what*—she was fucking.

Though shaken, Carly tried to play things off as the lust spell faded. If the others saw Carly looking weak, they might pity her, might push her to get the mental help she knew would not work. How could you explain an attempted alien abduction to your shrink, anyway? She would probably wind up in a padded cell and pumped full of pills to help her forget the fictional fantasy her parents believe she created.

Well, the last two weeks of crazy alien sex with that fine-ass tiger were very, very real.

Carly glanced again at her complexion in the mirror and fought a wry grin. This fling with an Earth-bound alien had to be borderline Stockholm syndrome, right? The padded cell might not be a bad idea.

Besides, she had always looked good in white.

She turned off the sink and returned to the spare bedroom. Krissik sat on the bed, studying his hands on his lap. He had partially retracted his curved claws, so that only the fiendish silver tips poked past his nail line, making all efforts to render his fingers as human and inconspicuous as possible.

Carly did not think it was entirely effective.

"I sorry we did this to you," Krissik said in broken English, and then looked up.

Carly took a deep breath.

Krissik's angled face had a square jaw and a full, straight nose. Dark brown stripes cut from his hairline across his cheeks and continued down his neck, back and arms. Thick lashes and heavy lids outlined gold eyes with tiger-like pupils. Short, reddish fur-like hair spiked off a deep widow's peak and feathered around the bottoms of his ears. He grimaced at Carly's pause, the hint of a pointed fang peeking from beneath his upper lip.

For a moment, Carly imagined him in a black, buttoned-up uniform—*their* uniform—his six-foot frame moving solidly beneath the slim-fitting material. The clasps on the front of his shirt stretched taught across his broad chest. His wide shoulders hunched forward as he moved about like a caged tiger, greedily staring at her with wild eyes and wearing the same knee-high boots that had chased her down the dark hallway.

She blinked, and Krissik sat beside her in heart-printed boxers with forlorn eyes.

"It's not all bad," Carly said, forcing a weak smile. "We met here at Samantha's, didn't we?"

"*Ri ist kas*. But I caused pain. I never want to do that. I never—" Krissik paused, shook his head. "I never thought. *That* is problem. I just do as told. How scared you are..."

"I'm not afraid," Carly said, a little more harshly

than she had intended. "It's just memories. They will go away. You help with that."

And Krissik had.

As a child, Carly's nanny had comforted her when she awakened to the roar of thunder or her parents fighting by rocking her back to sleep. Krissik had a similar, gentle tenderness to him despite the claws and sharp fangs. Their first night together, he had gently stroked her hair, kissed her shoulders, and simply held her—doing whatever he needed to drag her away from the nightmare's pull.

Carly appreciated Krissik's fond caresses and a seemingly endless supply of support. Still, she could not shake the knowledge that he was one of those creatures—that however sweet and caring Krissik acted toward her, the alien had come to Earth intending to bring back an unwilling woman to be his mate.

And to top it off, Krissik's first choice hadn't been Carly. He'd grabbed Samantha.

Carly sat on the bed beside Krissik, close enough to feel the heat radiating from his skin, but not quite touching.

Krissik knew better than to close the short distance. "You be all right?"

"Yes," Carly said. "I never have them twice in the same night."

"You want I leave?"

Carly knew he was being thoughtful, willing to leave her be if he felt she might benefit from some alone time. Carly considered the possibility of curling up in bed alone and dozing off beneath the blankets without the strong, warm presence she had become accustomed to. The thought was not comforting.

"No," she said. "You can stay."

Krissik tucked her in without another word, bringing the covers up to her chin and smoothing her curls away from her forehead. He dropped a soft kiss on the top of her nose. It was a tender, parental gesture, one he would no doubt learned recently during his favorite pastime of watching television. Carly had realized early on that gentle touches were not something taught on their alien planet. She smiled at him.

Good thing he's a fast learner.

Krissik's face was sad as he smiled back, and his golden eyes danced in the lamplight. "I be right here. Promise."

The light clicked off, and he climbed into bed beside Carly. He did not try to hold her again, instead, lying on his side just inches apart. His golden eyes glowed softly in the darkness as he watched her stare at the ceiling.

One clawed hand reached beneath the blankets and took hold of Carly's.

"I right here," Krissik whispered.

Carly closed her eyes, willing away the sudden tightness in her chest. When sleep came again, it was dreamless.

TWO

"Are you planning on staying long, dear?"

Carly pushed a curl back behind her ear, fiddling with her phone's Bluetooth earpiece as she did so. The small adapter had not quite worked right since Vegas, and her mother's voice sounded tiny and echoed.

Eventually, Carly gave up and just held the phone against her ear. "I am, Mom. Sort of. I was planning on coming back this week, but Samantha really needs the extra help getting things settled, so I'm probably going to stay a few more weeks."

Her mother clucked softly. Carly imagined her shaking her head. "As long as you're happy, dear."

They had had this conversation before when Carly had failed to catch the plane from Las Vegas back to New York and her parents' sprawling penthouse apartment after recovering from the hospital stay. Carly had hightailed it off to Samantha's ranch for answers. Carly's mother thought living on a farm was beneath her precious, college-educated trust-fund daughter, and Carly had made her opinion clear.

In some ways, Carly still thought the same thing—that her hands were made for photography and undressing her newest beau, not wrestling with horses, or bringing in crops. But there was something infinitely refreshing about the cool mountain air and the expansive sky over Samantha's Colorado homestead, and Carly could not help but feel a sense of satisfaction when she finished some hard, honest work.

Of course, there was also Krissik, but her mother was not ready to hear all about that.

"I'm just so glad you're *doing* something," her mother went on.

Carly managed not to roll her eyes—Mom could always tell when she rolled her eyes, even if she could not see it. "Something besides partying, you mean."

"Well, dear, I know you're young and having fun, but all those late nights and alcohol will age you terribly! You remember Auntie Dee, don't you? She's five years younger than me, and she looked twenty years older."

Auntie Dee did *not* look twenty years older, but she also did not look quite as good as Mom, who took great pride in her appearance. A lifetime of high-end makeup and cold cream ensured that she still looked fantastic well into her fifties. At twenty-five, Carly rarely worried about such things, but she supposed that reality might set in when she was thirty.

Until then, though...

"It wouldn't hurt you to learn to keep a normal schedule, anyway," her mother droned on.

They're just glad I'm trying something new.

Carly's parents, perhaps feeling guilty after years of putting her in the middle of their weekly all-out marital fights, had indulged her wild lifestyle for several years by handing out credit cards and refilling the tank of her BMW. Though, toward the end of college, they had started rumbling about cutting her off if she did not get serious and look for a purpose in life. Carly had not changed by graduation, and they had not followed through on the threat, but she was sure they would eventually try to force her to support herself. The fact that she was out here helping Samantha, on a *farm,* of all things, meant she was edging toward becoming a productive member of society. They were probably proud enough to burst.

Me, on a farm. Funny where life takes you.

"So, how is that new boyfriend of yours?" her mother asked.

Damn, she's perceptive.

Carly stood and walked to the giant picture window that let light flood into the spare bedroom she currently called home. From here, she had an exquisite view of the small farm: several horses trotted across the far pasture toward a tall figure standing near the paddock gate. From this distance, Krissik looked nearly human: broad-shouldered, with a thick, full head of auburn hair. Clad in slim jeans and a long-sleeved flannel shirt, he could easily pass as a vigorous young farmhand.

Carly let her gaze drift lower, to rest on his slender hips and perfect rear.

"Carly?"

Carly smiled. "Mom, he's not my boyfriend. He's a cool guy, but I don't think we're...y'know, meant to be or anything."

"Well, if you're staying at that God-awful ranch for him, he must be something pretty special."

Oh, he's special, all right.

Krissik's natural talent in bed despite his lack of knowledge—and the minty alien love-potion he bespelled her with—would probably drive any red-blooded woman off the edge. And Carly had thoroughly enjoyed coaching her inexperienced lover on all the tricks of the trade she had picked up over the past few years with ex-partners.

But even now, watching him play and romp with the horses with unnatural speed and grace that pulled at strings low in her body, she still could not see a future together.

"He's foreign, Mom, I told you. He's just here learning. You know, an exchange student. I don't think he'll be staying all that long."

Where Krissik would go remained something of a mystery. Krissik and his older brother, Rikist, would be wanted men in their homeworld if word of Rikist's location got back to their government after Rikist's renegade escape to Earth with Samantha. Krissik might not be in immediate danger, but as the younger brother of a military deserter wanted for high treason, he certainly could not just pick up his toys and waltz home whenever he wanted.

I wonder if he's staying for me.

Carly immediately banished the thought. The sex was great, but Krissik surely had other reasons for sticking around, most likely due to the almost guaranteed prison outlook if they went home. Perhaps he really liked the farm animals.

Or maybe he did not want to leave Samantha...

Regardless, Carly had been very careful not to commit to Krissik—or give him any reason to think she might *want* to commit. For surely, he was not entirely devoting himself to her.

...Right?

She could not tell her mother any of this, though. *See, Mama, I'm sleeping with an alien who happens to be Sam's ex-boyfriend* just would not go over well.

"Well, I hope you're having fun out there," her mother sighed. "And you'd best be wearing sunscreen!"

Carly glanced at the slight tan she had developed from being out in the sun all day. "Yep," she lied. "Tons of it. Anyway, Samantha's flagging me down."

"Carly."

"Yeah?"

There was a pause. "Do you need money?"

Carly hesitated. Of course, she did. She glanced

down at her nails, bare for the first time in years. She could so use a manicure after the weekend of helping Samantha on the farm. For once, though, she wanted to put her money to good use and help Samantha make rent and care for the two new men on the property.

"I'm alright for now," she sighed, looking away from a hangnail. "I gotta get back outside, Mom. Love you!"

She hung up and dropped the phone to the dresser with a clatter, at once relieved and mildly ashamed. Lying to her mother had never been her strong suit; theirs was an open relationship, and despite the rift between her mother and father, Carly had always been able to talk to them about anything. But no one believed her about Vegas and the invading abductors. How could Carly even *begin* to *think* about explaining Krissik?

She sighed and exited her bedroom, wandering through the open ranch house. She smirked at the hundreds of labeled neon sticky notes plastered over nearly every item to help Krissik—and Rikist to a degree—on memorizing English words.

Samantha had begun redecorating the place in the last week, adding feminine touches to take the place of her father's Wild-West decor. Samantha had begun repainting, putting up new pictures, and rearranging some of the furniture to make it homier. It was a big step forward from the girl who had wanted to leave the place intact as a tomb to her departed dad. Carly had never been prouder of her friend.

Outside, the hot Colorado sun beat down on Carly's neck and shoulders. The skimpy tank top she had thrown on this morning was better suited to a day of reclining in someone's back yard than actual hard labor, but she had not yet gone out to buy proper clothes. Mainly because Krissik had kept her heels up and spread in the air over the past few days—but also because she was not quite ready to transition from designer bags to flannels and boots.

Though I'm sure a quick search online would find something fashionable in plaid.

Carly joined Krissik out by the horses and leaned on the new pole fence. From the side, Krissik cut a striking figure. Even though she was several years his senior, Carly barely reached the alien's shoulder, and she knew the sort of strength that existed in Krissik's powerful frame. The lean muscles in his shoulders and chest stretched against the flannel material in all the right places to make Carly weak in the knees.

Krissik's tanned face twitched into a smile as he noticed her gaze. "How was mother?" he asked politely.

"Is. How *is* my mother," Carly corrected him, as she and Samantha regularly did to help his English grammar. "She's good. She just wanted to check on me. Make sure I wasn't doing anything too crazy."

Krissik turned away; his attention focused back on the horses. Carly knew he was still learning human behaviors, and while he had not fought Carly on leaving the room, the way he did not look at her suggested his feelings were hurt.

Carly bit down a sigh. "I'm sorry I kicked you outside. But you're very distracting, and I can't talk to my mother on the phone while you're pawing at me."

"But you like pawing." Krissik's expression did not change, though there was a glint of humor in his eyes. "You say every night how much you like."

"Not when I'm on the phone with my *mother*." Carly was not sure why she blushed when she spoke. Something about Krissik made her feel bawdy and restrained all at once. "That's just rude."

"Rude?" Krissik rested his arms against the fence, a cocky grin stretching across his face. "What is *rude*? Something new can try?"

Carly's giggle slipped out. "I'm sure we can work something out."

Krissik's grin turned thoughtful. "You have told mother about I?"

"*Me.* And yes, I have. She knows about you. Just not *all* about you."

Krissik knew better than to ask her why, though his displeased expression made his opinion on the matter clear. He locked the paddock gate and shoved his hands into his pockets.

"I finished all things," he muttered.

"Finished everything," Carly corrected.

Krissik ignored her. "So, we are done here."

Carly looped an arm around Krissik's slender

waist, and when he did not shrug her off, she stood on her toes and pressed her lips against the stripes on his neck.

"Kris," she said. "You knew it was going to be like this. We have to be careful."

"I know," he mumbled. One of his slender arms slipped around Carly and pulled her close. The curved claws that tipped his long fingers gently teased her side through the tank's thin material. "Just not like it."

A pinto mare ambled up to them, and her ears pitched forward. Interestingly enough, the horses had taken readily to the two brothers, allowing Krissik to help out in the stables. Carly was not sure if it was because the aliens smelled like the barn cats they resembled, but she was pleased that the horses seemed to lack the lingering fear the other animals showed.

Carly grinned. *The horses probably figure they're too big to be on the menu...*

She stuck her hand out, and the mare nibbled lightly at her palm, the velvety lips searching for a treat. "Sorry, sweetie," she said. "I forgot to grab carrots on my way out."

Carly leaned into Krissik and tipped her head upward. He did not respond, still looking at the horses. After a moment, Carly snorted and gave his jaw a poke.

"You're supposed to kiss me now," she said.

The gold eyes blinked. "Oh! My sorry."

"I think you mean *my bad*."

"Maybe?" Krissik smiled sheepishly. His English had improved tremendously over the past few weeks—Samantha had commented about Krissik being incredibly quick—but his occasional syntax slip-ups never failed to bring a grin to Carly's face. "My bad."

Carly rolled her eyes. "That's your *cue*, dear."

"Oh!"

Krissik kissed her properly, at least. His full lips covered hers, his tongue slipping between her teeth as if he were going to slide down her throat and roll against her insides like a furry ball of tenderness.

It brought heat between Carly's legs.

Krissik's moves had been a surprise to Carly; somehow, the virgin alien had been quite adept at the art of kissing despite his lack of experience in the bedroom.

Carly had not questioned things during their first encounter and still did not feel up to asking now. Someone in the alien world, maybe even Samantha—though Carly did not want to think about that—had taught Krissik how. Back in school, her classmates would have teased her for taking on Samantha's cast-offs, though Sam had assured her that there had been nothing real between them, at least not on her end. Though Carly felt Krissik must have been pretty enamored of Samantha to follow her to Earth despite Samantha describing the fascination as mere "kitty love."

Carly had accepted that answer and pushed the questions to the far corners of her mind, enjoying the fact the man's sexual advances were focused on her.

The alternative was too unsettling to think about, though it bubbled to the surface now and then at an unexpected comment or fleeting glance she managed to catch.

She broke away from Krissik's lips and snuggled closer to his chest, burrowing into his warmth and the smooth, slightly heady scent of warm fur and masculinity.

The horse shoved her head over the railing to nose at them again.

"Jealous," Carly observed.

Krissik's hand slipped down to the small of Carly's back, and he squeezed her ass.

Carly squeaked and jumped back. "Not while we're *working*, Krissik!"

"I say you, I finished." His breath brushed against her neck. "I want to shower."

Carly smiled. She knew showering with Krissik meant slathering up with much more than soap. Her stomach leaped in anticipation.

The rumbling of a diesel engine caught their attention. Carly turned to see Rodolfo's battered old pickup truck bumping its way over the dirt road from the farm next door. Rodolfo and Rikist had spent the last few days installing additional perimeter fencing and trail cams for better security to ensure nothing came onto the properties without their knowledge. From what Carly gathered listening in on Samantha and Rikist's conversations, Rikist was not convinced it would be enough.

The truck rumbled to a stop before the barn, and Rodolfo's tanned, weathered face poked out of the window in greeting as he shifted the gear into park. Rikist sat in the passenger seat with his eyes focused on the phone in front of him.

The butterflies in Carly's stomach wilted. Carly always felt a little uneasy around Rikist. Krissik was Carly's little clawed tomcat to roll around with in bed —a cute and huggable weekend distraction that made her heart purr. Rikist, on the other hand, seemed more a barely-restrained beast inside a man's skin. He always had a dangerous gleam in his amber eyes that narrowed to slits whenever he focused, and a thousand-yard stare that could drop a charging bull dead in its tracks. He was physically intimidating: standing around six-six and muscled enough to give a Norse god a run for his money. His wavy, auburn hair brushed just past his shoulders, and he'd let a rugged layer of red stubble cover his square jaw and neck. The fading stripes on his face and arms were not as noticeable as Krissik's behind his deep tan. However, a crisscrossing of white scars on his jaw, hands, and arms stood out starkly and gave testimony to his years in their military.

It was not that Rikist was particularly hostile toward Carly—sure, he was sarcastic and sometimes gruff and even downright crude—but his moods swung faster than Carly could follow. One moment he could be cuddling up against Samantha in the kitchen, and the next, he's baring his fangs and growling at anything that moved. Samantha had blamed Rikist's attitude on his recovering injuries, yet, while Carly had only known post-wounded Rikist, she had a hard time believing the man's disposition was anything new.

Carly had to admit that Rikist did have a few qualities she could respect. Rikist was nearly a decade older than his brother. After their parents had died when Krissik was around nine in Earth years, Rikist had filled both parents' roles to his little brother while juggling his budding military career. Then the wild lion-like alien had fallen in love with the petite Samantha, and Carly knew the man would move heaven and hell to do what he could to make her happy and keep her safe. So, Carly was just going to have to put up with the drama and try to make friends.

Carly lifted a hand to wave. Rikist looked up at the movement and offered a half-smile in her direction, which helped ease Carly's mood. She knew he had been trying, too.

Rikist jerked a thumb over his shoulder to the truck bed. "You two want a ride back?"

Carly nodded, and Krissik followed her to the back of the truck. Krissik held out his hands, and Carly smiled as he lifted her by the waist over the truck side and set her up on the truck. He followed by leaping effortlessly over the tailgate and settled down beside her against a hay bale.

They bumped back over the road back to the house. Carly ran her sneaker against Krissik's denim-clad knee, and he rested one hand atop her ankle, smiling. Krissik's smile—oh, that smile—made Carly's heart quicken, and when he circled the skin just above her sock line with one finger, she felt a sharp tightening in her center. Krissik had proven quite good with his fingers: a natural, almost, finding his way around her anatomy with little instruction needed.

"Many years building things," Krissik had said.

"Just right," Carly had responded breathlessly.

BY THE TIME they walked up the path to the ranch house together, the sun had officially started to set, sucking away the hot air of the late afternoon. Samantha greeted them at the front door, her dark hair pulled into a low ponytail, a dazzling smile on her face.

"I picked up another contract," she said, grinning from ear to ear. "Someone wants me to write a weekly column about sustainable farming and how anyone can do it!"

Rikist took the deep, sprawling porch steps two at a time, and swept the short brunette into his arms. A low rumble came from deep in his chest as he pressed his lips against hers, then he pulled back enough to shoot her a fang-laced grin.

"Guess we need to celebrate."

Samantha laughed as Rikist shifted his grip and hoisted her face down across his shoulder, butt in the air. "Rikist put me down!"

Rikist responded by slapping her ass and carrying her toward the house.

Krissik slipped an arm around Carly almost possessively. Carly leaned into his embrace but could not quite shake the idea that he was merely trying to put on a show.

Rodolfo made a slight grimace of distaste, and then touched his fingers to the brim of his cap. "I'll be going," he said. "Got to get back to Maria. She's been a bit under the weather."

Rikist turned so that Samantha could face the stairs.

"Do you want to take something back for Maria?" Samantha asked.

"Oh, no, thanks. We have leftovers." Rodolfo smiled at the girls, then left, calling "Adios, Rikist," over his shoulder before getting into his truck.

Carly knew Rodolfo did not particularly like Rikist, but he tolerated him. Krissik, he tried to ignore. That was clear.

Krissik stiffened on the porch, the slight noted. Carly rubbed his tense arm through the flannel overshirt.

Samantha struggled against Rikist, slapping at his firm back. "Enough, put me down!" She forced out a pitiful imitation of a growl when he refused. "Rikist!"

Rikist chuckled and pretended to drop her, gaining a surprised squeal, then caught her at the last moment. He set Samantha down gently and rolled his shoulders.

"I'm going to go shower," he muttered. He gave Samantha a knowing look. "And I'm starving."

"Make it quick, dinner will be ready in ten,"

Samantha said, winking. She turned to Krissik and Carly. "I picked up some good stuff in town today. I hope you guys like ham."

The tension below Carly's hand stilled as Krissik sniffed the air.

"What is ham?"

THREE

Dinner at Samantha's house tended to fall into two camps: Rikist and Samantha ate at the kitchen table while Carly and Krissik retreated to the den. The room held an upgraded flat-screen television—courtesy of Rikist's connections—and a jumble of mismatched furniture and decorations from Samantha's father. Carly knew better than to call it a storage room, but that was effectively what it had become.

Once Krissik figured out how to work the television, he had claimed the place as his own, taking it over every evening to practice his English.

Krissik made sure Carly was comfortable beside him, and then switched on BBC America.

"Time for *The Chemists*," he said, not bothering to restrain his glee.

Carly shook her head, not entirely understanding his obsession with the show. As far as she could see, *The Chemists* was about a bunch of British pharmacists who could not seem to keep their heads or their pants on. It was the sort of salacious, slightly deranged television she would have loved in college—and probably would have loved now, if life had not gotten quite so serious lately. But Krissik had discovered reruns of the show a week or so prior, and now he watched it religiously.

When the episode ended, Krissik turned to her with a smile. "That's ace!"

Carly held back an eye roll and reached out to ruffle his soft, red hair. Krissik leaned into her embrace, a slow, rumbling purr rising out of his chest. Carly shifted her attention to scratch at the underside of his jaw, and Krissik rumbled on contentedly, twisting his head to get her to hit the right spots. Carly grinned. The sound coming out of the gratified alien seemed like something she should have heard from a giant cat, a tiger perhaps, and it never ceased to please her.

"You probably shouldn't use a British show to learn your colloquialisms," Carly said. "Americans don't say *ace*."

"Maybe should."

The show ran its end credits, a montage of Big Ben, London Bridge, and some additional scattered scenery of Great Britain.

"You know, not all of these places are even in the show," Carly said. "They're just slamming them all in there to appeal to the average American."

Krissik sat up and looked thoughtful. "Are *you* average American?"

She thought about it. "No. I've been to London and the rest of Great Britain. Several times as a child, actually. I *know* all those places aren't in the same area. And you, well…"

"I am a purist," he said with a grin. "Learning about your world."

Carly smirked. "You mean a tourist?"

She ruffled his hair again, then began rubbing just behind his left ear when he laid his head in her lap. The purring started again, and Carly's smile widened.

A European newscaster came on, reporting on the business going on across the pond: something important in Rome, followed by the obligatory imagery of the Coliseum and the Vatican.

Krissik sat up very straight and leaned forward, his attention at once captured by the images floating across the screen. Excitement rippled off him in almost visible waves.

Carly almost laughed. *God, he's such a nerd!*

But such a cute nerd…

"Are these same places you show me in your pictures?" he asked, without taking his eyes off the Vatican. "The ancient holy places?"

"That one is."

Krissik had been a student of architecture in his world. He often spoke of his work there and had shown Carly some recreated sketches of projects he had been working on before coming to Earth. It had all looked very impressive to Carly, though her only experience with building anything had involved trying to create a pillow fort with her nanny back in grade school. Samantha had described Krissik as tremendously gifted—nearly a genius. Carly supposed it was not entirely out of the question for him to be interested in the architecture of Earth, which, he had told her, was far more graceful and attractive than the buildings in his homeworld.

We build for strength and function, he had said, *to withstand battles...your buildings, they such beautiful, as like dreamers designed them.*

The people of Earth fascinated Krissik; that much was clear. That a species could *dream* and create beautiful things was of tremendous excitement to him. Whatever concept he had previously formed of Earthlings before his stay had clearly been abstract.

"What did you think of the hotel you found us in?" she asked.

Krissik glanced at her in surprise. She had not brought up Vegas to him outside of their nightly rendezvous; the nightmares were quite enough. But while awake, Carly could block the images of the hotel hallways and the military invaders—and hoped that by finally addressing things in daylight, she might eventually heal. Besides, she was looking for Krissik's professional opinion about the structures, not his recollection of the transpired events.

Krissik thought about her question. "I did not see much. The place was dark, and, you know." He paused. "The bedrooms I saw—"

"Hotel rooms. Not bedrooms."

"The rooms I saw," he winked at her, "were nice. Very soft. Whole building is made for comfort. No weapons, no shields, no big walls to stand against blasts. Pictures and hanging cloths everywhere, water fountains... Very different from home." He watched the broadcast for another moment, his claws briefly stretching out before retracting, in what Carly had come to recognize as a sort of stimming mechanism. "People go to hotels to relax. My world had such places once. I studied them."

"How far back are we talking?"

Krissik shrugged. "Too far. I only see pictures. But I always want to build something like that...something more than just—just getting along?" He frowned, mouthing the words he had just said. "No, that is not what I mean. I want to do more. Our buildings were made to survive. Not to create beautiful things."

"I understand," Carly said. "At least, I think I do. You wanted more than the life you had?"

"No, I wanted more than the work I had. I did not think about life... until now."

Carly bit back a sigh. At least Krissik was not looking at her now, so he could not see her struggling to not close off from him entirely. She knew Krissik wanted more than she gave of herself emotionally. But the catastrophe with her ex, Andrew—even now, five years later, she cringed to think of his name—had taught her to build walls so high that even Krissik might not be able to scale them.

And even if I wanted to let someone entirely in, I don't know if I honestly could.

The Rome segment ended, and a Russian reporter in front of St. Petersburg continued the news coverage. Some sort of banking scandal, maybe. Carly was only half paying attention, running her fingers through the soft fur on Krissik's ears, and tracing the tiger stripes along his neck.

"I want to see these places," Krissik said suddenly.

Carly kept stroking his hair, considering his appearance. Rikist had ventured off the farm a handful of times since Carly had arrived, usually to meet one of the human handlers for intel, but always near sundown and behind sunglasses and collared jackets. Krissik could probably do the same with his golden cat eyes—contacts, maybe—but there was no saying his eyes could handle contacts at all. Krissik's fur-like hair could be gelled back into a more maintainable style...

But the stripes. The dark tiger stripes covering Krissik's skin from nearly head to toe would prove difficult.

Krissik sat up and twisted around to look at her. "Why you always so quiet when I talk about seeing your world?"

Uh-oh. He was onto her.

"We could travel together," he said. "It'd be a cracking good time."

Another *Chemists* reference. If Krissik was looking to television to improve his dialect, Carly figured he might have done better going after something more mainstream American...or maybe not. She was not sure she would live with herself if Krissik started talking like something out a reality dating TV show.

"Carly," Krissik said, a little more annoyed now.

Carly started, realizing she had spaced out for a moment. "Sorry. I was just thinking."

"What about?"

Was honesty the best policy here? She used another precious second to gather her thoughts. "Kris, we still haven't figured out all the specifics about...well, about what you're going to do here."

Krissik's mouth flattened into a firm line.

Carly continued. "You have to understand how difficult it is—I mean, your appearance—we can talk about things, sure, but..."

She was floundering now; she had never been much good at disappointing people. It had been easier to cut and run rather than stick around and watch those she cared about to realize she would just let them down.

"Can we talk about this later?" she asked.

Krissik sighed, nodded, and patted her hand. Then he rose and took himself out of the den without another word.

"Sorry," Carly murmured.

She heard the bedroom door close.

Carly picked up the remains of dinner and brought the plates into the kitchen. Rikist stood alone at the sink, washing the dishes. Even standing there barefoot, in jeans and a T-shirt, he was a formidable presence that seemed to fill the small space.

Carly hesitated in the doorway. For the most part, Carly made it a point to never be alone with the massive predator, which Krissik seemed to appreciate.

Probably still stinging from Rikist stealing Samantha away. He's probably still on edge.

In that regard, she knew Krissik had nothing to worry about. While she had to admit Rikist was drop-dead sexy, and the idea of being dominated by such an exotic beast twisted Carly's stomach into a frantic whirlwind of butterflies, the sheer intensity of Rikist's amber stare scared the living shit out of her.

Rikist's head jerked toward the sound of Carly's soft steps, though his hands never faltered. He offered her a faint nod.

"Hello," he said, his polite voice tinged with reservation. "Do you want me to wash those?"

Carly handed him the dishes. "Thanks. Sam putting you to work?"

"She's not feeling well." Rikist shrugged. "Said her stomach is upset."

Rikist scrubbed the dishes in silence for a moment. Carly considered following after Krissik but also felt some compulsion to talk to Rikist. It did not seem fair to just ditch him while he was trying to clean up after everyone. Besides, he *was* her best friend's boyfriend, and she *was* living in their spare bedroom. She ought to put in some effort to make nice.

"So," she said. "How's your leg doing?"

"Fine, for the most part."

"Does it still hurt?"

Rikist shrugged. "Now and then. Usually just when I overdo it."

Rikist had been seriously wounded during a battle on his home planet and exaggerated the injury during his and Samantha's escape to Earth. Samantha's ex—John, a veterinarian and an ally to the alien resistance—had patched up Rikist wounds and helped ease the pain. Over the past two weeks, Rikist had been finally able to get around without the help of crutches and had downgraded to a simple sports' knee brace. Carly had to admit that Rikist looked much better, and the freedom to move around had brought a shine into his piercing eyes.

Carly smiled. "How do you like living on Earth so far?"

Rikist scrubbed at an incredibly tough spot on a pan with the sponge, then gave up and used one sharp claw to scratch at the offending stain.

"Nice. I actually find farm life peaceful and very... not regimented." He made a face. "That is not even a word, is it?"

Carly shrugged. "I think that's probably true of non-military life in general, right?"

"No. Not where I come from."

The edge to his voice at once warned her away and lured her in. Samantha had recounted stories of the brothers' home while she was on their planet; many of the residences were shelled beyond habitation, nearly no vegetation surviving, and a strictly enforced curfew. Carly was quite curious to know more about the brothers' backgrounds, but Krissik seemed to dislike her asking too much, and so Carly had laid that topic to rest.

Though if Krissik would not talk, maybe Rikist would?

"So..." Carly leaned against the wall. "Your planet is in a civil war?"

"You could call it that." Rikist did not look her way. "It happens every fifty years or so, though this one is considerably larger... No one is happy with the factions in power, and with the disease and scarcity of females..." Rikist's scratching at the plate quickened, the thick tendons in his forearms flexing. "The leaders have become petty, ravenous bastards. Each attack against the citizens is just a flexing of power."

Carly stared. She knew Rikist's English skills were well above Krissik's, having been mated to a human before Samantha, but the outburst surprised her. In fact, she tried to recall another instance where he had said nearly as much in one sitting.

Rikist looked up as if catching himself. He chuckled, flashing fangs. "I didn't mean to explode like that. I guess I've been saving it for a while. There is no use in talking to Samantha. She thinks we are alone and safe. But I wish she would listen when I tell her I am worried."

"About them coming after you? Her?"

"Both. Or punishing Earth as a whole for my treason." He turned off the sink and grabbed a daisy-printed hand towel from the counter. "I did not leave on good terms."

Carly watched Rikist as he dried the plates and proceeded to put them into the cupboards in a casual and very domesticated manner. In Carly's opinion, it was an odd sight, considering the man's size and permanently extended claws.

Will Krissik's claws eventually be unable to retract?

She knew Rikist was almost ten years older than Krissik, and that physical changes—like the fading stripes and inability to purr—came with full maturity. She glanced again at Rikist's sharp fingertips and shuddered.

God, I hope Krissik's stays a little softer around the edges when he hits thirty.

Rikist finished drying his hands and leaned back against the counter. He slipped a cookie from the nearby rooster tin and winked at Carly, putting a finger to his lips.

Carly smirked. She had overheard enough of Samantha's comments about Rikist's obsession with her baking to know she had tried hiding the treats throughout the house. Though with the aliens' sharp noses, Samantha's attempts had been futile. Samantha had finally given up trying to be tactful and had begun nagging her mate about his sugar intake. Krissik took her words into full consideration. Rikist did not seem to give a damn.

Rikist sniffed the cookie before breaking it in half.

"So," he said. "What does my brother have up his ass this time?"

Carly stared at him. *How did he know we were fighting?*

"I don't—" she began.

"My brother is completely inept at hiding his feelings." Rikist tossed half of the cookie into the air and snapped at it with his teeth. "I am just assuming it has something to do with you."

"It's nothing," Carly sighed. "He's just... he's feeling cooped up here at the ranch."

Rikist studied for a moment, making Carly almost cringe under the intensity of his stare. The muscles in his jaw worked as he chewed. Then he frowned and shoved the second half of the cookie in his mouth and brushed his hands off on his jeans.

"Krissik cannot leave the farm. So, do not even entertain that notion of his."

"You leave," Carly noted.

Rikist's amber eyes narrowed, and a low growl emitted from between his snarling lips. "Krissik is not like me. Do not ever make the mistake of believing otherwise."

Carly's heart skipped a beat, and she took a step back. Rikist blinked, and he forced his face to go neutral.

"I am sorry. I am just a little on edge right now, and that was not fair." He dipped his head toward Carly and started toward the hall. "Good night, Carly."

Carly sputtered an affirmative and watched him go.

That guy is fucking crazy.

She stood in the kitchen for a moment, twiddling her fingers in thought. Deciding movement was better than standing alone, she retreated into the living room. She made sure the couch and coffee table were tidy and turned off the lights. Afterward, she headed down the hall to the two guest bedrooms. Rikist had given up his room to Carly and moved into the master with Samantha. Krissik had the third room—though he rarely slept in his room at all.

Carly's room was large, spacious, and pleasant, with several feminine touches, and right now, Krissik seemed to take up half of it. He lay on her bed, arms tucked behind his head, staring up at the ceiling. Carly closed her eyes.

Great. I've gone from talking to one brother about fears of military action to actually facing a war with the other. A battle we are both very ill-equipped to fight.

Rikist, she knew, understood how to fight on human terms, and did not seem to get bent out of shape when someone got emotional. As much as Krissik tried to act human around Carly, he had not yet figured out how females ticked, and their spats usually ended with him puzzling over Carly's behavior. He was far too used to everything being calculated and orderly, and any deviation on Carly's part seemed to confuse and frighten the hell out of him.

It's like I'm dating a striped Spock, Carly thought.

She closed the door behind her and leaned against the warm wood. "Kris," she said. "Can we not fight?"

"You are one who makes a fight," he said.

"Only because you don't understand."

"What is to understand?"

Carly groaned.

Oh, here we go again. Fine, if he wants a battle, well...I'll give him one.

"Krissik," she said. "You know you don't look human."

"I can wear some-gasses," he said. "Like Rikist."

"Sunglasses," Carly corrected.

This argument almost bubbled up a few days before, but Samantha ran into the room, needing help with one of the goats. Since then, it simmered; with Krissik obviously not forgetting.

Krissik frowned. "Why you not want us to go these places? Do you not want to show your world?"

"It's not that," Carly said. "I did show you some of them."

"Pictures," he said dismissively. "They just pictures, Carly. I want to *see* these places. View their arch-tech. Learn how they is made."

"And how do you expect to pay for all of this globe-trotting without a job?"

Krissik hesitated, pressing his lips together as he met Carly's eyes.

Carly crossed her arms and glared at him. "Of course—your sugar momma."

"Is not...I just want us to do these things together."

Us, us, us.

Krissik kept repeating that mantra as if it might stick—as if Carly felt the same. Carly could not entirely say she *did not* feel something for Krissik. Still, it had been so long between boyfriends that she could not quite tell whether she felt love, or just the addictive rush that came with excellent sex—and with Krissik, sex was *always* outstanding. But what about beyond that? The reality was that he was an alien; without a home, without a job, and seemingly without a daily purpose beyond dreaming of traveling the world and bedding Carly.

Is that what I want for myself long-term? A boy-toy who I have to keep hidden from the world and support for the rest of my life? I can barely manage myself, let alone another person.

"Because we just can't," Carly said flatly, with more force than she had intended.

Krissik sat up. "Why not?"

"Look in the mirror, Krissik!" She held out her hands, exasperated. "You have goddamn stripes and fangs, and golden eyes—"

"Rikist does it."

"You are not Rikist!"

The four words struck Krissik as if Carly had slapped him. His eyes widened, and his face blanched before he steeled his shoulders and shut his expression down.

Carly's stomach flipped, realizing her error.

Krissik sighed as if reading her thoughts. "Is all right. I no want to argue tonight."

"I'm sorry," Carly said, and meant it. "It's not that I don't think you're a great guy. But—this is hard for me. I don't know what they do on your planet, but here—"

"Yes, here you sit and think and try to make choice to be with this man or that man, or if what you feel is real feeling, or what is it word—passion?" He cocked his head to the side, stumbling slightly over the word. "That's ace, Carly, that's just ace."

Carly closed her eyes. "I don't think that's meant to be used sarcastically..."

Krissik choked down a howl and swatted angrily at a pillow on the bed, sending it flying into the corner. Krissik leaned over his knees and clutched at the top of his head.

"*Isk ti raka*," he muttered. "No luck at all..."

Maybe he was not over Samantha.

The thought gave Carly a start. Krissik had sworn again and again he was done with Samantha, but every now and then he pulled something in front of Rikist—from slipping an arm around Carly, to making sure to place a hand on her leg while they were eating, to the obvious kiss good morning in the kitchen. Maybe it was just about proving something to his brother.

But what if it was still about Samantha?

Why do I even care? Carly wondered. *We're not married or anything...even if he did care about Samantha more than me...*

Irrational anger temporarily flooded through her,

and she quickly shut it down. Samantha had nothing to do with this. Her friend had not asked to be abducted by Krissik in the first place and had made her feelings known upfront that she loved *Rikist*.

But Carly knew, from what Samantha had said, that Krissik had fallen for her quite hard. Samantha's later infatuation with Rikist had broken his heart and driven a wedge between him and his brother. Carly had known that much from the beginning and had not expected much of anything from Krissik, for that very reason. He needed a rebound, and it had been a while since Carly had let herself have a good time with a man.

So why does it bother me now?

Krissik kept his back to Carly. His entire body trembled with minute, almost invisible tremors. Carly hesitated as she watched him shake his head as if trying to clear away an unwanted image, and her shoulders sank.

He's already been hurt badly enough. He doesn't deserve me jerking his chain, too.

"Kris, I'm sorry," she said. "I'm...I'm all mixed up right now. Have been for a long time."

"Complicated," Krissik mumbled. "You females are *complicated*."

Carly nodded. "I think that's been a common complaint of men across the centuries—and probably all the galaxies."

Krissik snorted.

With a sigh, she placed her hands on his muscled

back. She felt the tension beneath her fingers shift. "Kris, don't do this," she said. "Don't get angry. You knew from the start we weren't... you know. A thing."

Krissik's shoulders heaved, and he swung around, his golden eyes blazing. The feral look took Carly's breath away, and then he brought his head down to hers, capturing her mouth in a hard, almost painful kiss so that his fangs nearly bruised her lower lip. He pushed her back down onto the bed, kneeling between her legs. Carly heard the distinct snapping of her jeans button, followed by the zipper as he pulled them to her ankles.

"I want to taste you," he said in a low growl.

Carly knew he was trying to end the fight, in the same manner that most of their arguments ended; by him winning her over with sex.

As if I'm that one-dimensional, Carly thought, frowning.

She let Krissik yank off her shoes, jeans, and underwear.

At least...I hope I'm not.

They practiced this position only once before. Krissik showed good instincts but dove in headfirst and full throttle—the concept of teasing seemingly quite beyond him. He messily dug in like a starving man at a buffet table, leading Carly to eventually prop herself up on her elbows to gawk at him, not entirely sure if he even knew what he was trying to do anymore.

"I'm ready this time," Krissik informed her. "I was reading some of Samantha's books."

Carly blinked. "Samantha has books about this?" She pictured a battered copy of *The Joy of Sex* hidden away under a floorboard somewhere.

Krissik's golden eyes twinkled, and his tongue darted out to touch his lips. "The books with the many strong men on the pictures."

Carly managed to choke back her laughter. She knew Samantha enjoyed reading the occasional romance novel on her tablet, but the image of Krissik curled up in the corner with an erotica novel made Carly want to break into giggles—probably not the sexiest thing she could do right now.

"They are *very* learning," Krissik went on, his face earnest.

"Oh, I bet they are," Carly said, trying not to laugh at his serious expression. "What are you going to do?"

He wiggled his eyebrows at her. "You see. And now, I shall explore you... honey pot."

Carly's sidesplitting laughter slowed as Krissik lowered his head between her legs. Carly tapped his hair, then paused when she felt his breath against her most sensitive spots.

"Gently," she said. "*Gently*, Krissik. Don't just try to touch everything at once."

He pushed her legs further apart, looking at her for directions.

"*Gently*," she said. "Just don't...bite this time."

Krissik's eager expression dimmed slightly. "I am sorry about that."

"I know." Carly smiled and ran her fingers along his forearms "I trust you. Go to town."

Krissik's tongue felt hot and strong, gently ribbed like his feline equivalents, and he traced her first along the edges of her outer thighs, leaving a warm, wet line that cooled in the window's breeze. He slipped in closer, his tongue flicking against her opening, and Carly nearly jumped off the bed at the sudden rush of heat.

He has been reading!

"Oh—that's good. That's *good*—"

Krissik's tongue slipped inside her, at once insistent and gentle.

"Just taste," Carly panted. "Just...taste..."

Krissik encircled her, flicking the tiny nub that made her jump. Carly squeaked, shoving a fist up to her mouth to keep from making too much noise. Who knew how thick the walls in this house were, with Rikist and Samantha in the room next door?

Krissik crawled onto the bed, kissing his way along Carly's body and to bury his face under her shirt. Carly propped herself up to yank her shirt and bra away, then settled back against the pillows. Krissik's hot mouth sealed shut around her left nipple, his fangs gently scraping against her feverish skin, and he gave a long, strong pull. Carly moaned softly as her nipple stretched until she felt it would tear away. Krissik did the same with the other side, pulling and stretching until Carly cried out. He squeezed both breasts together, forming an ample mound in the center of her pale chest, and let his hot tongue snake down her cleavage as his thumbs circled her reddened nipples.

Carly fumbled with Krissik's jeans as he reached into his pocket and took out a small glass vial, barely filled with a clear, sloshing liquid. Krissik uncorked the top, put the bottle to the tip of his tongue, and tipped his head back. Satisfied, he corked the bottled and set it on the bedside table. Carly closed her eyes as the scent of mint and kittens trickled down across her neck and face, and she breathed in the welcome aroma with a broad smile in preparation for the liquid's effects.

It took them a moment to get him to lose his clothing, and then Krissik's naked body pressed down against hers, the soft, white patch of fur in the center of his chest tickling her breasts. The scent of kitten and mint enveloped her senses. Krissik reared back to lick his way down her body, allowing her the opportunity to study him, to take in his frame.

Krissik's powerful shoulders and chest seemed to have grown in the past two weeks of working on the farm. Carly marveled at his form. The dark stripes that curved around his face and arms continued down his back and sides, accentuating the curve of muscles. Forget about a six-pack—she could have bounced quarters off his friggin' eight-pack.

Carly ran her hands down Krissik's slender waist, and her gaze alighted on the patch of fur circling the base of his cock. He was huge—bigger than any other man she had been with. Sam had murmured about Rikist's size during a late-night giggle session, and Carly could only surmise that the entire species was physically gifted.

Carly ran her fingers along Krissik's tip, a mischievous smile on her face as she slid her fingers further down to the soft fur on his heavy sack. God, what a remarkable specimen he was. Carly wanted to lick him, suck on him, make love to him until her body gave way, and they melded together into one boneless, copulating mess.

Krissik made a different sound as she stroked his velvety skin—not quite a purr, but not a growl, either. Some strange, alien sound that was entirely masculine—and it brought a surge of wetness between Carly's legs. She bucked slightly, longing for his hands on her.

"Kris..."

Krissik pulled Carly into his arms, embracing her, his weight pressing her hard against the springy mattress. Carly slipped her arms around his neck, kissing him, tasting her own essence on his lips.

Carly's vision exploded in a burst of golden stars and honey waves. Minty fire spilled between her lips as Krissik transferred the intoxicating liquid from his tongue to hers. Heat rose from Carly's groin, stroking between her legs and radiating up to her stomach and chest in a rush of wildfire that nearly left her senseless. She sucked in air, the fragrances of mint and kitten fur barraging her senses, and she felt herself running her fingers up and down his back in an almost frenzied rush.

"Inside," she hissed. She would not be able to hold on much longer.

Krissik reached between her legs, testing her readiness with his knuckles. He nudged Carly's legs apart a little more and began easing into her, inch by inch, letting her adjust to his size.

Krissik placed one hand on either side of her head and pushed fully into her. Carly gasped, lifting her legs up to wrap them around his firm backside. He slid in and out, and then lowered his face to her neck, puffing against her throat. She felt his hips pumping into her, his length sliding in and out, and she began to move with him, matching his thrusts, using her heels against his ass to push him deeper inside.

Krissik reached one hand down to grasp Carly's hip, squeezing almost painfully. Carly knew his claws were digging into her skin, bruising her, and she loved it, relished the sensation of *feeling* so much. Krissik drew back and pounded into her, stretching her open, flooding her with his very being. Fiery stars whirled around her head as honey waves rolled across her skin like ripples from Krissik's every thrust. Carly could not see, could not breathe, could only sense the heat from between her legs moving up through her body in powerful, never-ending shockwaves.

Krissik brought Carly to hurried, frenzied orgasm almost immediately. The first climax had just started to fade when she felt the second wave of golden honey begin, and Krissik drove faster in response to her strangled cries.

They came together, and he slid in and out of her a few more times, his face replaced by dazzling stars.

After a moment, Krissik withdrew and pressed his head against Carly's breasts.

Carly stroked his hair, running her fingers through the thick fur as the gold stardust slowly faded. Here, in the darkness, he could be any man—a perfect, human man—and no one would ever know the difference.

"Good job," Krissik said drowsily.

Carly blinked. "Did you just tell *me* good job?"

"Four out of five, I say."

"You're grading our sex?"

Carly felt Krissik smile against her breasts.

"You turkey," she said, because there was really nothing else left for her to say.

Krissik's tongue flicked out again, catching one nipple. "You like."

He was right, of course. She did.

She liked it too much. Every time he shared the minty, alien substance, Carly's brain simply stopped functioning, turning her into a wild, lust-crazed sex fiend, and every finale was more mind-blowing than the last.

"If you could bottle that stuff, you'd make a fortune," she murmured.

Krissik slid off, wrapped his arms around her

middle, and draped one leg across hers, effectively locking her against him.

"Good night," he murmured into her hair.

"Good night," she mumbled, already halfway into a dream.

The fight, for now, appeared to be over.

FOUR

Carly awakened early the next morning bruised and slightly sore, but utterly satiated. She glanced at the clock and almost groaned.

6:00? When have I ever woken up that early?

Krissik slept softly beside her, his chest rising and falling, the scent of kitten fur and man mingling into one heady soup. Carly was surprised she was up before him, considering Krissik was usually punctual to a fault; as long as she had known him, he had never slept far past sunrise.

Carly grinned proudly. *Guess I gave him a good run last night.*

Carly ran her hand along the small patch of fur on his chest, then slipped out from under the covers, wincing slightly as she set her feet on the ground.

Do I really like being with him that much, or is it just the pheromones talking?

Carly had learned the truth behind the devilish

little bottle, and Samantha's telling of her time on the other planet just helped to solidify what Carly had surmised after a few bouts of firework-mountain-moving coupling.

When Krissik and the other alien intruders had swarmed down onto Carly's hotel, they had been equipped with the same liquid-mint substance. The substance—genetically enhanced human pheromones—could bring down nearly any human girl's inhibitions, sending them over the edge and clawing at the nearest alien's fly, and had set off a mass orgy during the takeover of potential mates.

For Carly, the drug-induced high while going at it with Krissik made up for all of her uncertain feelings toward their budding relationship.

Most of the time.

It hurts so good...but what's it going to be like when he runs out of that pheromone? She glanced over at her nightstand, where the vial stood. There still seemed to be so little left, and she knew it was not going to last them indefinitely.

What happens when sex isn't enough?

She looked down at the sleeping Krissik. His mouth hung slightly open, and his hair stuck out awkwardly. His fangs gleamed slightly in sleep, but he seemed so harmless she did not feel her usual burst of apprehension. Asleep, he appeared less a grown man and more a dozing kitten.

A homeless, drop-dead-gorgeous raging sex kitten willing to try whatever Carly had up her sleeve.

Carly *had* always loved kittens.

A SHOWER and a change into clean clothes did not make things any clearer. Carly brushed her frustration out on her hair before going in search of Samantha. Maybe a little friendly insight into the situation would help calm her troubled thoughts.

She found Samantha in the kitchen, surrounded by random flours baking supplies, reading the ingredients for strawberry waffles. Carly leaned against the doorjamb, smiling. She watched her friend's struggling facial expressions as she studied the page between bouts of humming an indecipherable tune.

Samantha looked up and started. There was a touch of flour on her nose. "Oh, good morning. I didn't hear you." She paused. "Is everything okay?"

Carly flung herself onto the counter next to the mess Samantha had created. Her friend was usually a fastidious baker, following recipes a little too closely to make them her own, with never an item out of order. She raised an eyebrow.

"Maybe I should ask you that. You never make a mess like this."

Samantha lifted a hand to push the hair falling out of her bun aside. "No...I'm just feeling a little out of it. Nauseated, I guess. I don't think dinner sat well with me." She paled for a moment, and then snatched up one of the crackers on a nearby plate. She stuffed it into her mouth and then made a face.

"Rikist has some sort of announcement he wants to make at breakfast."

An announcement? Carly thought.

Rikist rarely made announcements. In fact, he pretty much made it a point to speak as little as possible to her and Krissik, so whatever it was he had to say was probably important.

"Where is Rikist?" Carly asked.

"He's outside somewhere, on another phone call," Samantha responded. "He's been working a lot lately. Always something going on..."

"You guys OK?"

Samantha's mixing faltered for a moment. "I just told him he needs to take it easy. I mean, his surgery was only a few weeks ago, and he's still taking a shit ton of ibuprofen and oxy at night..."

Carly watched Samantha cook for a moment, just enjoying her friend's presence. "Kris wants me to take him to Europe and show him the buildings," she said suddenly.

Samantha nodded without looking up from her batter. "We heard you guys arguing last night."

"You did?" Shame flooded Carly. She had thought they had been quiet, too, or at least settled down before their raised voices could disturb anyone in the house. "I'm sorry. He's just so insistent..."

They heard footsteps in the hallway and paused. A

moment later, the bathroom door closed, and the shower turned on.

Samantha wiped her hands on a paper towel and turned fully to Carly. "Kris can be... insistent. But he's also very upfront about his feelings, and I don't think he understands why you can't be open about yours."

"Well, some things are complicated."

"But he doesn't understand that, Carly. I don't know if his species... I guess maybe they don't think that way. Like they're not hardwired for it."

"But Rikist *gets* things," Carly insisted, propping her chin in her hands.

Samantha nodded. "Rikist is older, and he was mated to a human girl years before me, so he's had a lot more experience. He's better adjusted. But he's still not perfect, Carly."

"At least he's not using movie quotes as speech like freakin' Bumblebee."

Samantha laughed. "No, but there's still other things."

"Like?"

"Well..." Samantha thought for a moment. "Turns out Rikist is a real foodie, but the concept of pre-packaged food baffles him. Did you know he reads every label of everything I bring home?"

Carly furrowed her brow. "Everything?"

Samantha nodded. "Every label. And if he doesn't know what something is, he looks it up and then we have a long-ass discussion about it. That's why I've been cooking from scratch more. To avoid those conversations."

Carly smirked. "I never pictured him as a health nut."

"Really? Have you seen the amount of sugar that guy ingests? He's anything but. He's just baffled at the number of ingredients." Samantha counted on her fingers. "Rikist still doesn't understand the purpose of YouTube or social media. When we're watching movies, he's constantly asking if what's happening is based on reality or not." She smiled. "He still misunderstands my sarcasm, will drink out of the horse trough and can tell me exactly when my period's about to start just by my smell. Down to the hour." Samantha looked pointedly at her friend. "They're *not* human, Carly."

Carly groaned. "I know that! It's just... for the most part, they're so normal, and I think it's cute how excited Krissik gets about experiencing new things. But how long until he *gets* it? Until he understands personal space? How things work here and to stop and smell the damn roses once in a while? And that he can't just make everything better with sex?"

"Isn't that the pot calling the kettle black?"

Carly hesitated, tapping her chin with one finger. "Maaaybe...."

"I don't know what to tell you, Carly. Just be gentle with him. And maybe make up your mind."

The shower shut off. Carly shook her head; Krissik was always in and out of the bathroom at lightning speed, racing through what Carly had always considered a pleasurable experience. Who did not love a hot shower?

Mr. Practical, that's who.

"What was he like, on his world?" Carly asked. "Was he different?"

"He was a little less guarded," Samantha said, as she started pouring the batter onto the waffle iron. "That might be my fault. I hurt him."

Carly kept her mouth closed and made herself not think about Krissik and Samantha together.

She had asked, after all.

"He kept their apartment immaculate," Samantha remarked. "Everything inside had its place, and the decor was very monotone and modern. He was so obsessed with his studies... I think he mainly just worked and studied and ate. In that order."

"A creature of routine," Carly said. "Did he ever relax? Cut loose?"

Samantha chuckled. "I don't think their planet has much room for cutting loose. He wasn't dancing at clubs all night, that's for sure." There was no disapproval in Samantha's voice, just reminiscence. "Rikist smuggled in video games and junk food. But he always kept things from Krissik. Krissik's a pretty by-the-book guy. I'm pretty sure being here on Earth is the closest thing to wild living he's ever done."

Carly bit her lip. "He scares me sometimes, Sam."

Samantha gave her friend a look over her shoulder. "Why?"

"I don't know. He's open and willing to try things, he's just..."

How do I explain to my best friend that the creature I'm sleeping with has claws, fangs, and unimaginable strength that terrifies me and wakes me in the middle of the night—when that friend is in bed with a creature whose own alien attributes overshadow any demons I could ever conjure?

Carly wanted to talk to Samantha, wanted to tell her friend how scared she was, how deeply her fear had ingrained itself in her. It had congealed into a vast mountain in front of her heart, seemingly impregnable. The trouble was, she had locked herself in *and* shut Krissik out, and she was not entirely sure why.

Samantha paused in her cooking. "He's not Andrew, Carly. Krissik would never hurt you."

You know me too well, Sam.

Samantha had been there for the Andrew fallout, had nursed Carly's bruised face and babysat the drinking binge that followed, and then turned a blind eye when Carly started bringing home random guys just to take her mind off the pain. She knew better than anyone how hurt Carly had been after Andrew broke her heart and left.

Carly sighed. "I know."

Samantha looked ready to press the point, but then nodded and went back to her waffles.

By the time Samantha had gotten the waffles in the griddle, Krissik was dressed and waiting in the kitchen for a meal, his wet hair sticking up in multiple directions. He smiled at Carly, but there something missing there—a warmth she had grown used to seeing. Was he angry? Or just resigned?

When did things become so complicated?

Krissik greeted Samantha by taking her hand and rubbing his cheek and chin against the underside of her wrist, as was their morning custom.

Carly looked away. Krissik had never tried that particular greeting with her—maybe he had been too nervous to try—and she always wondered why. *Why* was it all right for him to rub his face against Sam? Carly had come to realize Krissik's species at times expressed themselves in ways that seemed more animal than human, but it seemed a strangely intimate gesture. Especially for two people with as much torrid history as Samantha and Krissik.

If Krissik was rubbing on anyone, it should be Carly. Hell, he already *was* rubbing just about everything else on her.

Man, jealousy is a bitch.

"Krissik," Samantha said softly, "can you please find Rikist and tell him breakfast is ready? Check out by the barn."

Carly forced herself to go to the refrigerator and pull out a carton of orange juice and the gallon of milk. Something to keep her hands busy.

Krissik's arms around Carly's middle from behind, halting her path to the counter. His warm breath huffed against her collarbone, and he placed a kiss against her neck. "Good morning."

"Morning," she squeaked.

Krissik squeezed her ass and released her before bounding out the back door. Flustered, Carly rushed the jugs to the counter before they slipped out of her hands.

"I saw that look." Samantha shook her head. "What's your problem now?"

Carly turned to a staring Samantha. "Nothing."

Her friend's narrowed eyes made it clear she did not believe her. "You're jealous. Why?"

It came out before Carly could stop it. "That... greeting shit. Why hasn't he ever done that with me?"

Samantha blinked and stepped back. Then she smiled as if she were about to explain the truth behind the Easter Bunny to a child. "Carly, it's because he considers you his equal."

"Then why—"

"Rikist is Krissik's older brother, and so considered the house head." Samantha spread her hands out. "I'm Rikist's mate, and that ranks me beside Rikist. The greeting is just a way of showing respect."

Carly's head spun as she tried to imagine the intricacies of the alien society. "You mean like alpha dog shit?"

"Pretty much." Samantha nodded with a grin.

"And you learned all this in the past month?"

"Three, actually. Time is faster on their planet, and I was there for almost four weeks, even though only two days had passed on Earth. But trust me, I don't know everything. I'm still learning."

Carly did one long, slow blink, and muttered, "What the fuck have I gotten myself into?"

Hinges screeched as the back door opened, and Krissik and Rikist strolled into the house, effectively ending the conversation. Krissik moved about quickly and helped Samantha set the table, as usual, while Rikist headed to the sink to wash his hands before sitting down.

At the head of the table, Carly noted, *with Samantha on his right.*

Carly mentally shook her head when she realized that their seating arrangements were always the same, as was the order of who was served first.

How is it I never caught onto the pattern? Maybe because I always stayed beside Krissik, and he knew his place in this whole mess.

The platters of eggs and waffles set on the table went quickly, despite the eggs being a tad undercooked and the waffles a little too toasty. Carly glanced at her friend as she sipped her juice. Samantha really *was* out of sorts to mess up this bad. Her gaze shifted to Rikist, who pushed the remains of his meal around his plate with an idle fork, and surmised that he was, most likely, the reason for Samantha being frazzled.

"I have waited too long already," Rikist said suddenly.

Samantha nearly dropped her glass, and everyone looked up. Rikist never did start out a conversation with something simple, like *I'd like to talk to you about this*. He just jumped right into things. Carly supposed she could appreciate the forthrightness, though depending on what he was about to say, she felt he could learn to use a little tact.

"We need to close the rest of those jumpgates," Rikist continued, "and we need to do it now. We've been lucky, and the intel I received indicates the war at home has intensified, so chasing after me is not a priority..." His gaze slid sideways to Samantha. "But I can't just sit here and do nothing."

The jumpgates.

Krissik had once tried to explain the technology around the jumpgates but had given up after Carly's eyes glazed over. There were just some things you could not understand unless you were literally a rocket scientist, and Carly was most certainly not that. Carly understood that through some sort of backdoor agreement with a branch of the U.S. government and the brothers' homeworld, the aliens were permitted to come through the jumpgates and steal women as a sort of peace offering. Officially, the women's absences were explained away as unsolved disappearances, car accidents, or, as they had in Vegas, victims of some manmade disaster—like a gas leak.

Vegas.

Even the word made Carly's stomach clench up, and she choked down the memories and sudden urge to lose her breakfast all over Samantha's pretty tablecloth.

Rikist leveled his amber eyes on his brother, like a

predator assessing its prey. "Krissik, you must protect Samantha and Carly while I'm gone—"

Samantha sat upright, her lips in a tight line. Her eyes blazed, and anger radiated off her in waves. "And when were you planning on discussing this with me?"

Rikist's stoic face stared evenly. "I'm discussing it now."

"No, you're telling me what you're planning to do. There is a difference."

"Samantha," Rikist let out a sigh, much like a yawning lion. "We've been over this before. You know that the gates need to be closed before something happens."

"What exactly could *happen*, Rikist? We're in the middle of goddamn nowhere here!"

Frustration took over Rikist's calm façade, and his claws tapped dangerously against the table, leaving marks in the lacquer. "Exactly what I warned you about last night. While I don't think they're actively pursuing me, if that *veterinarian*," he said the word as if it harbored something venomous and dark, "decides to say anything about our location…"

Samantha's face darkened. "That veterinarian saved your life."

It was an argument that had been repeated several times. Carly chanced a glance at Krissik, who seemed nonplussed with the whole ordeal as he plopped the last waffle onto his plate.

Carly dabbed at her mouth with her napkin. Sometimes, she almost preferred the open warfare that erupted between Rikist and Samantha to the concealed jabs she and Krissik seemed doomed to hurl at each other.

And lately, Carly noted, Rikist and Samantha have been fighting a lot.

Samantha placed her hand on the table, her own anger building. "You don't trust John because he's my ex. Fair enough. But you won, Rikist. I'm yours. Get over it!"

Rikist scowled and let out a low growl that rumbled along the floorboards and lapped at Carly's ankles, sending shivers up her spine. Then he rolled his shoulders as if to relieve tension and forced his claws to stop scratching the tabletop.

"He's loyal because of a hefty salary," Rikist forced out between clenched teeth. "Who's to say a larger buyer won't come by for our secrets?"

Samantha shook her head. "John told you the snatch expeditions to Earth have been halted while your government focuses on the war. They haven't contacted him for help in weeks—not since Krissik's jump. John showed you all of his emails!"

Rikist's fist slammed against the table, rattling the plates. "Can you quit saying his fucking name so much?"

Samantha sat back, startled, and Carly stared down at her plate.

Funny how things change.

Their entire trip to Vegas had been as a way to forget Samantha's cheating ex, John, who turned out to be working for the rebel organization Rikist is associated with. Samantha's tone toward John had changed after she'd realized the truth of John's secrets and had treated Rikist's injuries.

Rikist, perhaps understandably, had not enjoyed Samantha's change of heart.

Rikist looked away, taking a deep breath to control his heavy breathing. He roughly rubbed at the back of his neck. "Regardless of *how* they might find us, I am not about to sit on my ass and wait for them to come. At some point, they will realize the Vegas site is down, and it won't take them long to put two and two together that it was probably us to blame."

He paused and looked sadly at Samantha, who now kept her attention on her shaking hands.

"There are a few potential rally points a days' drive from here that I want to monitor. I will not be gone long."

Rikist's hand twitched on the table, slid toward Samantha, and then stopped.

"Krissik," Rikist said slowly. "I still have your laser. It's buried in a box behind the goat pen. I want you to practice before I leave. For just in case."

Carly raised her hand. Rikist looked at her with lifted brows, and then seemed to realize he was supposed to call on her. "Yes, Carly?"

"If you're really that worried, wouldn't it be better if you stayed here to help protect us?"

Rikist studied her. Carly did not much like the

steeliness in his gaze, but she refused to squirm until he finally nodded.

"Yes," he said at last. "It would be better. But I don't know what's coming, or if anything is coming at all. That's why I'm leaving to scout the area again." His eyes slid to his brother. "Krissik should be capable enough without me."

Carly sensed she would not get much further with Rikist, so she went back to mashing her breakfast together into a strawberry and egg-flavored pudding. The others sat in silence for a few moments, until Rikist stood abruptly, scraping his chair along the floor.

"Krissik, come on."

Krissik dutifully rose without a word, and the brothers left their plates on the table and stomped down the porch steps.

Samantha rested her head in her hands.

Carly stretched out a hand and brushed Samantha's elbow. "Are you OK?"

"I'm fine. I just wish he didn't have to be so involved with the resistance." Samantha sat up, wiping at her eyes. "I know he must, but it's just... he's been running around since the moment his leg could hold him, researching the gates and how to close them and...." She took a deep, shuddering breath. "It's like he's obsessed, and he spends so much time on the phone with his men planning and plotting. It's just... when is this going to be over? When do we get to have *our* time without worrying about another attack?"

It was the sort of thing Carly had never envisioned

her practical if somewhat hardheaded best friend. Frankly, it sounded like something out of a dramatic foreign film. Carly complained about needing space from her alien shadow, and Samantha just wanted to spend more one-on-one time with hers. Carly did not have an adequate answer, so for once, she kept her mouth shut and helped Samantha clear the table in silence.

THE DAY WENT by in a blur. Rikist and Krissik went over several items privately, and then after a few hours' crash course with the weapons.

Carly nearly limped on her way to the house from the barn, aching from mucking all the stalls and moving several bales of hay alone rather than alongside Krissik—and she came to terms with how much—or how little—she actually did when he was with her.

I guess I should probably start trying to pull my own weight a little more...

She looked up at a crunch of tires on the dirt road, as Samantha's SUV rounded the corner on its way off the ranch. It stopped beside her, and the window rolled down.

Carly was a little surprised when Rikist stuck his head out and leaned on one elbow.

"Are you all right?" he asked.

"Yeah, I'm fine," Carly panted. She rubbed her back. "I didn't know you could drive."

"I did manage a ship before this," Rikist smirked. "Rodolfo's been giving me lessons."

"Are you leaving?"

"Just getting gas," Rikist said. His face darkened. "Keep an eye on Krissik while I'm gone."

That seemed a strange statement from the man who had just told *Krissik* to keep an eye on *her*.

Rikist seemed to note her confusion, and he waved her away. "Tell Samantha I'll be back soon if she asks."

Carly watched the SUV disappear in a haze of dust. *Meaning you didn't tell her you were leaving.*

Carly thought Rikist was supposed to be the one in tune with his mate. He was either worried about an attack and not thinking straight, or he really was just an asshole.

Carly hobbled up the back steps and into the bathroom, splashing water on her face as she turned the shower on to heat.

"Carly," Samantha called out, "you might want to take a look at this."

Carly groaned and turned off the water. She stared at herself in the mirror, letting the water drip off her chin. She looked tired, somewhat more sun-kissed than usual, and she was still not used to seeing herself without her usual dash of mascara and eyeliner.

"Carly," Samantha called again.

Carly wiped her hands on a pale blue towel and left the bathroom, belatedly remembering to flick off the light switch as she left.

Samantha stood at the large picture window in the

den, blocking Carly's view of the outside. She had her hands on her hips. Carly stepped beside her, gave her eyes a moment to adjust to the lighting, and then had to cover her mouth to hide her laugh.

Krissik stood at the bottom of the steps with the sweet-tempered pinto mare that Carly always enjoyed feeding in the evenings. A saddle and bridle sat on her back, though the harness did not look entirely correct. The mare had lifted her head and was looking toward the door, and damned if she did not have a quizzical expression on her face, as if to ask, *what is this guy doing to me?*

"I told him if he tacked up one of the horses, he could learn," Samantha said. "I didn't think he'd actually do it. Guess I should have known better."

"He took it as a challenge," Carly said, a grin on her face.

Krissik stood with his hand on the mare's neck, trembling in excitement.

"Why does he want to learn how to ride?" Carly asked.

Samantha shrugged. "I guess he saw Rodolfo loping around on Foxy, and thought it looked fun. He also seems to have some idea that all gun-wielding men in the Wild West should ride horses and wear ten-gallon hats." Sam nudged Carly. "Wherever did he get that idea?"

Carly hid her smile. "I solemnly swear I did not make him watch a Clint Eastwood movie. Or ten."

"Anything to pry him off BBC, huh?" Sam shook

her head, giggled, and pushed open the screen door. "Well, at least get down there and fix that bridle, so Patch doesn't get a buckle in her eye."

Carly turned. "Me?"

Samantha winked at her. "I told him you'd teach him."

"What?"

Samantha smiled. "You used to ride all the time. You could at least put those years of expensive dressage lessons to good use. And I thought it would be good for you two."

Samantha trotted down the steps and joined Krissik and the mare. Carly sighed and followed and began fixing Patch's bridle, undoing several leather straps and buckling things as necessary.

"See?" Carly said to Krissik, "You do it this way... just make sure you don't go higher than this hole here, that'll pinch her."

Krissik only needed to be shown once. He picked things up so quickly—whether working the appliances, surfing the net, or repairing the tractor. Carly felt stuck between astonishment and a strange sort of envy at his skill. Though, to her own credit, Carly had to admit that Krissik was the exception. Even Rikist had ruined three batches of clothes trying to remember how to use the washer.

Though God forbid, Rikist's sacrificing my favorite pair of jeans was just not his way of getting out of laundry duty.

Carly showed Krissik how to slip his boot into the

stirrup and swing a leg into the saddle. Krissik did so after two tries. He smiled nervously, his lips twitching. For a moment, he appeared utterly vulnerable and unsure of the animal beneath him, as if second-guessing his decision to ride.

Carly had the sudden urge to calm Krissik's tense arms. To comfort him. She knew she could have walked away and let him figure things out on his own. That was usually her way of things.

Don't walk away, Carly told herself. *Try, for once.*

Carly gave Krissik a reassuring smile and patted his calf.

"Scoot back."

Krissik obediently shook his foot out of the stirrup, and Carly mounted up in front of Krissik. She ran her hands over Krissik's knees as a show of support and then moved his arms, so he grasped her waist before taking up the reins.

"Take a deep breath." Carly smiled. "Just relax."

Carly clicked the mare forward. She felt Krissik stiffen against her back, and she squeezed his arm with one hand. She led them in a wide arc along the pasture fence, through the gate, and toward the open field.

"Good," she whispered. "You're doing fine, Krissik."

Krissik's breathing had settled, and he leaned against Carly, so their bodies formed a solid, warm line. He slowly relaxed and rolled with the horse's rhythm, letting his hips sway gently in the saddle. Carly glanced over her shoulder at Krissik as he gazed over the field with a look of wonder on his face.

"This is as far I go on ranch," Krissik said softly. "Never here."

The longing and air of regret in Krissik's voice cut Carly deep in her gut. So often had Krissik vocalized his dreams of going out into the world that Carly had eventually just shut him down and stopped listening.

Suddenly, sitting in front of Krissik in the saddle, feeling the energy course off his skin, Carly realized how much she took her freedom for granted and how trapped he must feel.

Her dismissive attitude toward Krissik's needs had hurt him.

And in turn, it hurt Carly that she had been so unaware. So out of touch.

She tightened her grip on Krissik's wrist.

"Hold on," she whispered.

Carly kicked the horse into a canter, and once Krissik had caught the rhythm, pressed the mare into a full gallop. They flew through the grassy field with the wind in their faces, scattering butterflies and crickets in their wake.

Krissik tensed as they neared the property line and the three-foot-tall two-rail fence.

"Carly!" he warned.

Carly kicked the mare's sides and sat upright, pressing back against Krissik's chest, as she let the horse have the reins.

The mare lifted into the air and went up and over

the obstacle without a hitch. The heavy hooves landed in pace on the other side of the fence and continued forward at a gallop.

Carly led them past the edge of Samantha's land and through Rodolfo's wheat fields. The horses' hooves pounded against the earth as they turned along a row of oaks growing along a dry creek bed, and then up a hill to look down on their quiet little valley.

Carly slowed when they reached the crest of mound. A gentle breeze lapped at their faces and whisked the sweat off the panting mare. Up there, sitting among the swaying grass, their hidden homestead resembled something out of a fairy tale. Serene and untouchable.

Krissik rested one hand on Carly's thigh and gave it a gentle squeeze. He wrapped his other around her chest and buried his face in her hair.

"Thank you," he whispered.

The weight of his words burrowed themselves into Carly's chest. The gratitude was genuine, and Krissik's eyes flashed brighter and more alive than Carly had seen since he'd arrived.

Something sparked inside of Carly. A thin string tugged at her heart, pulling at the edges of her consciousness and wrapping around her center. She leaned into Krissik's back. She sat still, feeling the steady beat of his heart and enjoying the warmth of the sun on her skin.

For the first time since Vegas, Carly felt truly at peace.

FIVE

Dinner that night was different. Samantha had spent the afternoon in the kitchen, keeping herself busy while Rikist packed his things. She'd set the table for four, and for the first time since Carly had been in the house, they all sat together in the evening to eat.

Carly felt that calling the mood at the table tense was putting things lightly. Samantha picked at her food while Rikist kept his head down over his plate, chewing in silence. Krissik rubbed his foot against Carly's calf, giving her a small smile as if sensing her unease.

Carly shook her head. *This is fucking ridiculous.*

She excused herself from the table and stormed into the kitchen. She went straight to the cabinets over the coffee maker. She eyeballed the bottles of liquor she knew Samantha's father had left behind. Most were half full, some untouched. The majority was cheap vodka and rum, but there was a decent tequila and a dusty unopened Jack Daniels bottle. She grabbed the whiskey and then juggled four glasses back to the table. She set the bottle loudly in front of Rikist.

"Open that," she demanded.

Rikist looked up at her with annoyed eyes. Carly shoved a glass in his face and motioned to the bottle again.

Rikist sighed and took the bottle, opening the seal with a quick movement and took a sniff. He jerked his head back and sneezed. The edges of his mouth curled up in approval. He poured a half-inch into his glass and threw it back.

"Wow," he grimaced. "That's strong."

Carly took the bottle away and filled his glass halfway before pouring drinks for the rest of them. She hesitated and then poured a little more into Rikist's glass.

"Just like the testosterone in here right now," she muttered. She smiled at Rikist. "Too much for you?"

Rikist snorted. "You drink this?"

Carly gave him a sultry smile and drained a quarter of her glass. She smiled at the challenge in the big man's eyes.

Gotcha.

Rikist worked his jaw and mimicked her, visibly making an effort to keep his face neutral.

Carly stole a glance at Samantha, who sat glowing with humor. Carly knew Samantha was well aware of how hard she could party, and besting light-weight aliens at drinking was child's play at most.

Rikist blinked and cleared his throat. He swirled the liquor around his glass and nodded. "It's good."

Carly refilled Rikist's glass and then sat back beside Krissik, who had not touched his drink. Carly gave his thigh a gentle squeeze beneath the table. She did not think Krissik would follow suit and join in, but at least if Rikist lightened the hell up, then maybe they could finish their dinner in relative peace.

THE WHISKEY DID ITS JOB.

Carly's wits were settled, her belly warm from the alcohol, and she pushed her empty plate away and leaned sideways in her chair against Krissik's arm. She smiled as Rikist hooked his arm over the back of Samantha's chair, his fingers playing along her collarbone. Samantha smiled back at Carly, the tension around her eyes gone.

Rikist dropped his napkin on his plate and then used his thumb and forefinger to turn Samantha's face to his and kissed her.

"I have to get going," he said.

He kissed her again, holding his lips against hers longer than before, and then stood and pushed in his chair.

Carly sat up. "Where do you think you're going?"

Rikist stopped and turned, his brow furrowed. "Excuse me?"

Carly shot Samantha a mischievous smile, ignoring

the confused look on her friend's face. She felt Krissik's hand on her arm, squeezing gently in warning. Carly shook him off.

"We figured, Sam and I, since you are leaving, at least we can have a fun evening together."

"I have to pack."

"After you're done here."

Rikist glowered at Carly and then turned to Samantha. "You know I have to."

"Actually," Samantha said, "it would be nice to have you here for a little while longer."

"As a family," Carly added.

Rikist looked between the two women and then at Krissik. "Do you know what they're talking about?"

Krissik shook his head.

"Rikist," Samantha said softly, "please. Besides, you've been drinking, and the last thing I want is to watch the news as they scrape you off the pavement."

Rikist shoulders grew tense, and he turned to glare at Carly. The accusation clear in his eyes.

Carly leaned forward on her arms, giving him a proud smile.

Rikist looked ready to implode, and then he sighed and sat back down. He forced a smile and put a hand over Samantha's. "What did you have in mind?"

Carly squealed and stood up, clapping her hands. "Game night!"

Both brothers stared at Carly and then at each other, their faces blank. Samantha squeezed Rikist's hand. She waited with the men while Carly disappeared and later reappeared at the table and arms full of board games.

Carly dropped the boxes on the table and started showing off titles. "So, we have Monopoly, Scrabble, Trivial Pursuit..."

"Maybe we can keep things simple, Carly," Samantha said. She cast a smile in the brothers' direction. "I don't think trivia or other games requiring a lot of Earth knowledge would be appropriate."

Carly nodded. "Right. Didn't think of that." She scanned the options. "What about Uno?"

Samantha nodded. "Numbers are probably great."

IT TOOK LESS than five minutes to explain the game. Krissik, as expected, caught on quickly and was soon in the lead. His eyes lit up as he promptly depleted his hand. A smile pulled at his lips face as he held up his last card.

"Ono?" he asked.

"Uno," Carly corrected, her face glowing.

Krissik leaned over and gave her a kiss.

"You no!"

Carly laughed and glanced over at Rikist, still brandishing a hefty number of cards. Rikist glared at Krissik, and then went back to studying the deck.

"Hey," Samantha whispered. "You understand the game, right?"

"I get it," Rikist snapped the frustration evident on

his face. "How the hell did Krissik get all of those matching cards?"

"Do no be jealous," Krissik teased. His eyes narrowed, and a wry grin spread on his face.

Rikist snarled repositioned the cards in his hands.

Samantha leaned closer. "Let me look."

Rikist pulled his cards closer to his chest. "I have it."

"Rikist," Samantha admonished, "you have a ton of green cards right there."

Rikist's head shot up at the sound of Krissik's snicker. His eyes narrowed. "You didn't explain that."

Samantha and Carly looked at each other.

"What do you mean?" Carly asked. "I explained the rules at the beginning."

"No, not that part," Rikist glared at Krissik.

Krissik broke in laughter, but when no one else joined in, he settled and cleared his throat. He fought to keep the smug look off his face. "Rikist can no see green or red."

Carly spun around. "You're colorblind?"

"You never told me that," Samantha said.

Rikist tossed his cards down on the table. His hands were full of green and red cards. "Didn't think it would be an issue."

Samantha covered her eyes. "Oh, man, I'm sorry you should have just said something."

Carly glanced sideways at Krissik. "Why didn't you say something?"

Krissik chuckled again, obviously enjoying his moment.

Rikist growled. "*Isa ka ri trika,* Krissik."

Krissik's grin left his face.

Carly stood. "OK, OK. No need to get your panties in a wad." She gathered the cards and slid them back into the box. "Let's try something else."

Samantha frowned. "Carly."

"How about Jenga?"

TEN MINUTES LATER, both women sat on the sidelines with a glass of wine as the brothers battled it out with the tallest Jenga tower that Carly had ever seen. The blocks stacked precariously on top of one another, defining what seemed like every Jenga or natural gravitational law possible.

Krissik used a claw to poke at the tower and carefully slid a block near the bottom out at a painstakingly slow pace. Then he stood on his chair to gently settle it on top. The tower swayed and then stilled. He stepped off the chair and crossed his arms smugly at his brother.

Rikist rubbed the back of his neck and studied the tower. "Fucking architect."

Carly leaned into Samantha's ear. "The way they're going at it, you'd think they're competing for the super bowl."

Samantha chortled and then covered her mouth. "You know who's going to win," she whispered.

"I heard that," Rikist muttered.

The girls laughed an excused themselves into the kitchen. Carly was smiling ear-to-ear as they refilled their wine glasses. Samantha took a long sip and then wrapped one arm around Carly's side, hugging her close.

"Thank you, Carly," Samantha said. "I really needed tonight."

Carly smiled and rested her head on Samantha's shoulder, "You're my bestie. You know I would do anything for you."

"And the guys seemed to be enjoying themselves."

A sudden crash of blocks followed by a barrage of obscenities rumbled through the air.

Carly winked. "Well, mostly."

The men appeared in the kitchen. Rikist smiling and Krissik sullen.

Carly pulled away from Samantha. "Who won?"

Rikist opened his mouth to speak, but Krissik cut him off.

"He cheats."

Rikist held out his hands and shook his head.

"He sneeze on the tower," Krissik said.

Samantha put her hands on her hips. "Really?"

Rikist fought back a smirk. "I did no such thing."

Carly crossed the kitchen to Krissik and slipped her arms around his waist. "That's OK," she said. "We all know who would have won."

Krissik smiled down at Carly and over at Samantha for confirmation. Samantha nodded, getting a surprised look of betrayal from Rikist. Samantha waved him off.

"Oh, get over it, Rikist." She poured the remainder of the wine into two extra glasses and offered it to the men. "Truce?"

Rikist took the offered wine glass and threw back half of it before planting a firm kiss against Samantha's lips. "Fine."

Krissik held the glass on his hands, twirling a liquid around. "It stinks."

Rikist grinned. "Well, at least I know I can out drink him."

"You know, that's not exactly something to be proud of," Samantha said. She frowned as Rikist finished off his glass.

Rikist's smile spread, and he licked behind Samantha's gear. "You don't complain at night."

Carly glanced at Krissik, who purposefully stared into his wineglass and away from his brother. She gave him a gentle squeeze.

"You don't have to drink it if you don't want to," she said.

Krissik looked up, sucked back to the present from his inner thoughts. He smiled. "But it helps you relax?"

Carly nodded. "A little," she hesitated, "but I've gotten used to your slightly neurotic ways, and that's okay if you don't want to."

Krissik glanced sideways at his brother and then quietly set the glass back down on the counter. "Thanks, Carly."

Krissik brushed a curl behind Carly's ear and flashed her a warm boyish smile. It was a smile that Carly knew was all hers, and it melted a little more of her heart each time.

Carly smiled back and got up on tiptoe to give him a kiss. Krissik leaned down the final few inches down to oblige her.

THE FUN and games stopped when the sun began to set beyond the distant line of reddening mountains, signaling it was time for Rikist to leave.

Rikist readied Samantha's black SUV and strapped a gun to his waist, with another tucked under the passenger seat. Krissik and Carly sat on the porch off to the side while he set his duffle down and said his farewells to Samantha. Carly deliberately made it a point to look away, opting to give the couple some space. Krissik, though, seemed unable to keep his eyes anywhere else.

Carly had to admit that there was something sweet and romantic in how Rikist took Samantha's hands and pressed them to his mouth. The sight of the large, ominous beast towering over her friend in such a caring and almost submissive posture caught Carly off guard. She could not deny a slight sensation of envy: what would it be like to have someone who would do that for you? Who would give up his entire world to live in yours? She peered sideways at

Krissik, whose gaze was trained on the attractive couple like a tabby watching koi in an evaporating pond.

What would it have been like if I had been the one taken, instead? Would I be standing in Samantha's shoes?

"If Rikist closes all of the jumpgates," Carly said quietly, "there's no way for you to return home."

Krissik spared a glance at her, a slight smile tugging at one side of his face. "Now you think of I leaving?"

"Me," Carly corrected. "Think of me."

Krissik wrinkled his nose.

"No," Carly said. "I'm just wondering. You keep saying you might leave, but if there are no jumpgates—"

"It will take a long time to close all the jumpgates," Krissik said softly. "That is what he no say at Samantha. Is not just shut down, then come home. He will come home in between, but there are many sites. And some lost over time and forgotten, and he should get those, too, for be safe. Is no easy task and take a long time."

Carly's eyes widened. "How long?"

"Months. Years, maybe?"

Samantha had sounded so sad, so hopeful that they would soon have their time together. And apparently, Rikist withheld a great truth from her.

Damn you, Rikist.

Carly frowned. "He should tell her."

"Why? It will just upset Samantha. Rikist *must*

close the gates. They cannot be left open or more come here. Gallivanting with Samantha will no change that."

Carly felt her heart twist in her ribcage. "Where did you even learn that word?"

"Rodolfo. He say I is gallivanting with the goats."

Carly lifted a hand to her mouth to stifle a giggle. She could just imagine the old rancher snapping at the energetic Krissik.

"He may get trouble out there," Krissik went on. "I no think they is coming back soon for women. Got plenty last run." He hesitated, stealing a sideways glance at Carly as if realizing his slip. He cleared his throat. "But others can access to the jumpgates. I am sure that is why Krissik worries about."

Carly was not sure which element of Krissik's statement disturbed her more, so she picked a slightly less-frightening tangent. "What happens when one of you breeds with a human woman? What comes out?"

"Curious?" Krissik asked, slyly scooting a bit closer.

Carly leaned back, just out of reach. "Yes."

Krissik seemed grateful to have an excuse to look away from the couple on the porch. "Our species very similar. I no say for sure, but most families on my world have some human blood; best families do not. They are more pure. The artso... ari-crats..."

"The aristocracy," Carly suggested.

Krissik nodded. "Yes. Ruling class. Is look down on humans and see them as necessary but no equal. But our species *must* be very similar, maybe have shared ancestors, if breed so well." He paused as if rolling the idea around in his head. "I guess so, anyway. But is a reason more human blood is in family, is more human they appear."

"So, Samantha's and Rikist's grandkids might look fully human."

Krissik opened his mouth, and something flashed in his eyes. Anger. Regret. Pain. Then he shook his head, as if not wanting to address the subject at hand. "If have children, and then children breed with humans, then yes."

Krissik's pause puzzled Carly, but she let it go.

Rikist finally pulled away from Samantha. For a moment, it almost looked as if he would change his mind. Then he glanced toward Carly and Krissik and nodded once in their direction. Krissik nodded back; Carly lifted a hand to wave.

Rikist climbed into the rented SUV and drove off, blowing a kiss to Samantha.

"Good luck," Carly murmured under her breath.

Krissik nodded. "He is gonna need it."

SIX

Farm life, under normal circumstances, seemed a pleasant break from city congestion and fast-paced society.

Farm life under alien rule was something else entirely.

Carly did not know the first thing about sustainable farming, besides the fact that she liked its idea, and Samantha was not always the ablest of instructors. Krissik began rising earlier in the morning before the sun became a fantasy over the horizon. He took himself out into the fields with Rodolfo, helping the older man plant, sow, and weed.

Carly could feed the animals, at least. Samantha had a chart up on the barn door describing which group got which feed, and how much they needed. They had chickens, goats, horses, and the two new cows Samantha had bought the previous month. In particular, the cows were interesting; they stared at

Carly with their big eyes, chewing the grass in their pasture. Both of them looked pretty skinny, as far as cows went; they were young ones, apparently, not quite ready to start producing milk.

She patted one on the head. They were gentle and pleasant enough. She was not sure she would want to spend a great deal of time with them, but a farm had cows. That was the way of things.

"You no supposed be here alone."

Krissik's stern voice made her raise an eyebrow. She turned around and found him standing a few feet away, hands planed on his hips. He looked quite the annoyed cowboy in his jeans and a black work shirt with the bright sun overhead.

Carly gestured playfully toward the cows. "Think they're going to cause me trouble?"

"Is not them I worried about." Krissik strolled down to join her. "I think you and Samantha should work together. Under supervision."

"*Under supervision?*" Cary could not keep the laugh out of her voice. Whatever warm feelings she'd been nursing around their ride and dinner yesterday vanished. "What are you, my warden?"

"I need to at least be in shouting space."

Carly tried not to glare at Krissik. If it had been any other man, Carly would have labeled him a control freak and stormed away from that hot mess without looking back. But with Krissik, she had to consider his background. The females on his planet—human and not—were cloistered away, cherished, and under constant lockdown as private property.

Now, left in charge of two human females—both of whom had independent streaks—Krissik was probably trying to copy his brother's commanding presence. He had the intonation and commanding posture down, but it did not entirely sit naturally. He *looked* stern, but he also had a hesitancy to him, a *please don't hate me* gleam in his eye that made Carly want to do exactly that.

"Kris," Carly said, "if you start following me all over the farm, so help me, I'll deck you."

Krissik frowned. "Deck?"

"Punch. Pummel. Smack. You *cannot* treat me like some kind of prisoner. We don't even know that there's going to be trouble!"

Krissik's expression dimmed further. "We no know that there *isn't* no trouble."

"Krissik!" Carly left the cows to their munching and began walking back to the barn. She still had the chickens to check on, and she wanted to see how the goats were doing.

She heard him following closely behind.

"Krissik," Carly hissed, "I swear—"

Krissik's hands landed on Carly's shoulders, twisting her around roughly. "Do you know what you dealing if they come back? You see what happened in Las Vegas. You no stand a chance."

Images of green flares and glowing eyes roared to the front of Carly's mind. She was flying down the hallway, tripping over the people on the floor as Samantha disappeared and then left her behind, forgotten like always...

No! Not right now!

Krissik's alienness was suddenly real again. His words, his actions, his face. His face that she'd run from in the hallways of the hotel.

Carly's vision cleared, and she seized the next available emotion: anger.

"So, you'd rather I live my life in fear? That's not going to work, either." Carly wrenched free and walked away from Krissik, her emotions swirling in a pit in her stomach. "I know you lock up your women on your home planet, but that's not what we do here. If you want to protect me, then teach me to protect myself!"

Krissik followed, so close on her heels, Carly could feel his breath on the nape of her neck.

By the time they reached the chicken coop, Carly was ready to spin around and strike him. She whipped around and put a hand out to stop him, and it nearly slammed into Krissik's chest. She pointed at him as she backed into the coop enclosure.

"Stop," she said. "Stop following me. Stop *it*. You're not doing the same thing to Samantha!"

"She is with Rodolfo," Krissik said calmly. He hesitated. "And Samantha not my—"

"Argh!" Carly cut him off. She did not want to hear him say it.

Mate. I hate that word. Even if I were...that, I'd make him stop thinking of it that way!

Carly turned back to the chicken coop, the breeze kicking her blonde curls around her face. She dug into her pocket, retrieved a rubber band, and then shoved her hair back into an unruly ponytail.

At least she was safe for a moment inside the coop. Samantha had made it a rule the chickens were solely under the care of herself and Carly. The boys weren't allowed inside after Krissik had pounced and killed one of the hens his first night free on the farm. Carly didn't particularly like the chickens, she thought they reeked horribly, but at least the birds gave her a wider berth from her alien shadow.

The chickens pecked at the feed she scattered. One of the birds, a particularly robust little hen, waddled over and clucked at her feet. Carly was not sure if it was a friendly overture or a challenge. She smiled down at the bird.

Krissik had not moved.

"Krissik..." Carly buried her face in her hands. "This isn't going to work. You need to just back away."

"What else would you have I do? I need look after you." Krissik's voice took on a pleading tone. "Carly, if others come... we no nothing what can happen. I want you no harmed. I want you safe."

Carly idly used her foot to push away a particularly curious chicken and sighed. A part of her knew Krissik meant well, but his insistent attitude was suffocating, to say the least.

She looked about her and then reconsidered the chicken coop and its henhouse. The henhouse itself was original, according to Samantha, built before her father had purchased the farm. They had been discussing making some necessary repairs to it before the cold season came on.

And here they had an architect.

An architect who would probably follow her around until she bashed his head on the edge of the watering trough to escape his incessant pestering. An architect who would *keep* following her around, even after she bashed in his head because that was the only thing he knew how to do to protect a woman on his planet.

Carly knew Krissik loved research and history. Would it be so terrible to sit him down with a bunch of books about feminism and make him realize how insulting it was for a woman to be tailed? Or treated like property?

This isn't all his fault, Carly. He's doing the best he can. There was no getting out of this. But how to keep him from trailing her?

Her gaze settled on the henhouse.

"Could you fix this for Samantha?" she asked, pointing at the coop.

Krissik followed the line of her finger and frowned. "Is what wrong with it?"

"It's just old and kind of falling apart. I bet she'd appreciate it. We all would. And it would give us a project to do...together. All of us." She let the words hang. "You could keep an eye on us."

Krissik studied Carly for a few moments. He looked like he was trying not to smile.

"Part of *protecting us* means protecting the farm," Carly continued. "And if the farm doesn't run, guess what? The mortgage doesn't get paid. We have to keep things going here, Kris. So, work with me, not against me."

Krissik stepped up to the coop to look in on the chickens, his gaze raking over the henhouse. She heard him muttering to himself in his own language in a clicking, hissing tongue. After a moment, he gracefully hopped over the coop's fence. Carly tensed as the chickens scattered, but Krissik gave them no mind. He began pacing around the henhouse, touching the walls, checking the openings.

Taking measurements, Carly realized.

Krissik walked around the henhouse again, ignoring the chickens as they scolded him. "I will need materials," he said. "I could design quick enough."

Carly smiled. *I knew it!*

Krissik had slipped into work-mode, his enthusiasm for his craft far overriding his reluctant need to tail her. Carly pulled out her phone and began marking down the numbers he called out, along with his suggestions for materials and how long each part might take. Krissik asked several questions Carly did not have answers to. Still, she felt better working *with* Krissik rather than trying to escape him.

When he finished, Krissik vaulted over the coop fence again and wiped his hands off on his jeans. "Is will take a few days," he announced. "Maybe less, with Rodolfo's help."

"Well, look at that," Carly said with a smile. "See? Now we're getting somewhere."

WHEN THEY RETURNED to the house, Rodolfo's truck was gone, and Samantha was sitting on the front porch, a forlorn look on her face. "Maria called," she said. "She wasn't feeling well, so Rodolfo left. I was just about to take them some pasta I made."

Carly nodded. "Krissik has some ideas for the henhouse."

Samantha looked blearily at Krissik, and a faint smile stretched her mouth. "You mean that dilapidated old shack where I keep the birds? What do you want to do with it?"

"Build new one," Krissik said.

Samantha shrugged. "I'm all for that, as long as we can do it without outside help."

Krissik frowned.

Samantha realized her error, seemed on the verge of correcting it, and then gave up. "You know you can't be seen, Krissik," she said gently. "You *know* that. It's not that we're angry with you or ashamed of you. But if people saw you...do you know what kind of uproar it would cause?"

"People get used to this." He waved his hand toward his body. "I not a monster. Not like ones in your movies."

True, Krissik did not resemble the Predator or any of the other horrific characters depicted in the last twenty years of science-fiction cinema. Though Carly was not confident that it would be enough.

"You're a genius, Krissik," Samantha said plainly. "Don't insult your own intelligence by comparing reality to a movie."

Krissik glared at Samantha, then switched his gaze to Carly. "I want to come with you to deliver food."

"No," Samantha said. "Rodolfo isn't comfortable with you yet, you know that. We're only going to be gone a little while, and we'll have the truck."

"I need to protect you."

"For God's sake," Carly snapped. "Will you give me a little space?"

Samantha and Krissik both blinked at her. Then Krissik walked past her up the steps, disappearing into the house. He did not slam the door, but Carly wished he had. Some manifestation of anger would be better than resignation, she realized. Anger meant he was still upset; he was still willing to fight a little bit.

Resignation, though... she did not like the resignation.

Do I want him to fight? I guess I must. What could she hope to do, though, to help him?

She sat on the steps next to Samantha.

"What was that about?" Samantha asked.

They watched the breeze kick around dust on the road.

"He tried to follow me around the farm," Carly said at length. "That's his idea of protection. That's why he wants to go everywhere with us. So, he can save us from... I don't know. Tumbleweeds?"

Samantha sighed. "That sounds about right for Krissik."

"I wish he'd..." Carly trailed off. "I don't know what I wish he'd do. I know he means well, but it's exhausting. I can't stand anyone breathing down my neck, even him."

"It's all he knows," Samantha reminded her.

"I know that. But is he going to adapt? Rikist has."

"Rikist had a lot of contact with our culture for many, many years. Krissik was kind of isolated. He'll figure it out. He already *is*...he's changed a lot since he got here." Samantha glanced at Carly. "So, have you."

"Ugh."

"I know you don't want to hear it—"

"But you're going to tell me anyway."

Samantha's face split into a radiant smile. "Actually, I won't. I'm just going to say I like you two together, no matter how much you deny it."

Carly scratched at the back of her neck. She desperately wanted a drink—even a glass of wine would do—but that probably would not happen until after Rikist returned. All the thoughts of Krissik swirled around her head, and she briefly considered his smiling face again. She decided a change of subject was in order. "I hope you're okay with a new henhouse. I thought if we were working on projects together, I wouldn't get so angry about him following me around..."

"Oh, it's fine, it needs a new one." Samantha stood up and extended a hand, pulling Carly to her feet. "Come with me, I think a drive will do you good."

Somewhere, not far away, a horse whinnied, and Carly heard the wind kicking up again. She needed to reapply her sunblock, maybe run a brush through her tangled curls. Life on a farm was great for her cardiovascular system, but not for her overall appearance. She was starting to feel like a country bumpkin.

Worse, she kind of liked it.

SEVEN

Samantha's old truck rumbled up the drive to Rodolfo's house, the bench jostling Carly around. Samantha kept the thing in service because it had been her father's, but *in service* was not exactly the same as *properly functioning*. The truck needed a massive overhaul, and just about everyone within listening distance knew it.

They parked in front of Rodolfo's house, and Samantha shut off the truck. They climbed out, Carly quietly rubbing the small of her back. They had hit a particularly nasty bump, and the truck's lack of shocks had left her hurting.

Rodolfo had the door open before they could knock. "Hi, girls," he said.

Samantha held out the dishes of pasta and cookies. "How's Maria?"

Rodolfo peered inside the box and smiled, though he looked exhausted. "You think I can't cook for myself, *mija*?"

"I think you'll spend so much time fussing over your wife that you'll *forget* to cook for yourself," Samantha said, holding out the dish.

Rodolfo accepted it and invited them into the living room, which was decorated in bright reds and dark browns and photographs of Mexico City. Carly wandered from photo to photo, studying the buildings and the people in them.

Krissik would love this, she thought. *If only I could take him on some kind of tour...*

"And the cat? How is he?"

Samantha forced a light tone. "He's fine. He's going to help us rebuild the chicken coop by putting that architectural degree to use."

Rodolfo's gaze shifted to Carly, and she shuffled her feet. She knew he did not trust Krissik; he did not particularly care for Rikist, but the older brother had somehow managed to prove himself in Rodolfo's eyes. Krissik, though, was a wild card, a loose cannon, and by attaching herself to him, so was Carly.

Carly pasted a smile on her face. "He's perfectly safe, Rodolfo. I promise you."

Rodolfo shook his head. "You girls are too soft," he said. His expression and tone softened, and Carly saw the true worry behind the tough, flinty farmer. "You open up too soon. Rikist and Krissik seem good types, I'll give you that, but who knows what their compatriots are capable of?"

"Rodolfo..."

"Let an old man worry."

"You're not old," Carly said.

"Compared to you two?" He grinned at them and then waved off Samantha's hand. "It's all right. I won't say anything more about it. I just wish you two were more careful... but you're grown women."

Carly smirked. *Now,* she thought, *if only Krissik would realize that we'd be in great shape.*

"Thank you," Rodolfo said. "Let me know if you need anything."

Samantha smiled as she walked toward the front door. "You just take care of Maria for now; we can handle things."

Carly followed Samantha outside and climbed back into the truck, her back already tensing up at the prospect of more bumping and jouncing. Samantha slid into the driver's seat and locked the doors.

Habit, Carly noted. She had come to realize that Samantha had acquired the habit of locking every door behind her. The thought bothered Carly, and she could empathize with the sudden change in behavior after their shared experience.

She glanced over at Samantha, whose drawn features reminded her of Krissik's resigned look. "Are you sure you're okay?"

"I'm really sleeping badly," Samantha said.

"You miss Rikist?"

Samantha thought about it. "I do, of course. I don't know if that's why... maybe?"

Carly knew her parents no longer slept well without one another. Hell, maybe that was why they had staved off divorce—they could not bear to be alone anymore. Was that what relationships did to people? Make them incapable of sleeping on their own?

It did not seem like the kind of experience that would make someone a better person. Carly had gotten so used to standing on her own that the idea of depending on anyone—man, woman, walrus, whatever—seemed as alien as Rikist and Krissik. For a long time, she had thought Samantha might come to see things her way.

Now, though...

Now, whenever Carly closed her eyes, she saw Krissik and that resigned expression on his face. It did not seem incredibly fair to him, what she was doing, but it was a game she could not entirely stop playing no matter how hard she tried.

Samantha glanced at her. "What's wrong?"

"How did you do it, Sam?" Carly said.

"Do what?"

"Get over the alien part."

Samantha stared at the steering wheel and then started the car. "I don't know. I just... did. I mean, once I met Rikist, things just seemed to click, and then I kind of just stopped seeing him as *alien*. Make sense? Not human, but not... that different?"

Carly leaned her head back against the headrest as Samantha backed out of the driveway and turned onto the dirt road.

A sudden thought crept into Carly's head.

"Hey, with Maria sick, it made me think," Carly

said. "What would happen if Krissik or Rikist *got sick?* If one of them needed more help than John could give."

Samantha nodded. "I've been thinking about that, too. We were lucky with Rikist's leg. I was really worried at first about whether John could actually do the surgery on his knee. There's got to be other contacts that are real doctors."

"Rikist doesn't seem to want to contact a lot of people. He seems concerned about word getting back to his planet," Carly said.

Samantha nodded. "He's worried if word got back that there might be some sort of consequence... for Earth."

Carly turned in her seat to stare. "You mean you wonder if your tryst might lead to interstellar war?"

It got the desired reaction, at least: Samantha laughed aloud and pressed harder on the gas pedal. "Hell of a thing to go to war over, isn't it?"

"I don't know. Who was that Greek chick... you know, she left her husband, so the guy attacked her city with Brad Pitt—"

"Helen of Troy." Samantha turned onto their road. "And the person Rikist stole me from was Krissik, and Krissik *did* come after us, just without a thousand black ships."

Of course, Carly had forgotten that aspect of the legend and shuddered at the real-life similarities. "I only really saw it because of Brad Pitt," she admitted.

"So, if they were going to come after him, or them, or you, wouldn't they have done it already?"

Samantha shrugged. "I don't know. There's a lot I don't understand about their world, and a lot the guys just can't or won't tell me."

Carly trained her eyes on the approaching shape of the ranch house and the secrets it held.

"And you're OK with Rikist not telling you everything?" she said.

"To a degree," Samantha said softly. "It's about trust, Carly. Something you need to start putting in people."

When they pulled to a stop in front of the house, Krissik was waiting on the porch, his expression considerably dark. Samantha stepped out of the truck, swayed with a sudden rush of nausea, and brushed past him into the house.

Carly stepped out of the truck and shut the door. She turned and ran smack into Krissik's chest.

"God, Krissik... what?"

Krissik pressed a finger to Carly's lips and then took her by the hand.

"I want to saw this world," he said. "I want to saw the cities you have been. I want to saw them all, and I want to with you..."

He had begun pacing back and forth nervously. Carly watched him for a moment, frowning.

"Why are you pacing?" she asked.

"Is something I do." Krissik shot her a nervous glance. "I trying to say something."

"Well, stop moving."

Krissik forced himself to pause in front of Carly. He let his claws extend and retract at his sides.

"I can no live here as a prisoner like Samantha could no stay as a prisoner on my world," Krissik said after a breath. "If it is not possible for you to say I can leave this farm, to see others besides just this... then I should leave."

Carly bit her lip. Krissik's words made sense; she knew Samantha would have died being locked in that apartment in space. Yet, that still did not make them any easier to hear.

"Our species are too similar," he murmured. "We cannot exist in a vacuum any more than you can. I feel so many things for you, Carly, but if you do not feel these same things for me, then I will leave."

"Where will you go?"

Krissik's surprised face made it clear that wasn't the response he had expected. "I will meet with Rikist at a jumpgate, and travel home. There will be somewhere for me to go—is a big world. I might even join the rebellion."

He smiled, but there was no humor in his eyes. He hesitated. "Un...unless you say something else."

After a moment of silence, Krissik nodded and turned. Carly watched him walk away, his head hanging slightly.

Wait, she wanted to call after him. *Wait, don't go.*

Carly wanted to scream. To tell Krissik he was being dramatic, and that life here would be great and perfect and that he should stay. But what good would it do to keep him here? She could hardly make up for him being held prisoner for the rest of his life. She knew that wasn't a life either.

Carly climbed up the porch steps alone and walked into the house. Krissik had disappeared, likely to his room; the doorway to Samantha's room was closed. Carly almost knocked on the door to ask for advice, but her friend was already feeling poorly Samantha did not need to be burdened by Carly's whining over whether she wanted a relationship or not.

It's always the same, isn't it? Boys came and went. None of them held her attention for very long. Krissik, with his analytical mind and sweet smile, had fared the best so far, but it would only be a matter of time until she grew bored with him. No, she could not ask him to stay here with her, to make her his world.

She could not.

She *would not*.

Carly retreated to her own bedroom, still uncertain of her feelings. She undressed and then sat down on the edge of the bed, naked. Then, she lay down between the sheets, watching the shadows in her bedroom grow longer as the sun finally disappeared completely. The house was silent; even the animals were quiet outside as night fell and transformed Carly's bedroom into a silent tomb.

Carly felt the tears on her cheeks before she remembered starting to cry. She was not sure why she was crying, but it gave her a measure of comfort to just let go. Carly knew she put up a grand façade to others, that she was carefree and loving life. Still, she knew a big part of her throwing parties and one-night stands were just ways for her to control the situation, the relationships—everyone. Even Samantha hadn't wanted to go to Vegas, but Carly had insisted.

All of it was because of Carly.

And now she was going to lose Krissik.

Yet she had no idea how to turn it off. To not need to be in control.

Carly rolled over onto her side when the door cracked open. Krissik slipped in, his face lost in darkness. He paused in the doorway, his golden eyes sparkling in the darkness. Carly let out a sob and reached out a hand to him, and Krissik clasped it, crawling onto the bed to kiss the tears on her cheeks.

"I'm sorry," Carly whispered.

Krissik whimpered against her neck, his hands trembling as they encircled her into an embrace.

"Please, no cry, Carly." He rubbed the underside of his chin across Carly's shoulder as if scent marking her like a cat. "No cry."

Carly took a shaky breath and placed a hand on Krissik's chest. She pushed him back into the mattress. She fumbled with Krissik's jeans for a moment, finally freeing him from them, and climbed on top to straddle his waist, resting her hands on his chest.

Krissik hissed as he took in her form outlined in the dark and smoothed his hands up and down her Carly's, his breathing quickening. Gooseflesh broke out in their wake, and Carly moved lightly on top of him, her fingers nimbly unbuttoning his shirt. Carly swiveled her hips, rubbing against his bared flesh. A wry grin spread across her face as she felt Krissik squirm below her. She reached back, felt him hard and ready, and then lifted just high enough to rub his tip against her opening.

Krissik made a strained sound of pleasure. "We should stop," he said. "If I leaving."

Carly nodded and took him inside her. "We will."

It took a moment to adapt to the stretched fullness, to fully let Krissik sink in. Carly began moving on him, rising up and down, pushing her hips off and then enveloping him again. It felt *so* wonderful... and in this position, Krissik hit some juicy spot, causing a wave of pleasure each time Carly slid back down along his length. She rocked back on her heels, then bumped herself forward, getting used to this new position. She felt an entirely different range of sensations on top, and she tipped her head back, letting her curls spill over her shoulders.

Krissik's fingers trailed across her skin and cupped her breasts. He shifted his hips, rubbing a tender spot, and Carly froze, unable to move as a wave of pleasure stole her breath.

Why *hadn't* they tried this position before?

Krissik grasped Carly's hips.

"This no stopping," he said, his voice deep and guttural.

"We'll stop after this," Carly whispered.

It seemed a shame to just stop now when they were both getting riled up.

Carly quickened her pace, lifting up and then slamming down against him, Krissik gasping with each movement. He helped lift her up and down, his fingers sinking into her hips and pushing her up, guiding her along his length. Carly stuffed a hand into her mouth to keep from crying out as the pressure built.

Suddenly, Krissik's hands clamped shut entirely around her trim waist, and before Carly could protest, he had taken control. He lifted her up and slammed her down, pushing the pace until she was banging against him in a frenzied, desperate motion. Carly panted, her thighs trembling, as she surrendered to his greater strength, and felt her orgasm beginning to lick its way up her spine.

The climax roared into something marvelous, and Carly clamped down around him, her voice torn from her in a wordless sob of pleasure. She felt Krissik reaching his own release, thrusting firmly up inside her and beginning to shake. Warmth spread to every inch of Carly's body, filling and rolling around inside her like a wild creature suddenly freed from its cage.

Carly collapsed and sagged forward, barely catching herself against the pillows as she rolled off Krissik, tears streaming down her face. Warm hands pulled her close and enveloped her in a solid embrace.

Krissik lips trembled as he kissed her wet cheeks. "I will miss you, Carly."

EIGHT

Carly heard Samantha retching the instant she stepped out of the shower.

Carly wrapped a towel around herself and hurried into the master bedroom, where Samantha lay sprawled on the cold blue tiles of the master bathroom.

"Sam," she said, resting a hand on her friend's icy shoulder. "Sam, oh shit, *Sam!*"

"Don't get near me," Sam gasped, then gurgled and vomited again. "I'm sick."

Samantha's eyes bulged out, and she hurled herself over the toilet again. Carly grabbed Samantha's hair and pulled it away from her face. She leaned out the bathroom door. "Krissik! Krissik!"

"No!" Samantha waved a frantic hand. "I don't want him to see me like this!"

"You need water and some crackers," Carly said firmly. "And I need some underwear. *Krissik!*"

Krissik skidded to a stop outside the door, half-dressed, a T-shirt swinging around his neck. His stripes stood out starkly against the rest of his body. He took in Samantha on the floor, Carly in her towel, and the growing stench in the room.

"Oh, *bugger all*," he said.

Samantha choked, gagged, and then burst into hysterical laughter. Carly gaped at her for a moment to make sure she was OK and then allowed herself to laugh as well.

Krissik looked between them, confused. "Is not appropriate in this context?"

"Oh, Krissik," Carly whimpered, letting go of Samantha's hair with one hand to wipe at her eyes, "you have no idea how appropriate that was."

A HALF-HOUR LATER, Carly tucked an exhausted Samantha back into bed with some soda crackers and a bottle of water by the bedside. Samantha curled away from Carly—and from the bucket she had placed on the nightstand—and let out a heaving sigh. "I'm sorry about this, guys."

"Psht," Carly said. "We'll handle things. You text if you need us, okay?" She glanced at Krissik standing in the doorway. "We got this."

Samantha forced out a miserable smile.

Carly pushed Krissik out of the doorway into the hall and then shut the door behind them. Krissik moved without a fight, though his posture spoke volumes of his concern.

"What's the matter?" Carly asked. "Haven't you seen someone throw up before?"

Krissik nodded, his eyes guarded.

When he didn't say anything further, Carly fluffed her curls with her fingers and took a deep breath. "Okay. We can get all the animals fed on our own. But I don't know much about the crops, and I'm guessing you don't, either?"

Krissik shook his head.

"All right. We'll play it by ear. I'm going to call Rodolfo and see if he can just give us some instructions for watering, or whatever we have to do."

"*Or whatever*," Krissik repeated. "I think 'or whatever' is something Samantha wants hear when you say about her farm."

"Good thing Samantha isn't going to hear it, then, isn't it?"

Carly stared at Krissik until he bowed his head in defeat, and then she marched into the kitchen to pick up the phone. Rodolfo picked up on the third ring.

"Samantha, what's the matter?"

"Samantha's sick," Carly said.

Rodolfo sighed wearily. "*Maldición.*"

"Yeah, whatever you said. Can you tell us, I mean, is there a way to do what to do over the phone? We can handle the animals, but the plants—"

"I'm not going to spell out what to do with each plant, no," Rodolfo said. "But Maria is all right enough. I can come over for a couple of hours, show you what to do, at least, so you don't kill everything."

Rodolfo hung up. Carly stared at the phone. "Well, thanks for the vote of confidence, Rodolfo." She swung around to look at Krissik. "He thinks we're going to destroy the place."

Krissik shrugged. "He maybe no be wrong."

RODOLFO DROVE UP LATER that morning, his hat pulled low over his eyes. He barely acknowledged Krissik, instead beckoning for him to jump into the truck. Krissik did as he was told, though he glanced once over his shoulder at Carly, annoyed.

Carly crossed her arms. *Get used to it, Krissik.*

Frankly, Carly thought Rodolfo's reaction to him was somewhat muted, considering the stunt Krissik had pulled when he had reached Earth to reclaim Samantha. Hell, he had been in the wave of abductors at the Vegas hotel and *taken* Samantha to another world! Even if Krissik had come to realize the error of his ways, he had still participated in the event. Rodolfo loved Samantha like the daughter they never had, and Carly knew the man would do anything to protect her. She could understand the tension.

And yet, here I am sleeping with him.

For the most part, Carly had managed to squelch down her apprehensions against the alienness of Krissik and Rikist—well, not so much Rikist, but she was still working on it—enough that she was *almost* able to perceive them as normal.

Damn, a therapist would have a field day with her, for sure, though she could never actually admit to what happened: *Well, I had a crummy childhood, and then there were these cat-guys in a hotel...*

The thought of a perplexed psychiatrist prescribing a stay in a padded cell made her smile.

Even if some sort of interstellar peace treaty were reached *tomorrow*, and Krissik's people were permitted to settle on Earth, what could he expect? People feared what they did not know. They would fear him, and his tiger stripes and golden eyes.

Carly pulled on a spare pair of Samantha's boots and trekked around the farm to feed the animals. She made a mess of it: grain spilled everywhere, drawing every crow for miles, and she had trouble measuring out the correct amount of alfalfa for the horses, but no one seemed any worse for wear.

Carly finally stepped back into the house at noon to check on Samantha. Samantha was sleeping, breathing deeply and evenly in her bed. Carly rested a hand on her forehead, but it was cool to the touch. So, no never or chills. Carly frowned, wondering what sort of bug Samantha could be fighting. She made sure Samantha's phone was charged, that her bucket was empty and that she had a full bottle of water within easy reach. Then she tapped her fingers together, thinking what else she could do to be helpful.

I should make her some soup.

Carly ventured out into the kitchen and paused in front of the pantry chock full of food, none of which she had any idea of how to cook. Samantha made it look easy. She could slap ribs on the grill, bake up pastries the men loved, and throw vegetables and seasonings into a pot, and somehow, it became soup. Carly's parents had not cooked frequently; they'd had hired help for that.

For all the good my nannies did me.

Carly had never been required to take care of herself, let alone someone else. Samantha had always been there for her, though. Carly could be there for *her* now.

Carly reached into the cabinet and withdrew a package of instant ramen, and finally found herself smiling.

"Just add hot water," she read.

It probably was not ideal, lacking major nutrients and loaded with sodium, but it was something. She put a pot of water in the center of the stove on high and dropped in the packet contents.

The chorded house phone rang, making Carly jump. She answered, propping the headset between her ear and her shoulder.

"Samantha's phone, this is Carly speaking."

"Carly, hi." The vaguely recognizable male voice came through. "It's John."

Carly frowned as she wracked her brain. *John, John, John...*

Oh. *Oh.* The veterinarian. Samantha's ex. *That* John.

"Hi, John," Carly said cautiously. She knew

Samantha talked to John every week or so regarding the animals, and that Rikist dealt with him for his meds and knee therapy. Still, Carly had not interacted with the man since Samantha had broken things off. "What's up?"

"Rodolfo asked me to call. He wants to make sure everything is all right."

Carly sighed and rolled her eyes. "We're fine, John. Samantha's got some bug, but Krissik and I are handling things."

"How sick is she?"

Carly glanced toward Samantha's door. "She's been nauseous all morning and throwing up, but now that she's sleeping, she seems OK. Probably just the same stuff Maria has."

"Does she have a fever?"

"No."

"Chills?"

"No."

"Did she get hurt? Cut herself on something?"

"No, John. She's literally just nauseated." Carly heard John breathing on the other end. "You there?"

"Yeah," John said, his voice distracted. "How long has she been like this?"

"Carly?" Krissik called through the back screen door.

Carly heard the door squeak open, and boots stepped inside. Several pairs.

"I gotta go, John," Carly said quickly. "Thanks for calling!"

Carly hung up before John could protest and absently stirred the ramen. Krissik and Rodolfo stepped into the kitchen. Krissik's nose twitched, and the older man frowned.

"You're burning it," Rodolfo said.

Carly looked down at the pot. The ramen bubbled but did not seem particularly bad. "How do you burn soup?"

"I don't know, but that's what you're doing." Rodolfo pushed her gently out of the way, turned down the stove, and stirred the noodles. "Kris, you tell her about your idea."

Kris. Rodolfo had called Krissik Kris. Carly raised her eyebrows. That had to be a good sign, right?

"We could make big changes to the exist ear-gation system," Krissik said.

"Irrigation," Rodolfo muttered.

Krissik nodded. "Yes. Now is old, falling apart. Samantha knows and wants to replace, but not for a long time. I design something to water all plants and make Samantha happy, so we no need go all over the farm to feed these things. All easy."

Carly nodded slowly. "And how long is that going to take?"

"A month, maybe, with just us," Rodolfo said. "We would need to buy the parts, pull up the old irrigation system, and water by hand while those parts were out of commission."

Carly let out a low whistle. "Sounds like a lot of work."

"But worth it."

Carly looked at Krissik. "And you can do all this before you go home?"

The words flew out of Carly's mouth before she could stop them. Rodolfo, standing at the stove, raised an eyebrow. Krissik stared at Carly, the obvious hurt welling up in his face. Carly wished the kitchen floor would open up and swallow her.

"I would do before I leave," Krissik finally said.

Rodolfo took the pot off the burner, placed it on a cold one, and ladled the ramen into a bowl. "You're leaving?" he asked.

Krissik continued to stare at Carly. "Looks like yes," he said. "After work here is finished."

Carly felt a hot bowl shoved into her hands.

"Go feed Samantha," Rodolfo commanded. "She needs this more than you two need your—whatever the hell this is."

Rodolfo was right, of course.

Carly brushed past Krissik and tried to pretend she did not feel the jolt of electricity as their shoulders touched. She felt Krissik's eyes boring into her back as she walked down to Samantha's room, and knew Rodolfo was probably watching them both in turn, most likely shaking his head over the whole incident.

When Carly stepped back into the kitchen, Rodolfo and Krissik were gone again, handling round two of irrigation, or sowing the seeds, or whatever it was they needed to do to keep the farm running while Samantha was ill and Rikist was missing in action.

She brought them water and some dried fruit out in the fields. Rodolfo thanked her with a nod and sat down right in the dirt to eat. Krissik took the water but turned his nose up at the fruit. Carly shrugged and began eating his portion.

Rodolfo cleared his throat. "Even with the irrigation system Krissik proposes, we will need to hire more hands if Samantha wants this place to flourish."

Carly nodded. Samantha had made some noise about that earlier.

"We can manage for now, but when it was just Samantha and me, it was a problem. Right now, it's effectively just me...though Carly, thank you for helping with the animals."

She smiled. "Did I do it right?"

"Mostly."

Carly's smile faded. Rodolfo probably never set out to be mean about things, but he sure knew how to make a girl feel uncertain.

"What I need to know," Rodolfo said, "is when I can expect to be able to hire someone. There will need to be interviews... tours... we can't just hire someone with an alien hanging around."

Oh. *Oh.* Carly realized Rodolfo wanted to know when Krissik would be gone.

But what if he didn't leave?

"Kris," she said, "how long until your stripes fade some?"

"A few years, at least." Krissik paused, ticking off

numbers on his claws. Carly stared at them, her stomach twisting again. *Damn those claws.* "Earth years, Rikist is thirty-tree, and his fade maybe twenty-seven or twenty-eight. I think I twenty-two, so...five years? Maybe?"

Carly felt better Krissik was at least still talking to her. *A few more years,* she mused. She studied Krissik. Though even if the stripes faded from his face, there was something just angular enough about his features to strike an observant person as not being quite right. And those eyes would ultimately always be his undoing. Tiger eyes. Definitely not human. Though right now, they certainly displayed a range of human emotions.

Carly cleared her throat. "Let's wait until Samantha is better before we start hiring or placing ads. She'll want input on this."

"Samantha doesn't know how to run the farm," Rodolfo said, but then went back to his dried fruit without another word, as if to acknowledge victory. "Carly, are you enjoying your time out here? Big change from the city."

That was true. Carly felt better with a credit card in her hand than a bucket, but there was something to be said about the kind of honest, hard work she was doing—or at least trying to do. Carly smiled ruefully and took a sip of her water. "I do like it. It's gorgeous, that's for sure. I just don't know what to do, I mean, are there things that people do for fun around here? Besides cow-tipping?"

"I've never cow-tipped in my life," Rodolfo said, his face flat. "Are you interested in history?"

Carly smirked. *How much history could a place like this have?*

"Sure, I guess so," she said.

"There's plenty of history. This landscape is littered with old cemeteries, forgotten mining towns, things you would never find in a fancy city like New York."

Carly could not see anything exciting about an abandoned town. "Like a ghost town? Haunted?"

"Maybe." Rodolfo turned around and pointed at a mountain toward their left—close enough to be majestic, but far enough away to be somewhat elusive, almost mysterious in its swath of clouds. "That one right there, that one's got a creepy past. There was a mining town up there that lost half its population in the late 1800s."

"Did they get sick?" Carly asked.

"No one's certain. The records have been lost over the years, but the stories go back and forth. Some say it was a terrible plague year. Many speak of *fantasmas*. Ghosts. Others say half the town just up and left, like Roanoke."

"Roanoke?"

"An island," Krissik said. "A first colony. All the people famished—"

"You mean vanished?"

"—in one winter. No knows where they went. Many stories, but most believed, are they mated with native tribe after their people almost all died in one bad winter."

Carly and Rodolfo both studied him.

"Really...?" Carly asked.

"Yes." Krissik nodded enthusiastically. He seemed to be enjoying the undivided attention. "Is called Lost Colony."

"You are like a walking Wikipedia," Carly murmured. "Where were you when I almost flunked out of high school?"

"Likely studying Battle of Kst'kri Bay," he said.

Battle of what? "I...what's Kst'kri Bay?"

Krissik brightened further. "A legend battle in my home. A great naval *istraka* sank many sen...sent-trees..." he struggled with the word. "Long time ago."

"What do you think about your theory of Roanoke, Krissik?" Rodolfo asked. "You think there's any merit to it?"

Krissik twitched slightly. He glanced down and dug a toe into the dirt, making a visible effort at a nonchalant shrug. "I no around back then."

"But you have an interest in history."

"How do you know so much about Earth history?" Carly cut in.

Krissik looked up. "The television."

Carly could not keep a note of disbelief from her voice. "You learned about Roanoke from *The Chemists*?"

"Is not only show I watch," Krissik said, looking perturbed. "I also read much before I... got... Samantha. I wanted to know about her world, make Samantha more comfortable. I no realize there so many cultures, so many people." He shook his head. "I think I knowing much of her world scared her, I suppose."

Rodolfo tipped his head back to better study the alien. "Regardless, there are stories all over the world of disappearances that were never solved. I think of what happened to Samantha, what almost happened to Carly, and...I wonder."

Krissik's lip curled. "We no did Roanoke."

Carly almost choked on her water. She had not even realized Rodolfo was heading that in that direction.

"Are you sure?" Rodolfo asked. "It was centuries ago. And the local town disappearance. Your people have been conducting mass abductions for years; even John said as much. Why shouldn't we think some of them are connected?"

"Because is not!" Krissik bared his fangs, the skin around his mouth and eyes tightening as a low, rumbling growl rippled up his throat. "I people no destroy whole towns. No like this."

Carly jerked away from Krissik despite herself. His sudden change in demeanor both surprised and set her skin on edge, reminding her of his heritage.

Krissik noticed, and quickly smoothed his lips down over the sharp teeth. A blush crept up his neck and tips of his ears.

"Rodolfo," Carly said, her eyes on Krissik. "Let's not. Not right now."

Rodolfo jammed his hat down harder on his head. "If you both say so," he said. "Now. Can we discuss the logistics of this irrigation system? Assuming Krissik can finish the henhouse before... are you still doing that?"

"Yes," Krissik snapped.

Carly let the two men plot out the next few days' work and wondered when her life had begun to spiral so severely out of control.

NINE

Carly had hoped Krissik might sneak into her room again that night, and the next as well, but she awoke alone. Krissik was either too busy with his projects or too angry with Carly not putting up a fight about his leaving to try anything physical.

She sighed and rolled over, slipping a hand down between her legs. This was the second morning she had awakened aching and wanting. After two weeks with Krissik in her bed, the past two days felt like an eternity alone.

She slipped a finger underneath her cotton panties, hoping she could relieve some of the building pressure. She sucked in a breath when she felt the slick wetness already pooled and ready for her. She had not even had a dream about Krissik—just waking up thinking about him had been enough to get her hot and bothered.

She paused. Something was missing, and not just Krissik.

Vegas.

She had not dreamed about it last night—or if she had, she did not remember. She lay in bed, frozen, not sure what the absence of the dreams meant.

Am I recovering? Is this the first step?

Samantha called from outside the door, "Carly?"

Carly jerked her hand away and scrambled out of bed, then nearly tripped over her own feet as she made a mad dash for the hallway.

Samantha was out there, propped against the wall. Carly dashed to her, quickly looping one of Samantha's arms around her shoulders.

"I'm sorry," Samantha babbled. "I didn't realize you were still sleeping. I needed to get to the kitchen, but I guess I just got dizzy..."

Carly helped her friend limp into the kitchen and set her down in one of the nearest chairs. "You shouldn't even be up!"

"Yes, I should. I need to be managing this farm. A stupid cold isn't going to keep me down."

Samantha's color was much improved from the night before. Still, Carly feared that all that moving around might lead to some sort of hellish relapse.

"How are you feeling?" Carly asked.

Samantha cradled her head in her hands. "Better. Just nauseated. And bloated. My sweats are tight... like a period from hell."

Carly hesitated. She had not heard of a cold making anyone bloat up before. "Sam, is there any possibility..." Carly paused.

Samantha placed her head on the table and shut her eyes. "What?"

"Well, you and Rik have been... you know..." *Why was this subject so hard to bring up?* Carly swallowed and just dove in. "Are you pregnant?"

Samantha went so still Carly feared she may have passed out.

"Sam?"

Samantha jerked her head up to glare at Carly. "How could you even ask me that?"

Carly frowned and leaned back. Why did she sound so insulted? It was a legitimate question. "You said it's like a period from hell, and you're bloated and nauseated. The last time we talked, you weren't on the pill—"

Anger, and then abrupt sorrow, crawled across Samantha's face. She lowered her head to her hands and then slumped over on top of the table.

"Sorry."

Carly sat across from her, not sure whether she ought to check Samantha's pulse or shake her. "Samantha?"

"I can't have children," Samantha mumbled.

Carly hiccupped. "What?"

"They ran tests in the other world," Samantha explained. "That's how they make sure you're worth keeping. But I'm sterile, Carly. I couldn't have a baby if I wanted to." She was talking more to the table than to Carly, and Carly had to lean close to hear her words. "So Rikist and I have been going at it like damn rabbits.

No risk of me getting knocked up. Kind of freeing, I guess. Sad, too." Samantha turned her head and looked at Carly, her eyes welling up. "I always thought I'd want kids someday. And I know Rikist would love nothing more, but I can't."

Carly reached out, taking Samantha's clammy hands and gave them a reassuring squeeze. "Oh, Samantha." Carly swallowed down the lump building in her throat. "I'm so sorry."

"So, it's just a terrible cold," Samantha sniffed. She squeezed her eyes shut, and the tears leaked out anyway. "I didn't say anything earlier to you because I just didn't want to think about it."

"I understand." Of course, Carly did not. She could never understand that sort of pain, to have the decision ripped away from her. But she could understand by keeping silent, driving away the bad thoughts until they only existed in some tiny corner of her mind. "Just... just tell me if I can do anything?"

Samantha sat up, shook her head, and placed her hands in her lap. She wiped at her eyes and forced a smile. "Some water would be nice."

Carly nodded and stood, poured Samantha a glass of cold water, and then glanced out the kitchen window. Her mouth fell open.

"What?" Samantha asked. "What's out there? What's wrong?"

Carly made her jaw work. "Kris rebuilt the henhouse."

Samantha was back on her feet and at the window

with her before Carly could stop her. They stood together at the glass, agape at the new structure that Krissik had constructed overnight.

"Well," Samantha said at length. "He *is* a genius in his world."

"How did he get the parts?"

"Rodolfo?"

It had to be Rodolfo. Krissik was stubborn, but even he would not venture into town on his own if he wanted to; he couldn't drive.

"Let's check it out," Samantha said.

"You won't make it halfway down the porch," Carly said. "You sit here, and *"I'll* check it out."

"But..."

"*Stay.*" Carly stared at her the way she had stared at the family dogs growing up. "Stay. Or no cookie for you."

"You wouldn't dare withhold cookies from me, bitch!" Samantha grinned as she sat back down in the chair.

Carly raced back to her room, pulled on jeans, a bra, and a T-shirt, and rushed out the front door. It was already a hot day, and the sun beat down on her face and exposed neck. She kicked up some dust as she nearly skipped over the terrain, at last skidding to a stop in front of the chicken coop to gape at Krissik's handiwork.

It was not a henhouse. It was a hen *palace.* Carly would not have been surprised if the place had air conditioning.

Krissik opened the door, stepped outside, and glanced at her. "Good morning."

"Did you work on this all night?"

"No, could sleep."

It was such an easy excuse. When Carly had insomnia, she ate junk food, drank, or broke into her mother's sleeping pills. When Krissik could not sleep, he built fucking Taj Mahals. Even the chickens seemed awed by it; they milled around in front, occasionally tilting their heads to the side to regard their new home.

"It's big," Carly finally said. "That's going to hold a lot of chickens."

"Samantha say she want more birds," he said. "Instead than build addition later, she should have the space now. They will not mind."

No, they probably would not. Chickens were not deep thinkers, as far as Carly knew. She rubbed her eyes; still not entirely sure she was seeing clearly. Maybe this was still part of her dream: Krissik had not threatened to leave, and instead, he was making a living designing henhouses for discriminating poultry across the country.

"It's amazing," she said. "You just did this. Like, on the fly?"

"Thank you."

"But how did you do it?"

"I just did?" Krissik shrugged. "Some things is easy for me. Building. Designing. Simple. Other things are no as much. Humans... feelings is harder, I guess," he admitted. "No matter how much I *swot*, it no does stick."

"Swot?"

More British slang. God help them all.

Carly turned away from Krissik, uncomfortable with the sudden rush of feelings he prompted in her. Here was a man who, in other circumstances, would be an excellent fit. He did everything he said he would. He fixed things. With some prodding, he might be able to cook a decent meal.

Get on that, her girlfriends would say. *Lock it down.* The fact that he was from another planet should not have made *that* much of a difference.

Carly headed for the barn, intending to feed the horses, but paused when an unfamiliar coupe rumbled up the hill. Carly shaded her eyes, glancing back over her shoulder. Krissik was far enough away from the house that he looked like any other barn hand, so he was safe for now. Carly edged closer to the house, watching the coupe as it pulled up next to the front porch. A short, dark-haired girl popped out, looked around, and then darted up the porch steps.

A second later, she heard the joyful shrieks of reunification.

Mandy.

Samantha's little sister.

Carly had not seen Mandy in several years; once the girl went off to college, contact between them had been sparse. Samantha had missed her younger sibling, though, and spoke of her infrequently, especially after their father died.

Mandy was here.

Mandy did not know about Rikist and Krissik.

Mandy would want a tour of the farm...

"Krissik!" Carly barked, sprinting back to the henhouse. "We have to hide you!"

Krissik had already gone back to work on one of the walls, and his brow furrowed in cat-man confusion at her yell. "Hide? Isk ra ti?"

"Because Samantha's sister is here, and I don't think she knows about you!"

Carly barely waited for him to exit the chicken coop. Then she grabbed his hand and pulled him along behind her, making a beeline for the barn. Not that Mandy would stay out of the barn if she got curious about it—if Carly turned out the horses and hung an "Under Construction" sign in front of the doors, it might be enough to assuage her curiosity for the time being.

She shoved Krissik into the tack room. "Stay here," she commanded. "I'm going to turn out the horses, so Mandy can visit with them if she wants."

"But—"

"Stay!"

Krissik sat down on the floor.

Carly wedged the tack room door shut and looked around at the horses, all of whom looked back at her with pricked ears. She led them out two at a time, hoping they were all amiable creatures who would not cause her trouble. Fortunately, they were all happy to be turned out in their respective pastures, and within ten minutes, she was heading up to the house to figure out just how much trouble they were in.

Carly could hear Samantha and Mandy laughing even while she stood out on the porch. Carly had to squelch a stab of jealousy; Samantha had not laughed like that since Rikist left, and none of Carly's jokes seemed to elicit anything more than a vague smile and a chuckle. Carly forced herself to smile, strolled into the house, and found the sisters sitting close together at the kitchen table, hands intertwined.

Mandy jumped up. "Carly!"

"Hey, girl!" They embraced, Mandy's natural effervescence washing over her. Carly gave her a firm squeeze and pushed her back to have a look at her. She was Samantha's smaller and younger self, still, all tousled hair and pouty lips—a perfect little miniature.

"I didn't know you'd be coming up!" Carly said.

"No one did." Mandy plunked back down in her chair, a conspiring smile on her face. "I did tell Samantha I'd stop by when the semester was over, but I didn't tell her exactly *when*. Anyway, here I am. I didn't realize you guys were partying out here, though."

"Oh, we're not," Samantha said.

Mandy looked Carly's way; an eyebrow arched. "Really?"

It was a subtle jab, but Carly felt it nonetheless. "I'm working here," she said. "For a while, anyway."

This time, Mandy did not try to be subtle. "*You're*

working on the farm," she said. "You? I thought you'd be traveling around Rome or something."

"That was actually the plan, but after that nonsense in Vegas, I decided I might as well stay in the country." Carly looked Samantha's way, hoping for some help, but Samantha just smiled at her sister, obviously delighted to see her.

Mandy nodded and tipped her head toward Carly. "Well, I guess...that's great! I'm glad you're trying something new!"

Carly suddenly remembered why she had never spent a great deal of time with Mandy. Her best friend's kid sister had never approved of, well, anything she did. School was for studying, partying was for losers with nothing else to do, and so on. She had never *said* those things to Carly. Still, the slight disapproval in her eyes had always been enough to shame Carly into avoidance of telling her better stories.

I'm glad you're trying something new! Translation: *I'm so happy you aren't boozing it up in Paris again!*

Still, Carly could hardly pick a fight with her best friend's kid sister. "I like being around the animals," she said. "How long are you planning on staying?"

"A week or so, if you'll have me," Mandy said. "And it looks like *this* lady needs some serious TLC."

"It's just a cold," Samantha said.

"You shouldn't even be *up*," Mandy said.

Carly forced herself to laugh and patted Samantha affectionately on the head. "Well, if you can keep her in bed, more power to you. I'll let you two catch up and get back to feeding the critters—oh, and Samantha?"

Samantha looked up at her.

"The barn roof looks ready to cave in again. I moved the horses outside, but you're going to want to get a contractor out to take a look at things. I don't recommend going in there."

She held Samantha's gaze just long enough to get the point across. Samantha nodded slowly. "I wish that thing held together better," she said. "Thanks, Carly."

Carly grabbed two bottles of water from the fridge and her purse from the front foyer and trotted out the door, eager to be away from Mandy and her judgmental gaze. Still, it would be good for Sam to have her sister around. The two shared a bond Carly had always envied, even if Mandy *did* think Carly was Satan's offspring.

Krissik was picking at his bootlaces when Carly joined him in the tack room. He glanced up, but did not rise; if anything, his fingers increased in pace. At the rate he was going, Carly figured he would unravel the entire shoe. Carly sat down next to him, briefly overwhelmed by the scent of man, leather, fur, and the alfalfa in the feed bin. She set down the water bottles and the purse.

The pair of them sat in relative silence for a moment.

Finally, Krissik said, "What is happening?"

"Samantha's sister is visiting," Carly said. "Mandy. She's a few years younger than us, very studious."

Krissik nodded. "You no like her."

"More like she doesn't like me." Carly paused. "Is it that obvious?"

"You say about her like you say about your parents' accountant, Bill," Krissik said. "Same voice. Did something happen?"

"Samantha went through a partying phase after we met. She was never *that* bad about it, never like me, but I guess since I was there, Mandy began to see me as a bad influence and has ever since. Later, when Samantha calmed down, she didn't see why Sam would hang out with someone like me. We don't have a lot in common, after all."

Krissik looked at her sideways. "She say you this?"

"It's evident in her face. Body language. I can tell when someone doesn't want to be around me."

Krissik frowned, as if not quite believing her. "And Mandy does know about I or Rikist?"

"Nope. I don't know how Sam is going to explain it to her. Rikist, at least, if we get him contacts or if he put on shades, could maybe pass. But you..."

She considered the striping on Krissik's face, the thick hair on his head, the sideburns tapering down to his defined jaw. He was so *attractive*, it was undeniable. But those stripes...

"Can I try something?" she asked.

Krissik shrugged. "Take the biscuit."

Another gift from British TV, not doubt. Carly stared at Krissik, her eyes blinking slowly. After a moment he seemed to get the point and nodded.

"Oh-kay," he said.

Carly reached into her purse and pulled out her small makeup kit, sorting through it until she found a fresh sponge and her foundation.

I wonder if I have a cork in here somewhere large enough for his mouth...

Carly had not worn makeup around the farm after her first week here, which was a first. She sweated it right off and had resigned herself to the fact she had to be plain Mary Jane while working with Samantha. Besides, who was she trying to impress, anyway—the goats? She glanced up at Krissik, who stared at her patiently. There was no need to try to impress Krissik; in fact, she was not sure if there was anything—aside from keeping him prisoner on the farm—that she had to do to gain his attention.

Carly seated herself in front of Krissik, sighing.

Krissik had seen her apply makeup once and leaned away from her. I not liking this, Carly."

"You mean *I don't like this, Carly*."

"Yes. That."

"Look, barring an intergalactic peace treaty, the only way you're going out in public is with some kind of disguise. Makeup can do all kinds of things if you use it right. This will be too light for your skin tone, but I just want an idea of how we can cover you up." Carly held up the compact. "Okay?"

Krissik sighed and then leaned toward her. "Do the worst."

"Stop being so dramatic." Carly dipped the sponge

into the foundation and spread it across Krissik's cheek, flinching when she saw the tremendous change in color. He would need something several shades darker for sure, but then, this was just a spur-of-the-moment experiment. She blended the liquid into his cheek, taking care to brush onto the stripes that ran under his eyes and disappeared into his hairline.

Little by little and a half bottle of the foundation later, Carly had covered Krissik's face and neck. In about ten minutes, she had an extremely pasty, stripe-less ghost of a male sitting in front of her.

Oh, shit.

"You can open your eyes," Carly said, trying to hide her laughter.

Krissik's cat-like eyes fixed on her, the slit-like irises narrowing and widening as they focused: all the more unsettling in his new pallid, expressionless features. Carly lifted a hand to her mouth and coughed, torn between amusement and horror. Krissik looked down-right scary without his stripes—or maybe it was the amount of foundation she had needed to use to cover them.

"Well," she said. "They make better products for covering up scars and stuff...I know movie studios have fantastic things. I have some friends who work in the industry. I bet if we used one of their products, you'd never be able to tell."

"I see," Krissik commanded.

She shook her head. "Best if you didn't."

"I *see*." Krissik snatched the compact out of Carly's

hand, opened it, and studied his face in the mirror for a grand total of two seconds. The golden eyes widened, his mouth fell open, and he looked at her, utterly wounded. "Why you *do* this to me?"

Carly lost control of her giggles.

Krissik got up and stomped toward the row of saddles and bridles along the wall. He found a clean rag, doused it with water from one of the bottles Carly brought and began scrubbing at his face.

"Hey!" Carly called, "That was an expensive foundation!"

Krissik continued scrubbing his skin raw. Carly put her makeup bag away, and nearly doubled over, her laughter bouncing off the tack room walls. The more frantic Krissik got, the harder Carly laughed.

Krissik whirled around, his eyes wide and panicked. "Is your fault! I forever marked!"

"Oh, you're such a drama queen. Come here, and I'll help you."

Krissik crouched in front of Carly, and she gently dabbed the rag at a spot he had missed along his nose.

"You can't scrub at it; this stuff's so thick, you've just smeared it around," Carly explained. She pulled a travel cold cream out of her bag, applied some to his face, and rubbed *that* off, finally taking away the bulk of the foundation. "There, see? Much better."

Krissik pouted. Carly was not sure if he was about to yell or cry.

"Oh, stop that," Carly tutted, putting a finger to his lips to soften his expression. "You were adorable."

Krissik bit her fingertip, holding it between his fangs. He glared at her, and then closed his lips around her skin and slid her finger fully into his mouth.

Carly's entire body jumped to attention. Before she knew what was happening, Krissik's hands were at the front of her T-shirt, lifting it over her head. She let out a little squeal, and he buried his face between her breasts, his hot tongue flicking to one, then the other. His strong arms wrapped around her sides, and she heard the distinctive *flick* of her bra unsnapping. The straps fell from her shoulders, and Krissik cast the bra aside.

Carly thought it might have landed somewhere near the hay bales.

Krissik pushed her back against one of the saddles. His fingers played briefly with the fly of her jeans, and then he simply yanked them open and pushed them down to her ankles. He pulled out the small glass vial he kept in his pocket and took a sip as Carly stepped out of her jeans. Krissik placed Carly's left foot on his right knee and ran his fingers around her upper thighs.

Carly heard the smirk in his voice as he gazed down at her. "All ready, I see."

Carly's throat almost swelled shut, squeezing off her ready retort. She was practically dripping in anticipation.

Krissik bent forward, and his tongue touched her, lapping up the silk wetness.

Carly sank her fingers into his hair, smoothing the thick fur and massaging his scalp. Krissik teased her, his tongue venturing slightly inside, only to retreat. He leaned his head back to study her, to stare at her, and she saw the challenge in his eyes.

Krissik rose, his lips still slick with her desire. "You taste good," he said. He planted his lips firmly against Carly's, letting the minty substance tingle against her lips before breaking the kiss. "Turn around."

Carly turned around, her head spinning with golden starbursts and warmth building from her toes. She placed her hands on the nearest object in front of her—a saddle.

Krissik grunted. "No. Like *this*."

Krissik's hand landed gently but firmly against Carly's upper back, and he shoved her face down across the saddle until she was looking at the dusty floor on the other side. Krissik made a pleased sound, rubbed the small of her back, and then pushed her legs apart until she was spread-eagled before him.

"Perfect."

Carly heard him unzip his jeans, and the thought made her even wetter. She felt him rubbing against her, his hardness seemingly taking up the entire space between her legs. Carly whimpered softly, longing for him. "Please, Krissik," she whispered.

Krissik gripped her curly hair, pulling her head back slightly.

He slammed into her with near violence, shoving apart her legs even further, and planting her firmly against the saddle. Filled, Carly let out a delighted squeal, all the nerves in her body coming alive with that first stroke. His body crashed into hers again, then withdrew, and then came on again, hammering at her. Carly let out a moan as she leaned further over the saddle, her ample breasts bouncing and slapping against the cool leather in a frantic rhythm. Carly felt the pressure building low in her abdomen, and the scent of good leather, fur, and Krissik's own musk mingled in her nose, driving her to a higher level of ecstasy.

"Faster...faster...faster..."

The wet sound of their bodies slapping together was almost too much to bear. Carly's legs gave out, and Krissik grabbed at her waist, holding her up while she screamed and thrashed beneath him. Her orgasm rolled through her, a hot, rippling, golden beast that stole her breath and her voice, and left her nerveless.

A moment later, Krissik grunted his own completion, and his strokes slowed, growing gentler.

Carly stared down at the floor, boneless, her mouth dry. She was not entirely sure she knew her own name, much less what they had just done in Samantha's tack room.

"Thought you say no doing this anymore," Krissik mumbled into Carly's neck. His breath whooshed down her spine, and her nipples hardened into peaks.

Carly wriggled slightly, pushing her butt up against his groin. "Couldn't be helped. You were just so *ravishing* in your makeup."

Krissik reached down and slapped a hand against her ass. "Maybe you can practice it more?"

TEN

They lay together in the barn until the mid-afternoon sun reached its zenith, surrounding them in a pool of brilliant, golden light. Carly flung a hand over her face to ward off the harshest of the sun's rays. She turned herself so that she was nestled properly against Krissik's shoulder, using him as a sort of living, breathing pair of sunglasses. She ran a hand up and down the soft white fur on his chest, and then scratched at a spot low on his belly. She grinned at his satisfied purr as it rumbled through the shed. Carly thought it was adorable that he could make such a sound—something that Samantha had mentioned Rikist could no longer do—and it never failed to amuse her.

"Samantha will wonder where you stay," Krissik said, his voice a rumbling purr against her face.

"Unlikely."

"Samantha will wonder where you are."

As long as it was not Mandy who came after her,

Carly did not really care. She was comfortable here, snug and loved, breathing in Krissik's distinctive scent of male musk and kitten fur. She did not care if no one ever came looking for them. She could just stay in this tack room forever.

Carly's eyes snapped open.

Forever's a long time.

The spell at least partially broken, Carly sat up, running her fingers down Krissik's furred chest. She looked around the tack room, at the dust particles floating in the air, at the saddle they had so recently defiled. She could not expect Krissik to stay here, hidden away, any more than she would want the same thing for herself. This little tack room might be fun for an illicit tryst, but she could not hope to live out her days here, just as Krissik could not live out his life on the farm, never seeing anything of the world.

She wrapped her arms around her knees.

"Will makeup work?" Krissik asked. "I know I look foolish, but is functional, yes?"

Carly smiled again at the thought of his pallid, expressionless face. "Yes," she said. "We can probably cover your stripes with practice. I guess that's a good thing, isn't it? We just need the right color and the right technique."

Krissik ran a finger down her bare upper arm. "So, I maybe go outside one day."

Carly nodded, though she made sure to keep her gaze guarded. "*Might*, Kris. And you might always look a little off up close. If we can fabricate a story, that might be something. Like, say you're a burn victim or had plastic surgery."

After a pause, he said, "Is something."

Carly got up and pulled her underwear back on, then began the quest for her jeans. She found them hurled underneath a row of bridles and paused to dust off the denim before sliding it back over her legs.

Krissik watched her. "You never want a mate, do you?"

He was so matter-of-fact about it, Carly did not think twice before answering. "Nope."

"Why?"

"Men—mates—hold you back. I wanted to see the world, and do what I wanted when I wanted. In a relationship, you have to think of the other person—their feelings. I knew I would just end up hurting someone I was with because I've been hurt so often. So many times... so I avoid getting into relationships."

She pulled on her bra and T-shirt and frowned at the hole she found in the shoulder. Krissik had yanked it off her a little too hard.

"Where I come from, relate-ships is rare," Krissik said.

"Because there are no females?"

"*Few* females," he corrected her. "Most is royalty families. Matches be arranged. You do not meet and make choice in a pub."

Carly laughed aloud. "You don't want to meet a girl in a bar anyway, Kris. That's like the first thing they tell kids here when they start dating. If you go into a bar looking for a relationship, you'll find a girl like me."

"A girl like you?"

She bit her lip. "I'm trouble."

"You is," Krissik smiled. "But I like."

At least one of them did.

Krissik still had not started dressing. He studied her and then rose, his muscles rippling beneath tawny skin. Carly glanced down his powerful torso and fixated on that fabulous cock, which seemed to grow under her scrutiny.

She looked away. "Man, I just got dressed again."

"Do you care for I, Carly?"

Having this conversation while Krissik was standing there naked seemed like a not-so-great idea. "Of course, I care for you."

"Then why you no want to be with?"

"For the reasons I just said. I'm bad news in a relationship. I'm too walled off, I guess, is what I'm trying to get at."

Krissik frowned. "Even if I want to do same things? Even if I let you go do those things?"

Carly wished he would get dressed. "How is that fair to you? Relationships are about equals. Give and take. Two people sharing and building a life together. They aren't about someone waiting at home while the other goes from hotel to hotel, getting drunk and getting into trouble."

It was something Mandy might have said, now that Carly thought about it. She supposed that meant she was maturing, even if it was at a disastrously slow rate. Maybe at the rate she was going, she would be ready to *try* to have a boyfriend by forty, when she could not get into any of the fun clubs anymore.

Krissik pulled on his boxers and jeans, taking care to turn away from her while he tucked himself into his fly. "Strange world is this, where can turn away from real feeling and no feel guilty for it," he remarked.

"Feelings are a dime a dozen here," Carly said. "Kris, there are women here who would love to be in a relationship with you—"

Too late, Carly realized what she had just said.

Krissik pulled on his shirt and began buttoning the front. "But I can no go out to find these girls," he said. "I here. On the farm. With you." He gestured to the tack room. "Do I must stay in here until sister Mandy leaves?"

"I don't know. Probably. I think Samantha might end up giving her your room."

Krissik looked around the tack room, obviously sizing up his new digs. "This place is bigger, anyway."

At least now, they were back to a businesslike interaction. "Let me go talk to Sam, see what we can work out."

There seemed little else to do but leave him there; she could not very well bring him into the house, and with Mandy present, Krissik probably could not leave the barn, either.

Carly leaned out to kiss him. Krissik turned his head away, and Carly caught his cheek instead. The snub stung more than she wanted to admit, so she bowed her head and slipped out of the tack room and back into the barn before hurrying to the house.

MANDY WAS in the shower when Carly made it back inside. They were going to be squeezed in pretty tightly; for now, Mandy had the last guest bedroom—though she was, no doubt, wondering why there were men's items on the dressers. Carly wandered through the house until she found Samantha propped up against the pillows in her bedroom, flipping through the television channels with a slightly glazed expression on her face.

Carly perched at the edge of the bed. "News not doing much for you?"

"I keep worrying that I'm going to see something about him. That he's in some trouble... I guess he's not. Or I guess the government would hush it up, anyway." Samantha muted the television and turned to Carly, her drawn features even harsher in the dim light. "Mandy thinks someone is following her. That's why she came out here."

Carly was not sure why a ranch in a rural area was a good place to hide out—fewer people were around to see you if you were snatched. "Ex-boyfriend?" she guessed, even though Mandy had never so much as expressed interest in a man when she had known her.

Samantha folded her hands over the remote. "She

says it's a black van, or a black car. Usually, she's pretty oblivious to her surroundings, so I'd say it's a good bet she's right."

"Sloppy stalkers," Carly said.

Samantha flashed her an uncomfortable stare. "I'm not worried about *stalkers*, Carly. I'm worried about—well, you know."

She was worried about the very men Rikist had set out to stop. Carly could not help but recall her last conversation with him, standing in the kitchen that night as she dried the dishes.

The government in my world, what's left of it, is vengeful, he had said. *Samantha doesn't want to listen to it, but it's true. One of you needs to know.*

"How would they even know her? Did they have your ID or anything?"

Samantha shrugged. "I don't know. Rikist didn't want to explain how things worked there; I think he didn't want to scare me. And Krissik...I never got around to asking Krissik."

Carly supposed it was going to fall to her to do the asking. "Speaking of Krissik, are we just locking him in the barn until she leaves?"

"She's not leaving. I'm keeping her here until we find out who's following her and stop them."

"Then what are you going to tell her about Krissik?"

"I guess... I mean..."

"And when Rikist comes back?"

Samantha did not answer her.

"What are you going to tell her about your alien lover?" Carly asked.

"I'm sorry, but last time I checked you had one of those, too."

"Yes, but I'm a bad influence on you. That sort of craziness is *expected* from me. Carly and her cat-man." She grimaced at the thought, and then shrugged it off. "*You're* her sister. You'll have to explain it to her."

They sat in stormy silence for a moment. Carly found herself wondering if she was going to be able to get along with anyone today. At the rate she was going, she would piss off even the animals by the end of the afternoon.

Samantha folded her arms across her chest. "Rikist can pass. We'll put in some contacts. He'll be unusual-looking, but she probably won't notice."

"And what happens when they bump into each other in the middle of the night, looking for the bathroom?"

Samantha scowled at her. "Why are you so unpleasant?"

"Why are *you* so irrational? You have two aliens living on the farm, Sam! This isn't *E.T.*, and they're not going home. They're *living here*. They intend to stay!" At least, one of them did—but Carly was not about to get into specifics about that. "It's *me*, Sam. You can be a bitch to me if you want, but don't let it screw up everything you've got going here."

Go easy on her, some distant, logical part of her brain cautioned. Samantha had been through a rough time, and she was still pretty sick. That bad of a flu, coupled with the lingering news about her sterility, could make anyone irrational. But then, Samantha had never exactly been the most sensible one when confronted with bizarre situations. She had not needed to be—she had been the good student, the hardworking girl she had been brought up to be. It had been Carly who had gotten into all kinds of shenanigans.

But locking Krissik in the barn and not telling Mandy about Rikist just seemed like begging for a loud, possibly destructive confrontation.

The shower stopped. Carly bit her tongue; Mandy could come waltzing out and burst in on them at any moment.

Samantha looked at the television. "I don't want to deal with this right now."

"So, you just want to...what? Sit here and pretend it isn't happening? What are you going to do if Rikist comes back tonight?"

"He won't."

The flat tone in her friend's voice indicated the conversation was over. Samantha had effectively shut down; Carly sighed and turned away from her. "I'll have Kris stay in the barn tonight."

"Tell him to watch for any visitors."

"I'm sure he'll be glad to guard your farm, despite being kicked out of the house," Carly snapped.

She stomped away, knowing she was acting childish, but not quite able to stop herself. Samantha was going to have to come clean about Rikist at some point, especially if she intended to keep him around for the long haul.

The long haul. That was a laugh. When was the last time she had thought of any sort of haul—be it long, moderate, or short? Carly lived from moment to moment, enjoying her life as she could. Planning ahead only got in the way.

The news about Mandy being followed was troubling, though. Mandy had always been a good kid, had always kept her nose clean. There really were not that many people out there she could manage to upset, tick off, or even attract the attention of. That left the unsettling idea of someone in the alien world looking for revenge.

There was nothing they could do about it now, of course.

Carly put together a basket of food—some leftover ham from the other night, a few bottles of water, a slice of the cake Samantha had made a few days prior, and some other odds and ends in case Krissik decided he wanted a late-night snack. She tossed in some magazines, and then popped into her bedroom to collect the book he had been reading.

Krissik's regular room—Mandy's room now, she supposed—had the door shut. It was just as well that Krissik had pretty much moved in with Carly; all his stuff was already in her room. Not that Krissik had all that much, anyway. Interstellar travelers tended to pack light.

Carly carried the basket and some blankets out to the barn.

She did not see him inside. "Kris?" she called.

His head appeared, upside-down, from the hayloft. "Hello."

"What are you doing up there?"

"Looking for where to sleep. It smells nice here." He rolled over and stretched out a hand. "Come up!"

Carly hefted up the basket.

Krissik stretched one long arm down for it. She passed it up, and then climbed up the ladder into the loft, pausing once to sneeze as the sweet, fragrant scent of hay filled her nostrils. It was warmer up here, and the air was somewhat staler, but Krissik had found himself a very nice stack to relax against. He flopped into it now, grinning at her.

"I always wondered what one of these looked like," Carly said. "I've been all over the world, but never up in a hayloft."

"I like how is smells!" Krissik stretched out, rolling around in the hay like a big, satisfied barn cat.

Carly had to bite back a smile.

"How is Samantha?" Krissik asked.

"She's not feeling well. She gave Mandy your room."

Krissik helped Carly stretch some blankets over the pile of hay and then began rummaging through the basket while she stretched out on their makeshift bed.

"Kris," she said.

"Hmm?" He held up a magazine with a reality star on the cover. "Are lips normal?"

"Doubt they're real. Hey, Mandy thinks she's being followed."

Krissik put down the magazine immediately.

Carly sat up. "Is it possible—I guess, I mean, what's the likelihood that it's from your world? Could they track her because of us?"

Krissik sat down opposite her.

"Women is no preselected," he said. He paused, perhaps to consider his next words. "The ones at checkpoint—"

"At *the* checkpoint."

"Fine—whoever is there, we take. Samantha no have her diver's license at my apartment—"

Diver's license? It took Carly a moment to figure out what he meant. "Oh. Driver's license."

"Yes, that. I see no way to track her, or her sister. Officially."

Carly digested that statement. "Officially?"

"Our planet do work with some of your government," he said. "Is no hard for them to know who is taken from the hotel and track down family members... your technology is very similar to ours."

Carly nodded. Samantha had talked about being able to use the aliens' television, and most of the tech in Krissik's apartment had seemed like heavily upgraded versions of existing Earth appliances.

Maybe they were.

"Do we get most of our technology from you?" she asked. "Tablets and stuff?"

Krissik grinned. She took that as a *yes*.

"So, it's like a trade? Women for tech?"

"Sort of." He worried at his lower lip, one gleaming fang catching some of the light from the first floor. "Your government is afraid of us, I think. Rikist would know more about the pacific."

"Specifics?"

Krissik paused and then nodded. "But they do as we say, because we have jumpgate power. They fear if we were angry."

Carly puzzled over that last statement for a moment, and then returned to the matter at hand. "But Mandy *could* be followed by—I don't know, Men in Black?"

Krissik's brow furrowed.

"Ah, shit, I'll have to show you that movie. I mean it's possible that someone in our government is keeping an eye on her?"

"Yes," he said. "Though I no know how likely."

"I'm working on a freaking *farm* and Samantha has two aliens squatting on her couch," she pointed out. "I feel like we passed *likely* a while ago."

Krissik smiled at her sarcastic tone, though his slightly puzzled stare indicated he didn't quite understand everything she said. That was all right; Carly had had enough of rational, worried thinking for the day, and wanted something useless and trivial to distract herself with.

"Maybe you can give Rikist a call in the morning," she said, "For now, do you want to learn about gossip?"

"Gos-sip," Krissik repeated.

Carly moved over so she was sitting next to him. She stretched the magazine out across their laps and tapped the face of the reality star with the giant lips.

"This is a very famous person in our world."

"Why?"

Carly shrugged. "Actually, I don't know. She has a film crew following her around, taping her daily life. A lot of people do this. For some reason, millions like to see her lounging around in her beachfront mansion."

"But why?"

Carly had no answer for that. "Because humans are illogical?"

Krissik nudged her. "You don't say."

She smiled. "Smartass."

"Did I say correctly?"

"Yup." She let him fold an arm around her shoulders. "You definitely did."

ELEVEN

"And it is just *so gorgeous* out here."

Carly's eyes snapped open. Who was talking? Why did her back hurt? And why did her bedroom smell like the barn?

"Yeah...I'll be back soon enough...just want to relax awhile, you know, get back in touch with nature."

Her eyes focused on the bale of hay directly opposite her. Oh. It smelled like a barn because she was *in* a barn—that made sense.

"Sister Mandy is talking to a friend," Krissik whispered in Carly's ear. "She is been outside at least fifteen minutes."

Krissik had much better hearing; it stood to reason that he would hear someone speaking much sooner than Carly would. Even so, he should have woken her up. Carly sat up, brushed some strands of hay from her hair, and shook her head. "Sleeping in a hayloft is definitely best left to teenagers. I feel like someone punched my spine."

"I feel most excellent." Krissik hopped to his feet and extended his hand, then pulled her upright. Carly flinched, her back creaking loudly as she straightened up.

"I know..." Mandy was still talking on the phone with her friend. "It's just really great to get away from school...from everyone...yeah...yeah, there's a barn!"

"Uh-oh," Carly said.

"I dunno, Samantha's friend said there was something wrong with it, but let's see..."

There it was: the sound of Mandy fiddling with the latch.

Carly shoved Krissik backward toward the giant stack of hay in the center of the loft. "Hide in there!" she whispered, shoving fistfuls of hay across his face. "Don't let her see you!"

"But—"

Carly pushed bales of hay in front of the pile, and then sprinted for the ladder, swinging her way down it just as Mandy pushed the door open.

The two women stared at each other for a moment.

"Good morning!" Carly chirped. "Did you sleep well?"

Mandy nodded. Then, into her phone, she said, "I gotta go—call you later!"

She slid the phone into her pocket. "I thought I would come to see the horses," she said.

"Oh, they're all turned out. I told you last night,

remember?" Carly raced through all the varied excuses she could possibly dream up.

I left something in here. I come here to meditate. I like the smell of hay.

"So, what are you doing in here, then?" Mandy asked.

None of her excuses sounded plausible.

"There's an alien in the hayloft," Carly said.

Mandy's eyes widened slightly. "Right," she said.

Carly smirked. *She probably thinks I'm high.*

"I still need to clean out the stalls," she said. "The horses are out, but we can't just let the manure fester. Then it *really* starts to stink."

Mandy cocked her head to the side, her gaze focusing on Carly's neck. "You have a bruise, it looks like."

"Huh?"

Mandy whipped out her phone, switched around the camera to forward-facing, and handed it to Carly. "There. On your neck. Looks kind of like a hickey."

Carly stared at the blotchy, reddish-purple mass on her neck. Two smaller bruises were on the outside—fang marks, no doubt. It looked kind of like a hickey because it *was* a hickey. The fang marks, at least, were sufficiently throwing Mandy.

"Damn," Carly said. "I don't know what that is. Some of the goats get a little rough—I wonder if one neck-butted me."

She regretted the comment immediately. Getting

neck-butted by *any* animal did not seem like an event that would slip from memory anytime soon.

Mandy, that sweet, miniature version of Samantha, seemed willing to let the subject drop. "So, the horses are outside?"

"Yeah, in the paddocks."

Someone sneezed.

Mandy glanced upward, toward the hayloft. "Was that...?"

"Barn cat," Carly said.

Krissik sneezed again.

"I didn't know cats sneezed," Mandy said.

"All animals sneeze." At least, she hoped they did.

Mandy shrugged, apparently deciding the conversation with her sister's weird friend had gone on long enough. "I'll go see the horses, then...see you at breakfast!"

She started for the door. Krissik sneezed again.

Carly covered her mouth and nose with her hands. "Sorry, that one was me."

"Bless you," Mandy said politely. She left in a hurry.

Carly waited until the girl's footsteps retreated from the barn, and then she scurried back up the ladder. Krissik poked his head out of the pile, his eyes and nose reddened. "Nose is—" He sneezed again. "Is *wrong* with me?"

"Apparently, submerging you in hay is a bad idea." Carly pulled Krissik out of the pile and began tugging long pieces of hay out of his hair and clothing.

"Sorry. We're going to have to figure out what to do with her."

Krissik sneezed again.

Mandy fished around in the basket, came up with a tissue, and handed it to him. "Here...use this. And why did you give me a hickey?"

"Hick-ey?"

Carly pointed at the mark on her neck.

Krissik, to his credit, gaped at it. "Not remembering," he said. "I maybe been asleep..."

Marvelous. Carly was sharing a bed with an alien who chewed on people in his sleep.

"Try not to do it again, will you?" she asked. "She might not buy the goat story next time."

"Buy?" Krissik's brow furrowed. "She pay you for what?"

Carly stared. Was Krissik trying to mess with her? Sometimes, it was hard to tell.

No, she sighed. From the look on his face, Krissik was dead serious.

Krissik grew alert, lifting his head into the air. His nostrils flared as he sniffed, suddenly a bloodhound picking up a scent. Carly was not sure whether to pet him on the head or back away.

"Samantha is coming," he announced.

"You can smell people?" She could not keep a note of astonishment out of her voice.

He tapped a finger to his nose. "Useful."

If he could smell people approaching, what else could he smell? Carly imagined the myriad scents he must be exposed to daily, and almost blushed. Was *that* how he knew what to stroke and poke?

The barn door opened.

Carly stepped to the edge of the hayloft so she could see Samantha. Her friend looked up at her, shook her head, and then closed the barn door. "I was going to ask why Mandy thinks you're is shagging some mysterious stable hand," Samantha said. "But that thing on your neck pretty much explains it."

Carly slapped her hand against the mark on her neck. "It was a goat. A goat, I tell you."

Krissik sneezed.

Samantha's eyebrows went up. "She also said he probably had allergies... Krissik, that's not subtle at all."

Carly started climbing down the ladder. "Is she gone?"

"Yeah. She ran into town to pick up some more of the shitty pink stomach stuff." Samantha leaned against one of the stalls, a hand resting on her middle. "I'm still not feeling good."

"You no smell right," Krissik offered, climbing down the ladder behind Carly.

Samantha sent him a sour look. "Appreciate that, Krissik. Nothing makes a girl feel better than slamming the way she smells."

"So, what are we going to do?" Carly asked. "Leave Kris in the barn? Limit Mandy to certain parts of the ranch?"

"She won't like that." Samantha appeared to ruminate over the possibilities. "Give me another day to get over this bug, and I'll talk to her about what really happened. She's going to meet Rikist at some point, anyway, and she'd know something wasn't quite right about him."

"What are you going to tell her?" Carly asked.

Samantha shrugged. "It'll have to be the truth... I just don't know how she's going to react. This is going to be a huge shock."

Ya think? If Carly had not experienced the hotel invasion herself, she would not have believed a thing. She would have packed Samantha off to the nearest psych ward and crossed her fingers that some miracle medication could help erase her friend's crazy hallucinations. Mandy might try to do the same thing when she heard Samantha was housing two tiger-men from outer space.

Tiger-Men from Outer Space. It sounded like a fabulous, cheesy B-movie.

Or a porno. Depending on the time of day...

"I think what I'll do is tell her; and then, Kris, you'll be waiting in the wings."

Krissik frowned. "I no have wings."

"It's an expression...you'll be ready to come out and be our display model. Show her what you are."

Krissik nodded.

Carly agreed it might be better to go with Krissik instead of Rikist. Krissik was tall and intimidating, but not quite the hulking specimen that Rikist was. He lacked the military bearing that could be terrifying on its own. It took time for Rikist to warm up to people, but Krissik, who borderlined bubbly, would probably appear warmer and much more approachable. His random knowledge of historical Earth might even prove endearing.

Or Mandy might run away screaming. That was what a practical person would do.

Carly cleared her throat. "So. What if she runs?"

Neither of them answered.

"Sam..."

"I know, I know I need to think about these things." Samantha drew the back of her hand across her eyes and took a breath. "If she runs, we'll stop her. I don't like it, but we have to be practical here. I don't even know who she'd tell, or what she'd do... but it's for her own good, and for ours. Okay?" She directed that question at Carly, who nodded.

"I'm going to head back into the house." She eyed Carly. "You might want to take a shower. Krissik, if you can quick..."

Krissik bowed his head at her apologetic tone. "I understand, Samantha."

Carly watched Krissik's claws flex, a sure sign that he was not happy. But for now, he seemed to be tolerating the situation.

Carly gathered her purse and walked back to the house with Samantha as Krissik hung back.

"I had the strangest dreams last night," Samantha said.

"Yeah?"

"Just weird and disjointed... I don't remember

them, but they were strange." She glanced at Carly. "Did you dream?"

Carly shook her head. "If I did, I don't recall them."

Whether Carly was too tired to relive her memories or Krissik's presence had driven them off, she was not entirely sure. But she had not felt so rested in days, despite the ache in her back.

"I can't believe you slept in the barn," Samantha said with a grin as they climbed the porch steps.

"Me neither. I'm going to regret it later."

INSIDE, Carly locked herself in the bathroom, stripping off her clothes and leaping into the shower before it had fully heated up. *Yes.* This was what she needed: a thorough scrubbing and some flower-scented shampoo. Bits of hay continued to fall out of her hair, and she scrubbed at her hands and face until the water ran dark and her skin glowed pink and raw.

How did I get so dirty sleeping outside for one night? It was really kind of astonishing. *Mom would be so horrified right now.*

It was a good kind of dirt, though. She could not quite put her finger on it, but Samantha's farm was starting to feel like home.

Maybe Carly would be able to let it stick this time.

TWELVE

By mid-afternoon, Carly had fed all the animals, cleaned out the stalls, collected eggs from the henhouse, and brought Krissik and Rodolfo sandwiches to eat out in the fields. She shambled up the front steps, exhausted, her feet dragging against the floorboards.

Inside, she heard Mandy coaching someone through something. "You just pee on it."

"I'm not pregnant, Mandy," Samantha said. She sounded tired. Carly paused, but both women turned to her when she paused in the kitchen. A few bags of groceries were on the counter, along with odds and ends from the big pharmacy in Grand Junction.

Samantha held a small, rectangular box with elegant pink lettering on the side. Carly knew instantly what it contained; she'd had enough pregnancy scares during college to personally finance First Response. Somehow, her period had always shown up, and in junior year, she finally got herself on birth control. But Samantha—practical, calm Samantha—had probably never had the pleasure.

"The flu doesn't make you bloated," Mandy said. "And you were talking about that new boyfriend. Just take it."

"I don't want to."

"Please? For me?"

Samantha turned to Carly, the plea for help evident in her eyes. Carly could not even shrug at her; what could Samantha say that would not lead to some sort of interrogation, and then an explanation? Mandy was just the concerned younger sister right now. If Samantha broached the infertility subject, Mandy would seize on that and want to know where she had been, who had done the testing. All the other questions no one was ready to answer.

Carly offered her an apologetic smile. "It's pretty easy," she said. "Look, at least it'll be one less thing on your mind, right?"

Samantha's expression suggested Carly would regret that statement later on. Still, she offered them both a clipped nod and took the pregnancy test into the bathroom with her.

Mandy hovered outside the door. "You have to pee on it," she called.

"I'm well aware of how they work," Samantha snapped. "Now, will you go back into the kitchen? I can't pee while I can hear you breathing."

After a moment, Mandy retreated to the kitchen.

She and Carly looked at each other, silence stretching between them. Why was making conversation with Mandy always so hard?

Come on, Samantha, Carly thought. *How long does it take to take a whiz?*

Carly considered reaching for the radio; some noise would be better than none, after all. But Mandy might perceive that as rude. So, she smiled and said, "How was town?"

"It's great. I understand why Dad loved it so much." Mandy paused. "I do kind of like cities, though. Grand Junction isn't exactly my idea ...well, of a good time."

Well look at that, we've got something in common.

"Me, too. I like it here, though. The fresh air, the animals, seeing the stars at night...." That was something of a lie; she had been so busy with Krissik since coming out here that she simply had not been bothered to look at the stars. But she had seen them last night when she trundled out to the barn, and she knew there was less light pollution out here in "the sticks."

Mandy nodded but did not have anything to add.

The toilet flushed. Mandy and Carly turned as one toward the hallway. The bathroom sink turned on, ran for thirty seconds, and then shut off. Then the door opened, and Samantha stepped out.

She was holding the test stick, her expression unreadable.

Carly waited for the inevitable. *See, Mandy, I'm not pregnant; it's just the flu.*

But Samantha did not say those words, and Carly realized that her blank stare was not from lack of emotion. It was an expression of shock.

Mandy edged closer, her head canted toward the test.

"Oh," she said.

"Oh?" Carly crossed the distance between herself and Samantha. There were two pink lines across the test. Samantha's hand was starting to shake. "Oh, fuck."

Carly and Mandy caught Samantha just before she collapsed to the ground. Carly helped her to a kitchen chair, and Mandy took the test, her brief triumph quickly evaporating into uncertainty. What was one supposed to say in these situations, anyway?

Mandy sprang into action first. "We need to call your boyfriend," she said. "What's his name? Rick?"

Samantha still possessed enough fortitude to look despairingly at Carly.

"No," Carly said. She had to keep this going as long as she could. "First off, Mandy, did you get another test?"

Mandy shook her head.

"Then go into town and grab one... get two more. And bring food, will you? In the meantime, I'm going to book Samantha a doctor's appointment, so we can know for sure. *Then* we're going to tell Rik."

Samantha slumped back in her chair.

Mandy wavered. "But, we need to call him..."

"We want to make sure this is for real. False positives happen." When Mandy raised an eyebrow, Carly sucked it up and closed her eyes. "Look, I know, okay? Let's not scare the hell out of Sam or her man before we have to. Go get those damn tests."

Mandy grabbed her keys and purse from the counter and bounded out the door. Carly turned to Samantha, not entirely sure what she ought to say, or whether her commentary would be welcome.

Samantha shuddered and then lifted her head. "Do you think it could be real?" she asked.

"I don't know." Carly paused. "Does Kris...I mean...did he...?" He was the only person Carly could think of who might know what was going on, but Carly did not want to go to him if it meant betraying Samantha's trust.

"He knows," Samantha whispered. "It's the reason Rikist had to get me out. The sterile women there... they do terrible things to them..."

"Things?" Carly asked.

"Let's just say that Rikist saved my life."

Samantha shook her head. Apparently, it was too much to even discuss.

Carly's stomach knotted into a cold ball of churning rose vines. She sat with her friend for another few minutes, her hand resting atop Samantha's cold fingers. Samantha herself shivered, her teeth beginning to chatter together.

Carly stood up. "Let's get you back to bed."

"No. I can't stay another minute in there. Just... help me to the couch?"

They made their way to the den, and Carly found a heavy blanket to wrap around Samantha's shoulders.

"Okay," Carly said, handing Samantha the remote. "I want you to focus on ridiculous trash shows for a while. Keep your mind off of things. I'll go talk to Krissik. You *can* get in touch with Rikist, right?"

Samantha shook her head. "He calls every now and then, but always from a different number. He had Rodolfo pick him up a bunch of disposable phones...."

Carly nibbled on her lower lip. That would make things difficult. "Okay. So, if Mandy asks—and she will—you just tell her he's traveling for work and can't always be reached. Oil rig or something like that. I'll be back as soon as I can. Okay?"

Samantha squeezed her fingers. "You're a good friend, Carly."

Carly warmed briefly at the sentiment, then hurried out of the house.

The air felt more alive now, warmer, even electric.

Samantha's pregnant.

They had talked about children once, during a drunken night back in the dorms. Carly had never been sure about kids. Samantha had very much wanted them—at some undisclosed point in the future—and the information about infertility must have been a crushing blow.

But if the testing on the other world was wrong...

"Krissik!" she burst into the barn. He was not there; she had shouted into empty box stalls and particles filtering through the sunlight. Of course. He was out in the fields, tending to the fruits and vegetables. Carly scampered out to the back of the barn, and held her hands over her eyes, scanning the fields.

There: a pinprick of motion.

She took a breath and ran.

Her lungs burned. Running had never been her forte; the last time she had really run had been in Las Vegas, and again, the green-tinged mist threatened to close in on her consciousness. *No. Go away.* Samantha might be having a baby. That was so much more important than Carly's fear-laced memories.

This isn't about me, it's about Samantha.

Krissik either smelled or saw her coming and ended up meeting her halfway.

"What?" he demanded, grasping Carly's shoulders. He held her upright as she tried to catch her breath. "Is wrong? The farm? Is there—"

Carly waved a hand, shook her head. "No," she rasped. "No, it's... Sam took a test... she's pregnant...."

Krissik's face froze, and his hands remained rooted to Carly's shoulders. "Pregnant," he said.

"Mandy made her take a test. She's gone into town for more to retest to be sure. Samantha said your doctor said she couldn't—I guess what I mean is—could it be wrong?"

Krissik's eyes lifted, his gaze moving past Carly, focusing on something behind her—the house, perhaps, and its lone occupant.

Something flashed in Krissik's eyes, something feral that Carly had not seen before in her sex-kitten's face. She swallowed as she felt the tips of Krissik's claws nip at her skin, and his breathing quickened.

Krissik forced the words out. "The test he gave could been wrong. Humans is different than us. I wanted a retest. I begged for one, really." He spoke slowly, choosing his words with great care. "I never... Samantha, I mean... yes is possible."

Krissik lifted his hands to the sides of his head and held them there as if he were trying to cover his ears. Carly stared at him, not entirely sure what to make of the gesture. His eyes squeezed shut, and he briefly turned away from her, breathing deeply.

Carly stepped back, feeling she was intruding upon something intensely private. Krissik's shoulder's trembled, a silent bout of emotion raging under his skin.

When Krissik returned his attention to her, his face was guarded. "Yes, is possible," he announced. "Though we must know for sure. And... I wonder when it happened...."

There it was: that stab of jealousy. Rikist had what Krissik wanted—the mate, the baby, all of it—and it might have all been Krissik's, had life played out a little differently.

Had an earlier test not given a false negative.

Carly looked away, her eyes stinging. She dug a toe into the dirt. "Are you OK?" she asked.

"Yes," the word came out as a hiss.

Krissik did not sound okay. Composed, yes; but not gleeful. Maybe he was just as shocked as Samantha.

"If you want to talk about it, or something...."

Then what? I'll say, 'I understand,' and give him a hug? I don't understand. I cannot possibly understand.

Carly's good intentions would splatter in front of her, as they usually did, and she would wind up alienating him and leaving her alone. She never had been much good at giving advice.

Krissik rubbed the back of his neck. "Let us go back to house," he said. "We is company... we will keep her company," he corrected himself.

"And Mandy?"

Carly saw the *Oh, shit* expression pass over Krissik's face.

He shrugged. "If Samantha pregnant, Mandy will need to know. Rikist will come back right away."

"But until then—"

A growl built in Krissik's throat. "You want me stay in barn? Talk to Samantha on phone, maybe?" His voice grew clipped, angry. Frustration and sorrow had mixed together, taking a toll on his English conversational skills. "I do that. OK."

Carly reached for his arm, but Krissik stepped back. "That's not what I meant, Krissik, and I think you know that." Carly gauged the amount of time Mandy had been gone. "Come to the house. You can talk to Samantha. If Mandy comes back, you can hide in my room until she's distracted, OK?"

Krissik just stared at her, his cheeks red. His nose twitched.

She almost smiled. It must have been one of Krissik's frustrated ticks, but it was something she had never seen on him before. She was glad for the sudden distraction from the pain in his eyes.

"Fine," Krissik said, heaving a sigh. "Fine, fine."

FOUR MORE TESTS, four more positives. Samantha held up a hand when Mandy tried to press the fifth one on her. "I'm all for covering our bases, Mandy, but I can't pee anymore today."

The three women looked at the arrangement of tests on the newspaper that Mandy had brought back from town. The first test had a place of honor in the upper corner, right above the news about a corrupt local politician. Five tests, five positives. It was probably time to break out the burgers and fries Mandy had brought back along with all the tests.

Samantha let out a sigh. "Well, girls, I guess I'm knocked up."

Mandy seemed at a loss for words.

"Congratulations?" Carly asked.

Samantha's smile was thin but genuine. "You don't have to walk on eggshells. This is a lot earlier than I would have liked it to be, but it's good news...." Her hand drifted down low to rest over her abdomen. "I'm having a baby. Holy shit!"

Carly clapped her hands together, eager to be of use. "Okay. Do you have a card for your doctor? Let's get you in and get you all checked out and find out how far along you are... *do* you know how far along you are?"

"Um...." Samantha tapped her fingers in the air. "It couldn't be more than a month or two?"

Mandy's jaw dropped. "How long have you been seeing this guy?"

Carly rolled her eyes. *Oh, here comes the judgment.*

"We'll deal with that later," Carly said, eager to get them back onto safe ground. "Samantha, where's your doctor's card?"

"In the address book near the phone."

It took Carly five minutes to reach the doctor's answering service, and she managed to book an appointment in two days. That meant Samantha would have to live in a state of suspense, but Carly figured that *five* pregnancy tests really could not be wrong.

Carly thought of Krissik locked away back in the barn, and her heart sank. Krissik had come inside briefly before Mandy returned. He asked Samantha a few questions: how she was feeling, what, exactly, the doctor in his world had said to her, if anything—and if she was pleased. Samantha had answered in the affirmative and had then asked if Rikist would be happy.

Krissik had smiled and gently touched the side of Samantha's cheek. "He will be thrilled," he had said, while his own heart seemed to break as he disappeared outside.

Carly blinked away the vision and turned back to

the girls. "Tuesday at ten o'clock," she announced. "One of us can drive you."

Samantha nodded.

Belatedly, Mandy glanced at the bags of takeout, still sitting on the kitchen counter. "So... victory dinner? I figured no one would want to cook, but it's probably cold by now."

"Sure. I'll just nuke them in the microwave. Mandy, can you set the table? Samantha, you just...sit there and supervise."

They managed to get the food on the table within five minutes. The mood lifted as the fries and shakes were distributed.

Carly took small bites of her lukewarm burger. She figured she could save half of it for Krissik.

They ate in silence for a few minutes before Mandy asked, "So, how long have you been dating this guy?"

Carly appreciated Mandy at least she reined in her disapproval when it came to her sister. She was not sure how much more confrontation Samantha could handle in her admittedly delicate state.

"A few months," Samantha answered. "It got serious, really fast."

"How'd you meet him?"

"Traveling," Samantha paused, her eyes averted.

Carly could see the wheels turning in Samantha's head.

Samantha smiled at Mandy. "I met Rick's brother first, and we met through him."

"Cool! What does he do?"

Mandy was trying so, so hard, and Samantha seemed at a genuine loss for words. Carly kicked herself for them not working out a story yet—there had not been time, no one had cared enough, and besides, they had this idyllic existence at the farm. Carly had known it would come to a crashing halt—all good things did—but even she had thought there would be a little more time.

She tuned the others out as Samantha fabricated this tale of Rikist—or Rick, as she called him—as a self-starting market strategist who traveled a lot for work. Her mind relaxed as the old Samantha came back, and her love of writing and novels shining as the lie grew.

By the time the others had finished their small talk, Carly had wrapped up her burger and tucked it into the fridge. She helped Mandy clean up the kitchen, and then checked the clock on the microwave. Eight o'clock.

Carly excused herself and retreated to her bedroom, closing the door softly behind her.

Carly sat back on her bed and let out a breath. She could not hope to understand what Krissik was feeling right now, just as she could not hope to understand Samantha's present condition. She could be there for both of them and listen to their problems, but as for what they were going through....

Carly had never felt so lost.

She stood and opened her bedroom window, letting in the evening breeze. The air was still hot, but at least it licked the stale sweat off her skin and helped release the pressure pounding against her temples.

For a brief, wild moment, Carly considered just letting Krissik sneak in and sleep inside. Mandy would not be coming into her room, right? And Krissik could come in through the window.

Then Carly quickly dismissed the thought; if Samantha needed something in the night, Mandy would not hesitate to burst into Carly's room without knocking. It would be bad enough if Mandy caught some random man in Carly's bed, but Krissik with his distinctive eyes and stripes would blow their newly-constructed lie right out of the water.

Carly rubbed her eyes with the palms of her hands and turned away from the window. No, she'd be sleeping alone tonight. For all Carly knew, after today's revelations and Krissik's reaction, she could be alone for a very long time.

She sniffled and gathered some of Krissik's things from the dresser, shoving them into a tote.

Safety first, even now.

THIRTEEN

When the house grew quiet, and Carly was relatively confident that the sisters were either in bed or visiting quietly in Samantha's bedroom, Carly made her move. She left her window open, thinking she would enjoy a gentle breeze the next morning, and closed her bedroom door, tiptoed to the kitchen, and grabbed her half-burger and a bottle of water. She could not risk heating the meal—someone would hear the microwave and come out—and she hoped Krissik would be okay with eating it cold.

Outside, the crisp, cool nighttime air soothed her lungs. She took the porch steps in a single hop and paused to look up at the stars, the Milky Way's thin ribbon winding its way through the bright celestial beings. Krissik's homeworld was out there, somewhere, close enough to be real but yet so far out of reach for her lover.

If I'm feeling alone now, she thought. *I wonder where that puts him with everything.*

Carly found Krissik lounging in the hayloft again. She tossed the burger and water bottle up and then climbed up the ladder to join him. Krissik had draped additional tack blankets over the hay bales and the big pile in the center, effectively stifling some of the scent and dust particles floating around in the stale air.

Carly looked around and gave him her best smile. "I like what you did with the place."

Krissik watched her, no humor in his eyes. He pointed at one of the blanket-covered bales. "Sit?"

Carly sat on one of the covered bales out of Krissik's reach and tossed him the water and burger.

Krissik caught the items without his eyes leaving Carly's face, his reflexes instinctive.

Carly stared back. In the darkness, Krissik's eyes glowed brighter, more reflective. The dark stripes on his face and neck camouflaged him with the shadows, and his face moved in and out of her vision as he lowered his head to inspect what items Carly had offered.

Krissik unwrapped the burger and took a long sniff. He lifted the bun off, and his tongue darted out, lapping gently at the burger patty. He replaced the bread and took his first bite. He chewed thoroughly, swallowed, and twitched his nose.

"Is good," he said. His nose twitched again.

"You've had burgers before, right?"

"No."

"Mandy went to the good place. They have grass-fed beef and some kind of secret marinade."

"I can no compare good or bad." His eyes flicked to her and then away. "No get outside much."

Carly's smile faded, and something tightened deep in her chest. Krissik was not the only one with super senses.

Carly could tell when a fight was brewing.

She swung her legs to straddle the hay bale. She pressed her body down against the bale, trying to mimic one of the back-stretching positions her mother was always using. She heard something pop in her neck, and faint relief trickled down her spine as her muscles relaxed. She slumped and stretched out on her stomach, her head cradled in her folded arms.

Krissik ate loudly, his lips smacking together as he devoured the burger. "Is something I say," he began through a mouthful of food.

"Eat, then talk," Carly said. "It's the human thing to do."

Actually, the human thing would have been to babble right through his mouthful of meat, but Carly was not sure she could watch him gobble and try to have a discussion at the same time. Even Krissik could not make chewing with his open mouth look sexy.

Plus, it gave her a few moments to steel her emotions and prepare for whatever he was about to throw her way.

Carly heard Krissik crumple up the wrapper and suck the last of the juices off his fingers. She closed her eyes as Krissik's footsteps approached, and then she felt the whisper of a touch as he straddled her waist, his fingers touching her back through her T-shirt.

"You are tense," he said.

"Hmm, wonder why."

Krissik dug his thumbs into Carly's shoulders first, rubbing and stretching the muscles before moving down to her waist. Her muscles slowly untangled as he worked.

"More in shoulders," he said.

"More what?"

He thought a moment. "Twists?"

"They're called knots. It's... stress."

Krissik's hands stilled, then fell from her back as he stepped away. "Carly, we need talk."

Carly sighed and then sat up, crossing her arms. "About?"

Krissik took a seat on the bale next to her, his hands folded in his lap. "I am sorry," he said slowly. "For I... *my*, action earlier. About Samantha."

Tears stung at Carly's eyes. No, he did not get to apologize right now and move on just like that.

Suddenly, it was she who wanted to fight.

"What part? You mean you pouting about having to stay in the barn for a few days or the feral spark of rage that her baby isn't yours?"

Surprise and anger flashed over Krissik's face. "You no nothing about—"

"Oh, I get it." Carly nearly leaped to her feet, her hands shaking. "You followed Rikist here, pissed that he took something that was yours. And now that you're stuck here, you've moved on with me because you think you have another shot. And you were OK with that shot because you thought Samantha was damaged goods."

Carly wiped at her eyes. She glared at the alien sitting still before her.

"But you're not over her, are you? I've seen the way you look at her, even still. The way your eyes shoot daggers at Rikist's back whenever he touches her." She let out a single, choked sob. "Be honest, she broke your heart, but you'd give all the little pieces back to her in a second if she wanted you."

Krissik covered his face with his hands and then abruptly stood and grabbed Carly's shoulders. His cheeks burned in the darkness, the moonlight glinting off his wet skin.

"I love you, Carly," he hissed. "I do. I did love Samantha and is part of me that... I no know the word... is a part that wonders how things would be if different. If I was home, mated, with a family."

Krissik took a shaky breath and released her, spinning away. He hugged his arms to his chest. "I understand how you feel when we came to the hotel. I feel it now." He turned back to her, his face distraught. "I hurt, Carly. I miss home. I miss my life." He sniffed and wiped at his eyes.

Carly shook her head. "And I'm what, a rebound? Someone you're stuck with here?"

"I choose you."

"Because you can't leave!" Carly shouted. "Would you still choose me if you left? Would you come back?"

"I know!" Krissik roared. "I know I no leave, I no have other choices."

Carly stepped back, her knees bumping against the hay bale as Krissik advanced on her. Krissik's claws extended and retraced as he towered over her. He bared his fangs as he hissed in her face.

"I want to leave this place. This farm. I want to saw things. Cities. Buildings. But no can. And no will. I no want to without you." He looked to the ceiling, blinking, and then met her eyes. "I happy with you, Carly. *You* make me happy. Samantha never could. Not like this. But you no feel back same, do you?"

Carly's chin trembled. The barn walls felt suddenly heavy and oppressive, despite the desert cold creeping through the old wood. She shivered and sat on the hay bale, pulling her knees to her heaving chest.

Carly's mind stared into the warm pool of swirling honey below, wanting to make that leap from the dark ledge where she crouched. Her heart ached to be held, caressed, without worrying about the past or the constant hurt. She mentally reached out, calling to him, but something held her sleeve, jerked her back into the shadows. Krissik was beautiful, innocent in a way, and a piece of her would die if she tainted that perfect heart of his. He deserved better.

"I want to, but I don't know if I *can* love, Krissik," she sobbed. "I have been hurt so, so much. And I'm tired of being hurt. Of being disappointed."

"I will never hurt you, Carly."

"Everyone hurts me," she whispered. She rested her forehead on her knees. "Everyone eventually leaves."

Carly felt Krissik kneel beside her. Felt his trembling hands cover hers. His warm breath rolled over her skin as he kissed her knuckles, her wrists, her arms.

"I never leave you, Carly," Krissik said, his voice thick. "If you can have me, I never leave."

Carly raised her head to meet his eyes, inches from her face. The sat for a long moment, their noses close enough to touch, just staring, soaking the other in as the crickets chirped in the distance.

Don't jump, Carly. Just let yourself fucking fall.

Carly let out a long breath and leaned forward over the golden abyss, pressing her forehead against Krissik's. She felt him shudder, and then Krissik collected her into his arms and sat on the bale behind her. He cradled her to his chest, rocking her gently.

Carly twisted in Krissik's arms and wrapped a hand behind his neck, pulling him down. Krissik kissed her, his lips hot and hungry. His mouth moved from hers to kiss the tears away from her cheeks, then down to her neck.

Carly let her head fall back as Krissik's teeth nibbled at her throat and collarbone, and her hands reached for the buttons on his shirt.

The bang of a gunshot roared through the barn. Carly jerked away, and Krissik fell sideways, landing on his hands and knees beside the hay bale. Carly crouched, tension running up her spine in hot electric waves.

"Help!" A voice screamed from outside. "Someone help me!"

Carly's heart skipped a beat. *Mandy*.

Krissik leaped from the hayloft to the barn floor and raced out the door. Carly was able to skitter down the ladder and run after him, but he was already halfway to the house by the time she got outside, his legs carrying him across the ground at a ridiculously fast clip.

Tires squealed in front of the house. "Look!" Carly called out. A black van flicked on its lights and tore out of the drive, barreling at high speed toward the road that led out of the farm. Carly sprinted the rest of the distance to the house and found Samantha curled up on the front porch, a shotgun in her hands and tears streaming down her face.

"They took her," she sobbed. "They *took her!*"

"Who?"

"Men. Men in suits..." Samantha fumbled across the porch. "They *took her*...."

Krissik held out his hand. "Keys."

Samantha shook her head at him, speechless and in shock. She lifted a shaking hand and pointed to the house.

Krissik raced past her and into the kitchen. He appeared a moment later with his keys in hand and a large black duffle over his shoulder as he sprinted toward Samantha's old truck.

Something cleared enough in Samantha's face for her to look toward Carly. "Carly... he can't drive...."

Carly could not quite say what drove her to race toward the truck and leap into the passenger seat after him. He had the ignition turned on immediately, and after a brief survey of the equipment, he unlocked the parking brake and correctly put the vehicle into drive. It lurched forward, nearly slamming Carly backward against her seat.

"Right pedal is gas; left pedal is brake!" she instructed.

"What is *brake*?"

"It slows you down!"

"Oh." Krissik nodded. "I no want to do *that*."

He stomped down on the accelerator, and the truck hurtled down the road, chasing the rapidly diminishing rear lights on the black van.

Holy shit, he shouldn't be driving.

Carly reached for her seatbelt, and it took her numb fingers several tries to properly make the thing work. The sound of the engine blazed all around her, filling the passenger compartment with its buzzing hum.

Krissik leaned forward, his knuckles white around the steering wheel.

Carly's mind raced. *He doesn't know how to drive. He doesn't know how to dive.* Why hadn't they taught him? *Oh, because we figure he has nowhere he can go, anyway.*

Rikist knew how to drive. Carly knew how to drive. Krissik did not need to.

Except now, he was—and it was really, really bad.

Carly made herself talk, as much to calm herself as to instruct him. "Okay, Kris? Turning the wheel left makes it go left, and right makes it go right."

"I have saw *The Fast and the Furious*," he informed her.

Carly's eyes went round. "That doesn't make me feel any fucking better!"

They bounced over a pothole. Krissik yelped and jerked the wheel left out of reflex, and the truck nearly went up onto its left wheels.

Carly clung to the oh-shit handle overhead. "It's *sensitive* at higher speeds! Don't yank it around!"

I should have driven. I should have driven. Who am I kidding? I've never been in a high-speed chase before!

The rusty truck hurtled headlong down the freeway. They were keeping up with the van, but not enough. Carly did not know her vehicles very well, but she was sure something that old should not have a ton of power.

"Kris," she said, still hanging onto the handle, "who are we dealing with?" She assumed they were humans; Samantha would have told them otherwise.

Krissik did not answer.

The engine crept up to redline, and the mysterious van's lights disappeared completely.

"You're going to kill the truck," Carly said. "And us."

"We need find her. We can go fast—"

"Not without a freaking engine!"

Krissik kept driving another minute. Carly silently prayed to whatever god might be listening.

He sighed. "How I... slow us..."

"Hold the wheel. Take your foot off the accelerator, but *don't* push the brake. Let us just coast down." The engine's roar eased, and the car began decelerating. Carly held her breath. They moved slower, slower—down to seventy now, sixty-five—

"Okay. Now apply the brake—gently!"

The truck screeched and jerked. Krissik lifted his foot off the brake immediately, then tapped it again. They hustled and jolted to a staggering, exhausted twenty miles per hour, and Carly pointed wordlessly to the side of the road. Krissik pulled the wheel to the right and managed to stop the car entirely.

Carly would have melted right onto the floor if the seatbelt had not kept her upright. Her heart crashed against her ribcage, and hot tears pricked at her eyes. She had never gone this fast in a car—least of all with an inexperienced driver.

Krissik reached into his pocket.

The truck lurched forward.

"Brakes!" Carly screeched. "Brakes!"

Krissik slammed his foot back down onto the brake, and the truck halted. Carly leaned over, shoved it into park, and then switched off the engine entirely, pulling the key from the ignition. Krissik stared at her for a moment, then bowed his head in what she thought might be thanks.

"It is stopped," he said.

"Yes. You can do whatever it was you were doing."

Krissik reached into his pocket and withdrew his cell phone. His fingers shook; he had to breathe for a moment before he could punch in a string of numbers.

"Calling the cops?" Carly asked, before realizing what a ridiculous question that was.

"Rikist."

Oh, even better. Carly blinked. "I thought he would be calling us from disposable phones."

"We had back-up."

"A back-up what?"

"A continent... contingency. Just in case."

"And you didn't tell us, why?"

"Did not want to scare."

Carly guffawed.

Did not want to scare.

Well, we're in a world of shit now, boy howdy.

Carly heard the warm baritone of Rikist's voice on the other end of the phone, and suddenly Krissik was all business. "Rikist," he said. "Sister Mandy is been taken..."

Carly heard Rikist shout but could not make out what he was saying. After a moment, she realized he must have been speaking in their native language.

Krissik glanced at her, appearing to weigh his options, then said in English, "Carly is with me."

Carly heard Rikist's cursing over the phone. "Put it on speaker," she said. "Maybe I can help."

Krissik pulled the phone away from his ear and inspected it for a moment. Carly took it from him, set the speaker option, and set the phone on the dashboard.

"Hi, Rikist," she said. "We're in a bit of a pickle here."

"Do you know who took her?" Rikist asked.

"They were in a black van." Carly reached for her own phone, and then realized it was back in her purse —in the barn. "I didn't ask Samantha if they were human...."

"They probably were." Rikist let out a long, frustrated sigh. "I feared this would happen. Portions of your government are very sympathetic to mine. They will work with each other as necessary... if that is the case, then Mandy was likely taken by human men on the orders of someone from our world."

Carly bit her lower lip. *When did my life turn into a freaky sci-fi movie?*

"How did they *find* Mandy, though?" Krissik asked.

Rikist seemed to lapse into thought. Carly heard a distinct tapping sound that probably indicated his claws clicking against something. She stared at the bright screen of the cell, and the bars indicating how much service they had.

"Does anyone have any ideas?" Carly asked.

"We're just sitting right now. No plan." No one answered her. "Rikist? Military man?"

Rikist cleared his throat. "I just thought of something."

"Yes?"

"Krissik, did you keep your translator."

Krissik lifted a hand to the back of his ear, then paused. "*Isk?*"

Rikist's growl rippled across the dashboard. "You did, didn't you? Fucking idiot, Krissik! I told you to destroy it!"

"I..." Krissik looked helplessly at Carly. "I no mean anything."

"It means they're targeting us, not Samantha," Rikist went on. "But they saw a young woman and couldn't help themselves."

"Translator?" Carly asked. "Will someone explain this?"

Krissik switched on the overhead light, then bent toward Carly and pushed his thick auburn hair aside. She saw a tiny silver implement sticking out just under his first skin layer. She touched it and realized she had felt it many times before but never gave it much thought.

"A translator," she said. "So, that's how you can understand us?"

"Initially," Rikist said through the speaker. "Until we learned English."

"Ah."

"They can be tracked," Rikist said. "It's difficult;

without a paired mate, they would have to track it down by manufacturing number and the embedded signal. That would take weeks to figure out. But since I don't have one.... They must have figured they'd take a shot and go after Krissik. And it paid off."

Krissik had his hands on the steering wheel, his face long and sullen.

Always take a gamble, Carly's father had told her when she was younger. *Even if you lose, at least you tried.* The aliens must have been celebrating that mentality right about now.

Meanwhile, she and Krissik were sitting in the car. At the same time, Mandy got further and further away, trapped in the clutches of some very vindictive aliens.

"Rikist, you know where they went?" Krissik asked. He must have been thinking the same thing. "Is must be a jumpgate or base here, somewhere...."

"Didn't you come here through a jumpgate near here coming after Samantha?" Carly asked Krissik.

"Yes," he said. "Near Whitewater. Is was first jumpgate Rikist shut down. Is must be another."

Rikist was silent for a moment. His claws tapping against what sounded like keys. "I found some references to an abandoned jumpgate up in the mountains near Independence Pass. They pulled people during the 1800s, or so it said. Place is a ghost town now. But the gate would have been shut down decades ago, even a century—"

"Is must be it," Krissik said.

"I did register activity south of me on the scans a

few hours ago…" Rikist hesitated again. "I don't know, Kris. Even if it were still functioning, they would have had to—"

"You betray them, Rikist!" Krissik shouted. "You know how they are! They resourceful. Vindicated."

"You mean, vindictive?"

Carly waited a moment to make sure Rikist was finished. "We need to get her, Rikist," she said. "Can you text Krissik the location of the jumpgate?"

"Let me call in some old favors. I may be able to get some help out there."

"We don't have time."

"I'm just outside of Denver, about three hours away from the pass," Rikist said. "The gates take time to charge, and if they came through today, we probably have time. I can be there soon."

"We'll meet you there."

Rikist grunted. "Fine. Wait for me when you get there."

"Got it."

Carly clicked off the phone and turned to Krissik. "We're not waiting for him."

Krissik nodded and extended his hand. "May I have keys, please?"

Carly shook her head. "I'll drive."

Krissik tightened his grip around the wheel. "Let me do this."

"Krissik, you're going to kill us."

"I can do this, Carly!" Krissik shouted, his claws

extended from his fingertips. "This all my fault, Carly. Please."

Carly stared at his hand and swallowed.

After a second, Krissik retracted his claws. "I sorry. When I upset...."

"I know." Carly placed the keys into his open palm.

The phone vibrated, and they both looked at it. Rikist had sent them an image of the vicinity and the spot where he expected the jumpgate might be. Carly noted the landmarks and surrounding towns and transferred that information to Krissik's map program. It informed her that their probable destination was just under a two-and-a-half-hour drive into the mountains.

Carly blew a strand of hair off her forehead. "We can follow this road, and then turn onto CO-82 toward Aspen. The pass looks pretty windy...."

"Then they no be going fast, either." Krissik turned on the truck. "Call Samantha and say her what we doing."

They pulled back onto the road, and Krissik managed to keep the car to a comparatively sedate seventy miles per hour. Carly dialed Samantha's number, but the call went straight to voicemail. She hoped her friend was not curled up in a ball on the front porch, alone and afraid.

"Sam, it's Carly. We think they're taking Mandy to a jumpgate in the mountains. They were probably looking for Krissik or Rikist. I'm on Krissik's phone, mine's at home. But we're going after her. We'll get her back, Sam. I promise."

She then scanned through Krissik's tiny list of contacts until she came up with Rodolfo's number.

"Yes, cat?" Rodolfo answered, sounding like he was in the middle of a yawn.

"Rodolfo, it's Carly. We've got a situation here." God, she sounded like her mother calling the family psychologist whenever her father slipped up and looked at another woman. Carly quickly soothed her voice. "Mandy's been snatched by—we're not sure—we think government workers in league with the guy's homeworld. We're going after her. Samantha is alone at the farm. Can you take care of her?"

Rodolfo's voice blared through the speaker. "Why would you leave her *alone?*"

"Because I make poor life choices!" Carly snapped. "Get to her!"

She hung up and dropped the phone on the center console, her fingers quivering. Good grief, when had she turned into a jittery wreck?

It's just your adrenaline crashing. You'll be fine.

But she was not fine. She was exhausted, and Mandy was gone, and she *had* left Samantha alone on her farm, with no one to turn to. The tears rolled down her cheeks, and she swatted at them, nearly hitting her cheekbone with her fist.

Stupid girl, stop crying and get it together. There's shit we need to do.

After a few moments of silence, punctuated only by her occasional hiccupped sob, Krissik said, "Samantha is be fine, Carly."

"They won't come back for her?"

Krissik shook his head. "I no think so."

There was that, at least, though Carly would be on pins and needles until Rodolfo or Samantha called her back. She looked at the battery charge on Krissik's phone and fumbled in the glove box until she came up with a charger.

"Just in case," she said, when she saw Krissik eyeing her. "I want a full charge in case there's news."

THE MILES ROLLED BY.

"Rikist said they used to take people from the mining towns," Carly said. Anything to break the stifling silence.

"I no know about that, exactly," Krissik said. "It was easier to take people in past. So many sicknesses, so much... nature? Things could get you outside. Wolves may attack you, other beasts. Or people can wander off and freeze somewhere. Now everyone connected...by the social thing."

"Social media," Carly supplied.

"Newspapers, phones. When you disappear, you are noticed. My people know this, and they worry. So, they trying take more and more at once, in case something happens, and we can take no more." He paused, and then corrected himself. "And *they* can take no more."

"Is that why they tried to take so many at the hotel?"

"Yes. Numbers matter."

Mining towns. Why did that set off a warning bell in her head?

Then she remembered: *We did not take Roanoke.*

"Kris, that story Rodolfo told us about the town up the mountain, where we're headed," She fumbled with the phone, doing a web search on the ghost town Rikist mentioned. She found it immediately, a mountain attraction already closed for the season. "He said everyone vanished, one winter. Was that because of your people?"

He steered down the road, staring straight ahead into the darkness. "Before I would say no. But now knowing is a jumpgate nearby? Maybe. Probably."

Carly let out a low whistle. "That's ballsy."

"Things is different."

"Did our government help you out?"

"I no know pacifics."

"Specifics."

"Just yes, your government agreed cooperate with us in exchange for technology. And again, was easier in past, not to have to explain things, not to have to... people disappeared anyway," he finally amended. "Easier make excuses then."

Carly stared out the window. Every now and then, they passed a smattering of lights—a farm, maybe, or a small town sleeping through the night. *How could they do that to us?* She did not even know who *they* were—a nebulous, abstract group of individuals willing to trade the lives of others for some bits and pieces of technology.

Technology.

How much was one human life worth? How much was an entire town? What had their government—the one sworn to protect them—given up for something like a touchscreen phone, or the Internet, or new medicine? How many of humanity's accomplishments were nothing more than compensation from the aliens as gifts to keep them quiet?

She rubbed her eyes.

"They no are all bad people," Krissik said, as if reading her thoughts.

"Who?" Carly turned in her seat. "Your government, or my people helping them out? They're kidnappers, plain and simple, selling women into slavery!" She pressed herself against the locked door, trying to put as much distance between her body and Krissik's as she could. "You were involved! You knew!"

"I know."

He did not reach for her, at least. She was sure she could not bear his touch in that instant.

"I no did know—I did no *think*," he corrected himself. "I, and many others like, we know only what is told about Earth. Leaders keep it quiet, perhaps to keep from thinking of people we take. I no think when I brought Samantha back... I no think when I came for her... I did still understand her as... as mine, I suppose, because that is how we is trained. We look at you as you look at..."

"Pets?" she asked.

He shook his head. "No... there is no word for it I know. Pets is not same. Belongings is not same. Maybe now, with new government in charge, a pet is similar comparison but...."

"I don't want to hear it," Carly muttered.

"OK."

They drove on.

"This my fault—*my* fault, because I no let Samantha and Rikist just be happy together. I come here, they follow me and catch Many, and now Samantha is suffering."

He balled up his fist and slammed it against the steering wheel. It was a purely human gesture, one that Carly appreciated all the more when his claws and fangs did not immediately follow.

"I have to bring her back," he said.

Carly opened her mouth to speak when Krissik's phone rang. She glanced at the caller ID and picked it up. "Hi, Rodolfo."

"I've got Samantha cleaned up and drinking some tea," the man said through the speaker. "Seems like these guys came in through the house."

"They break a window? I saw shattered glass."

"No—Samantha shot at one, and *that* broke the window." She heard Samantha's voice in the background, muffled, explaining something. Rodolfo continued: "They came in through one of the back bedrooms. A window was open."

Carly's gut twisted into a fat, intricate knot. She wanted to roll down the window and vomit out onto the road, hyperventilate into a bag, chug water until her stomach burst.

They came in through my *window.*

She swallowed and made her mouth work. "We're going after them," she said.

"You and Krissik," Rodolfo said slowly.

"Yes. We know where they're headed. We're going."

She imagined Rodolfo nodding. "We will be here," he said. "Good luck." He hung up.

She supposed there was not much else he could convey to her. It was not like he and Samantha were going to call in the cavalry, or show up in a helicopter, or somehow sprout superpowers and save the day. No one was going to help out with this particular rescue mission. No cops, no army, no special forces. Just Krissik and Carly, with not one superpower between them.

She put the phone down on the seat beside her. "They came in through my window," she said. "I left it open."

She held back the anger. There was nothing she could do now. Nothing. It welled up inside her anyway, surging against the colossal wall she had erected against her feelings long ago. Anger, helplessness, and something she might have once called despair

—all of these feelings mixing into one potent stew. Her eyes watered.

Krissik placed a hand on her knee. His claws were retracted, but she could just make out their silvery tips. "Is no your fault," he said.

No, it's your fault for coming here, and going after Samantha—and you know that, you alien prick.

But she could not bring herself to say the hateful words. Krissik deserved much better than that.

Besides, it was Carly who had left the window open. If she had bothered to close it, the men might have had to break in, alerting Mandy and Samantha, alerting Krissik and Carly. There would have been more noise. They would have had a chance, at least, to stop all of this before it had been set into motion.

Instead, she had left the window open, and now they were chasing Mandy into the mountains of Colorado, with only the vaguest idea of where they needed to go.

What a couple of royal fuck ups we turned out to be.

FOURTEEN

Krissik pulled over at a wide shoulder on the highway somewhere around one o'clock in the morning.

"I need help," he said.

"Yes?"

He pointed at the nub beneath his hair behind his ear. "This needs be removed. If they track usage, is means they see us coming."

Wouldn't want that. Carly slipped off her seatbelt and rubbed her hands together.

"Wait, will you be able to understand me without it?"

Krissik nodded. "I English is good enough."

Carly smirked. "Okay," she said. "What do I do? Do I need pliers, or a screwdriver, or—"

Krissik's fingers squirmed beneath his hair. His claws scraped along the edge of the device, the skin healed and adhered from years of use. He winced, made a soft meowing sound, and then moved his hand aside. Blood trickled down his neck. "Just take and pull. I loosened, but I no can get out. Going to hurt."

So, he wanted her to do it. *Ugh.*

Carly leaned toward the device. Krissik had indeed worked it out, at least partially; blood smeared his neck, and bits of skin and flesh stuck to the exposed portion of the translator. She grasped it with her thumb and pointer finger. Krissik tensed, his hands wrapping around the steering wheel and his knuckles turning white.

"I may let out claws," he said softly. "Just warning you."

He knows. He knows it bothers me.

How could he not? Carly went rigid every time she saw them; Krissik, being deeply attuned to body language, would, of course, have noticed. She blinked back unexpected tears—of what, gratitude? Or understanding?—and then locked her hand around the nub and pressed her other hand against his neck for leverage.

"One," she counted. "Two..."

It popped out before she said three. Krissik yowled, and the leather steering wheel wrap split as his claws shot out. He quickly controlled retracted them back and clamped his right hand down on the bleeding wound.

Carly searched the truck for a rag, finally came up with a sweater from the back bench seat and shoved it at him. "Hold this on it," she said. "We must have a first aid kit in here—"

"Later." Using one hand, Krissik got the truck back in gear and pulled back out onto the highway. Carly held her breath, but he seemed capable of driving while putting pressure on the new wound. She held the translator in her bloodied fingers and held it up to the overhead light. There were no lights, no fancy beeping sounds to indicate they were being tracked.

"Throw it out window," Krissik said.

Carly rolled the manual window down and hurled it out. She imagined it bouncing across the asphalt to be smashed to pieces by the next car that came along.

Krissik breathed through clenched teeth. "Thank you."

"You're welcome."

Krissik removed his hand from his neck and wiped it on his jeans, leaving a scarlet smear across his thigh.

"Do we have a plan?" Carly asked.

"No yet. I thinking."

"How many do you think there'll be?"

"Hard to say. Could be just two. More likely, eight or ten. If is reconnaissance squad..."

Carly knew by his tone that a reconnaissance squad was no good, but she could not exactly figure out why. "Kris, maybe you'd better just lay out what's going on for me. I kind of get why they came after Rikist, but everything else..."

"Communication between our worlds is no good," he said. "Is mainly occur through the jumpgate. If this is an older gate, as Rikist said, is means is not manned on both sides. Then this maybe an exploratory mission.

They came to look for me and Rikist... and if they tell those on the other side—"

"In your world," Carly said.

"Yes. If report our location is here then action may be taken."

Carly's throat went dry. "What will happen to Mandy?"

"They will question Mandy. They have Samantha's blood in file. If scan Mandy, is will match."

Krissik did not need to elaborate on what they might do if they wanted to extract Mandy's information. Carly's feet turned to ice. She kicked off her shoes, curled up on the seat, and turned up the heater. It was ridiculous to feel so cold on a warm night, but it was all she could do to keep her teeth from chattering.

"Then," Krissik continued, "or maybe same time, they decide what they want to do with me and Rikist. Remember, right now, we escape but missing. Maybe dead. If we is alive, living with human women is the highest treason. And my government makes... samples?"

"Examples," Carly whispered.

"Yes. Make examples. They want Rikist, and they will take me, and if is any scattered cousins remaining, they take them, too. They take those closest to us."

And that's probably Samantha and me.

Krissik glanced at her sideways, confirming her thoughts.

Carly rubbed her temples. And Samantha was pregnant. What would they do with the pregnant wife of a traitor? To their child? Would they go after Rodolfo, as well? John? How far would their net reach in order for them to stop?

"Our planet is in civil war," Krissik said. "Is possible that they wish to send force to make example of Earth."

Carly frowned at that thought. "Take out a whole planet just because of your brother?"

"Would give our planet something to focus on. United. If not fighting each other, our world maybe can recover, and perhaps...." He shook his head. "I should not wish for such things. Our fortune is directly tied to your misfortune."

The politics of Krissik's world were more confusing than ever. Carly wriggled her toes but could still barely feel the vinyl of the seat beneath them.

"Do you really think they'll launch an assault like that?" she asked.

"No. But is possibility. Depends on mood at home. Things change quickly there." He appeared to mull over his words and dared to take his eyes off the road and glance skyward. "On the channel I watch, they talk about European countries fighting with diplomacy, arguments... is like this at home all times, except we use weapons instead of words."

Carly shoved her hands beneath her arms and shivered harder.

This is all so much bigger than me now.

And all because she had left the goddamned window open.

"What can I do to help when we get there?" she asked.

Krissik shook his head, as much as Carly had expected he would. "No, Carly."

"I don't know that you're in much of a position to turn down any help," she said.

He sighed. "I no want put you at risk."

"It looks like I already *am* at risk, so you might as well let me try to help." She sat up, trying to rub some circulation back onto her feet. "I did take a shooting class when I was younger, so I might be able to handle a gun."

"Carly—"

"And I can talk my way out of pretty much anything."

"Carly—"

"I have to do *something!* I left the window open!"

Krissik's hand landed on her thigh, and Carly felt his claws biting into the fabric of her jeans.

"Is not your fault," he said. "They would have come in, either way, like Rikist warned. We were not prepared. We might have heard them crash through, but then we might have run in and been killed."

He cut himself off and breathed deeply for several moments, fighting for composure. "Please, Carly. No blame yourself. I blame myself for so many things, for so much."

Carly placed her hand over his, ignoring the feel of his claws under her fingers. In the darkness on the road, he was just a man, and she was just a woman, and they needed to work together to do something, to find their way to redemption. Mandy was alone and afraid somewhere, stored as chattel to be transferred to live as a slave in some alien world and they needed to work together to save her.

It could have been me, Carly thought suddenly. It could have been her back in Las Vegas. Could have been her sleeping in Samantha's spare bedroom if she had not gone out to see Krissik.

That terrified her. Had she escaped her fate twice? Was the world trying to tell her something, *Final Destination*-style? She could have easily been snoring away in her bedroom, not realizing something was amiss until she was being carried out in that van.

Instead, Mandy had been in the house and had paid the ultimate price. Carly had gotten too comfortable. She had not thought about what could happen, what might happen.

Rikist had known. Rikist had been worried.

Why hadn't we listened to him?

"Kris," she said, "I will hate myself forever if I don't do something."

He smiled faintly. "So, will I," he said. "I mean, I hate myself. Not you."

Carly smirked. "You have to let me help."

She was not sure how she could help, of course, or in what capacity she could manage to do so. Fighting off a potential alien invasion seemed best left to soldiers and tough girls like Sigourney Weaver. Carly

Nichols, globetrotting party girl, was not equipped for this sort of shit.

Krissik squeezed her thigh and then went silent for several minutes.

On the plus side, I've definitely got the brains of the operation with me, she thought.

"We go in," Krissik said. "We go in, and we find her and take her back. We must destroy the jumpgate somehow... I sure is ways to do it—"

"We can call Rikist."

"He will want us wait. And I no know how many there is, or how we should best handle them." He paused. "I no want to harm many."

That was a forlorn hope; no matter what they did, someone would end up harmed. They might manage to minimize casualties, but even that seemed unlikely.

Carly turned the cell screen back on and glanced at the maps again. She forced her mind to concentrate, to recognize the various dots and lines that symbolized villages, mountains, passes, and trails.

She was not what some would call an *outdoor girl*. Searching for a path to an abandoned mining town was something quite out of her comfort zone. But she could spot a pair of heels on sale at Nordies, and she knew how to travel across Europe to get to a party that had just been announced one day prior. She could handle this.

There. She touched a small red dot and zoomed in. There was not much there; more of a stopping point than an actual location, but it was a start.

"There's a town at the base of the mountain," she said. "I don't know what sort of reception we'll get once we're there. We can ask for directions and get fuel before we head up."

Krissik smiled. "You two steps ahead of me."

She was not sure she liked the sound of that. Planning some kind of military mission was the last thing Carly had ever imagined herself doing. It was definitely multiple steps above her pay grade.

But here they were.

"You know," she said, "I'm still deciding if it's a positive thing, but my life has gotten so much more interesting with you in it."

FIFTEEN

They stopped in the town an hour later at the base of the pass.

Carly showed Krissik how to fuel up the truck in the dim light of the yellow Shell sign. The lone employee tucked away in the store was busy on her cell phone and paid them no mind as Carly explained running the credit card and topping off the tank. Krissik had a decent grasp of money, but he seemed surprised by the total cost to fill up the tank. He gaped at the numbers as they spun up.

"This is crazy!"

The fueling line made soft, reassuring chugs as it transferred gasoline from the tanks beneath the station to the truck. *Glug-glug*, it whispered. Carly knew that sound, taking heart in the familiar noise. It was probably the last normal thing she would experience this evening.

Glug-glug.

"You fill tank like this how often?"

Carly made a face.

I keep forgetting he hasn't been off the farm.

Hell, Krissik had not even *driven* before this evening, though he had improved so rapidly that he seemed to have been doing it for years.

Carly contemplated the truck, and then looked at the numbers they were running up. "We're at twelve gallons now," she said. "As long as we're not going into Grand Junction or heading into the mountains, I think Samantha can fill it up every couple of weeks? The faster you drive, the more fuel you burn, stuff like that. I actually don't know how internal combustion engines work."

"But is so much *money*. And you must drive places."

"It ain't cheap being an Earthling these days," Carly said. "What do your vehicles run off of?"

"Solar power." Krissik shrugged. "They charge while is idle."

"Does it really work? We have solar tech, but it seems kind of imperfect." At least, that was what Carly had heard.

"Yes."

Glug-glug. The truck happily choked down more gas. Carly thought about cutting it off and sparing her wallet, but she had no idea how much fuel they would burn getting up the mountain, or whether they might need to pull a daring escape, or—any number of other things. The last thing she wanted was to run out of fuel during a high-speed chase.

She could only imagine how convenient properly working solar power would be. "Gonna share that technology with us?"

"I believe we tried...." Krissik paused. "Outside interests no accepting such help."

Carly blinked. *Oil lobbies are more influential than aliens? Wonders will never cease.*

"You said you mostly walked places," she remarked. "Back home."

Krissik nodded. "The places I need go is easily accessible. Is more sensible to walk."

I wish we had that luxury. Out here in Colorado, she *had* to drive places. In Europe, or in denser cities like New York, she could walk around, but most of America was stretched out, an absolute haven for a car enthusiast.

She glanced at the shop again and saw the girl standing there behind the counter. A rack of sunglasses sat on the counter beside her. Krissik had always wanted to venture away from the farm, and now, here he was, driving the freaking car in what would soon be broad daylight.

Carly patted Krissik's shoulder. "Can you wait in the truck for a second? I'm going to get us some supplies."

He peered at her. "But we have guns."

"Not that kind of fortification. You figure out how we're going to handle that jumpgate."

The store was cool and almost damp inside. The girl behind the counter did not give Carly a second look, allowing her to browse the racks in complete peace. She found a pair of sunglasses that would probably fit Krissik, grabbed a second for herself, and then loaded up on snacks and sodas—anything she felt would help give them some much-needed energy at his hour. What, exactly, was one supposed to eat before charging off into an uncertain battle? Beef jerky and Skittles would not be her first choice, but they were among the handful of appetizing things the store had to offer. A few browned apples were available, and some frozen fruit, but that would not do them any good. She also was not about to risk their stomachs on the ready-made, vacuum-sealed pies or wannabe MREs stored toward the front. This was not some camping expedition—this was saving Mandy.

And maybe the world.

God, that's an intimidating thought.

The cashier rang up her tallies. "Twenty-five seventy-nine," she said, glancing at her phone again. "Oh, I think I just got another high score."

Carly started to fork over her credit card, thought better of it, and dug into her purse for cash, instead. The odds of some alien sitting at a bench and watching her ring up expenses was probably slim, but she might not want to give anyone—alien or otherwise—any added impetus for tracking her.

Damn, she thought. *I should have done the same for the gas.*

The cashier gave her some change.

"Hey," Carly said when the girl reached for her phone, "is there an old mining town up in the mountains?"

"There's places," the girl said.

"Places?" Carly repeated. "Can you be a little more specific?"

The girl rolled her eyes and folded her hands on the cool beige countertop.

I must seem so old to her, Carly thought. *At twenty-five, old and demanding of her time.*

"You going up to the mining town?" the girl asked.

Carly nodded.

"I thought so. That's the only real reason people come through here at all. There are a couple of places you can pull out. Vista View, or something like that. It's real pretty if you're just hanging out there... but it's pretty sketchy driving up there at night."

The girl sized Carly up; her manner clearly indicating she didn't think Carly was the type to tough it out long in the sticks. If you don't drive properly, you'll end up sliding off a cliff."

Plunging into an abyss did not hold a lot of excitement for Carly. She would have to remind Krissik of that. "I think we'll be okay," she said.

"Good luck." The girl waggled a finger at her. "Remember, slow down on the turns. That's when most people go plunging off the side."

What the hell is wrong with people in these mountains?

"Thanks," Carly said, picking up her bag. "You've been really helpful."

The girl went back to her phone, and Carly slipped out of the store.

Krissik was sitting in the truck bed, the open duffle by his feet, mucking around with something long and silver. Carly paused, the bag of goodies from the shop still clutched in her hand. "Is that what I think it is?" she asked.

"This gun is done," he grimaced. "Rikist took good ones for himself. This one, my father ruined years ago. But some parts still work. I brought as backup with when I came to get Samantha. Was going to make her come back."

"With a non-functioning gun?"

Krissik smiled ruefully. "*She* no know it was non-functioning."

Ah, the ever-working mind of the master criminal. Carly edged closer to him, then perched next to him on the lip of the trunk.

"I got you some sunglasses," she said. She pulled them out of the bag and held them up. "You'll want them in case where' still here when the sun comes out."

"Thanks." He tried the glasses on, and then set them aside. He removed a circular object from the gun and held it up to the station's harsh fluorescent lighting overhead. "The charge is still good. If can make it combust, we in business."

Carly had never been one for making things combust, except maybe in bed, and figured it was probably best to let Krissik do his thing. She opened the Skittles and propped the bag between them, occasionally grabbing a handful while Krissik fiddled with his parts. Ten minutes later, Krissik held up a flat, Frisbee-shaped object.

"What is it?" Carly asked.

"A bomb."

She looked around quickly, but they were still alone.

"If we can plant on jumpgate, is *should* put end to it," he said. "Of course, is no way to test... but we can try."

Carly balked slightly at the idea.

"No worry," Krissik assured her. "Is will not go off until we trigger."

Even so, Krissik set the device very carefully in the duffle and then tied it down against the wheel well. He hopped off the back, offered a hand for Carly to join him, and then closed the tailgate. They migrated forward to climb into the truck, and Carly did not miss the girl looking out the window.

Shit.

How long had they been distracting her from her cell phone game? The kid did not seem concerned, only mildly interested; for all she knew, the two of them had been playing a video game or checking Facebook.

Hopefully we aren't bringing more hell on us than necessary.

"I'll drive," Carly said, taking the keys. She jumped

into the driver's seat. "I have a little more experience with winding mountain roads than you." She could thank teenage visits to her uncle's vacation home in the Rockies for that. She had hated the drive at the time: the winding roads, the plummeting drops directly below her. She was reasonably sure she could handle a trip up to some old mining town, narrow and potholed roads notwithstanding.

Something clicked next to her. She glanced over at Krissik in the passenger seat and found him examining a small firearm—a pistol of some sort. "I should have checked these earlier," he said. "But is seem to be mostly functioning. I can fix."

Carly marveled at the man sitting beside her.

Sexy as hell, checks pistols, builds bombs out of spare parts in the back of a car...

If they survived all of this, she would sit Krissik down and make him watch a few seasons of *MacGyver*. The man really *was* a freaking tinkering genius.

She reached across the seat and caressed Krissik's striped cheek.

Krissik purred softly, leaning into her hand.

Carly smiled and shoved the keys into the ignition. "So, we're just going to go in there, guns blazing, and stick the bomb on the jumpgate?"

"Is depends on how many is there. I no think there will be many. Is no can be a large jumpgate. It could not handle so many at once...." Krissik frowned, trailing off.

Carly wanted to ask how many men a jumpgate

could handle, and what they needed to know—but the last time Krissik had tried to explain anything vaguely scientific to her, his narrative had dissolved into a complicated array of mathematics, numbers, decimal points, and something about light speed. None of which Carly was equipped to handle.

Though if it were anything like Vegas, Carly knew they'd be royally screwed.

"There won't be too many," Krissik finally said.

Their headlights lit up the road as they peeled out of the station. Carly did her best to focus on the miles disappearing under their tires and not the vision of driving directly into an ambush.

VISIBILITY FADED as they climbed higher. Carly was not sure if they were moving into cloud cover, or if some mountain storm was coming their way. Carly flicked on the fog lights, slowed her pace as much as she dared, and kept both hands on the wheel.

There had been no phone calls from Samantha or Rikist. Nothing from Rodolfo, either. The silence from all directions scared her. Why wouldn't they say something?

But then, what could they really say? *Good luck? Don't get killed?*

At least her feet were warm. She blasted the old heater as high as it would go.

"Kris," she said.

"Hmm?" He looked up from his latest bit of tinkering.

"If your people took an entire town—it wasn't a town of women, obviously. Why would they...?"

Why would they what? Take them all? Do this?

She could not formulate the thought she wanted to ask, that was for sure. She could only hope Krissik could understand what she was asking and figure out a way to answer it that did not leave her more confused than before.

Krissik lowered the gun into his lap. The flat, silvery surface dully gleamed in the overhead light. "Stealing women for mates is recent thing," he said. "I know Samantha say you some of our history. Human females been welcomed in our world before. Men too, for time."

"But why would you take an entire town?"

He did not answer her.

Red flag, Carly, red flag!

Krissik tended to go quiet when he knew he was going to say something Carly would not like. But Carly had to know. If they were going to make some kind of stand, she needed to know her enemy, needed to anticipate the way they might fight. It was the same sort of logic she used when attending a Black Friday sale at Bloomie's.

Andy Carly always wanted to come out ahead.

Krissik seemed to make up his mind. "My planet is been at war for centuries," he said. "You must understand before I say you anything else. We fight each other, Carly. This is what we do. Is so many *things* is... we no seem to get along. Ever. If our species is ever studied elsewhere in galaxy, it is because we fight so much with ourselves."

Carly nodded, urging him on.

Krissik looked out the window. "We fight and fight and... we have always fought this way. Is all I ever know. Is all any have ever know. Your planet has its wars, but they are more localized. They are not like what we endure."

Carly nodded again, her breathing picking up speed.

"Sometimes our wars is bad," Krissik said. "We forget about Earth for time, though we have known about you for millennia. Our cultures is no so different. Is been enough interbreeding over the years... my species is filled with human DNA."

"That's why you look so similar to us," Carly cut in. "Your DNA's been watered down."

Krissik glanced at her and nodded. "Our species fall in love or drawn to one another naturally. Is how stories say it." He looked back out the window as they climbed, staring off the side of the road and into the canyon below. "But then came sickness... so many men died in war, and sickness killed females. Targeted them. We is no sure if nature, or if created in lab...."

Carly shivered. *This is some creepy stuff.*

Krissik faced her. "Our species faces extinction. We know we can breed with humans, and so became necessary."

"So, you started taking them."

"A little." He nodded slowly. "Then more and more."

The gentle uphill slope of the mountain grew more pronounced as Carly drove.

Krissik went on, "Before we knew, our government sanctioned jumps. All stories of old love disappeared. By time I in school, humans is described as similar to us, but less intelligent, with less self-awareness. Though instant I met Samantha I knew all was untrue."

Carly tried to imagine Krissik's first encounter with her feisty friend and had to smile. This discussion, disturbing as it was, kept her from thinking too hard about what they were about to do, and helped her steer along the road.

"What was your first thought when you met her?" she asked.

Krissik stared out the window, his breath fogging the glass slightly. "I thought she was beautiful," he said softly. "The most beautiful thing I had ever seen."

Carly's hands tightened around the wheel. *I shouldn't have asked.*

Krissik seemed to catch the movement and he frowned. "I amazed by Samantha. I thought finally, I have someone for myself. Then Samantha fight me, yelling at me and I could only think I make a really terrible mistake." Krissik laughed, returning his attention to Carly. "Was so *difficult*. As a child, I taught humans females is easy, Samantha would want me immediately. When Samantha fought I... I could not understand."

"Well, maybe you shouldn't kidnap people," Carly said before she could stop herself.

Krissik reached across the center console as if to touch her, then hesitated. "I trying to say you how I raised... I thought what we did is right. For survival of our species. I never realized females would come... willingly. I was wrong about many things, Carly. I know this now."

Carly supposed he was referencing her. She braked a little too late and took a hard left turn, skidding precariously close to the edge of the road.

Krissik cleared his throat. "There is some who did no like what we did. Our government sanctioned the relocation, they say it."

"Relocation," Carly repeated. Like they were moving refugees from one planet to another. "That's a merciful spin."

"They say us that without my species, yours would be left alone in the void. That was the way they sold it to us?" He glanced at her to see if he had used the right phrasing, then continued at her nod. "Is other things out there, Carly. Other species. Bad ones. We is no so bad. Not great, looking now—but no *bad*. I always told we rescuing humans from a worse fate, from an invasion that might come, something your planet can no fight."

Carly almost jammed her foot down on the brake. "What? Invasion? Other species?"

"We not alone," he said. "In universe. Our government has say yours what is outside, and your people afraid. Is why they let us take what we want, because without my planet's protection, without weapons, your world is dust. Your leaders is afraid, and so they let us—let *them*—take what is wanted."

Carly had to stare straight ahead at the road. The wind was starting to kick up; the clouds overhead looked like they promised rain. She felt around the controls, making sure she knew where the wiper blades were. For a few moments, the only sound was the engine's steady thudding as it gunned its way around the winding road.

We could be out here at the end of the world, and no one would know.

Would Samantha send a search party after them if they did not come back? Rikist would try to find them, she knew; but if he could not reach them in time, if they ran up against some adversary they could not outsmart or outfight...

Well, then it would not matter. Carly and Krissik would disappear, and that would be the end of it. Carly wondered what Samantha would tell her parents.

"So, there's a risk for interstellar war?" Carly asked because talking about something was better than talking about nothing.

Krissik chuckled humorlessly. "War? Your species no be able to put up much fight." He sighed, inspecting the gun in his lap. "In truth, neither can we. We no very big in universe. But we say to your leaders otherwise. Is let us get what we want."

"Back up to *alien invasion*."

"Is no happening."

"But you just said—"

"I say we threaten Earth. Is other bad things out there in universe, Carly. Much badder than us. But they no concern themselves with Earth. You are... inconsistent?"

"I don't know if that's the word you want." Carly thought about the various words he might be trying to say. "Inconsequential?"

Wow, she thought. *Sometimes I impress even myself.*

"Yes. Earth is too small. But Earth no know that, so Earth is afraid and lets *my* world do as wants." He looked at her, the earnestness in his voice almost frightening. "Do you understand?"

Giant drops of rain splattered against the windshield. The beginnings of a late summer storm. Carly turned on the wipers, setting them to their slowest speed, and tried not to think too hard about Krissik's revelation.

Both of our species are small fish in a big sea, she reasoned. *I don't go chasing after ants unless they get in my way. Why would a bigger alien species come after us?*

Then again, holy shit. There's all kinds of shit out there—what if one of them does *decide to bloody our noses, one day?*

Krissik did seem to excel at turning her world upside-down.

"Do you guys talk to other species?" Carly asked.

"Some trade, but mostly stay ourselves." He grimaced. "We is no liked very much."

Ah, great. We couldn't have teamed up with the schoolyard bullies to keep Earth safe?

Were humans and even Krissik's races really that low on the totem pole?

"And everyone thinks humans are dumb?"

"No just like children, almost. Little ones." He played with the gun barrel, his tone growing gentler. "When Rikist and Lindsey paired, I no know what to make of her. I no understand her humor... she is—*was*—very sarcastic is the word, I think. I no did understand why she say things certain ways, or why Rikist finded it appealing. The translator no allows some things going through. Rikist learned English through military, and he understood."

Carly thought translators seemed like a wonderful technology. It was a pity they included built-in tracking devices. "But you got used to it."

"Eventually a little, but no really. Now, spending time with you and Samantha, I understand more. Is bothers me what is done to this world and Samantha." He cast her a sideways glance. "And you. What maybe still happen to people here... people I care for."

He did not have to say, *and that's why I'm doing this.* It was implicit in his speech. Carly let go of the wheel long enough to reach across the seat and rub his knee. Krissik's hand covered hers, and he squeezed her fingers gently, his thumb tracing over hers.

They were going to rescue Mandy, shut down the jumpgate, and bring themselves home to Samantha. It was the only option—the only thing they *could* do. Carly's heart pounded.

Are you crazy, woman? You can't pull this shit off. Let me phone in my shrink to get some medication to take that heroic edge right off.

"People change," Krissik said.

"Yeah," she murmured, a lump building in her throat. "People do."

SIXTEEN

The abandoned mining town of Independence passed by on their right.

There was a sign indicating a stop-off point; Krissik shook his head when Carly began to slow, indicating that she should keep driving instead. She ignored him and pressed on the brake, pulling over to the side. She shifted into park and leaned across the passenger seat for a look.

Krissik's hands twitched in eagerness. "We have to go," he said. "Are you waiting for Rikist?"

"I just want to take a look."

Maybe a look at the town would give her some clue, some insight about what they were facing, or what they would face. Maybe she just wanted a glimpse of a town decimated by alien abductions long before society even had the time to create such conspiracy theories.

Theories that turned out to be true.

Rain dribbled down from the heavens, splattering against the windshield. Carly turned on the wipers again, and they slapped across the windshield. The rest spot where she had pulled over was quickly turning into mud.

A sign just to the right of the car read INDEPENDENCE, and below the letters were smaller, indecipherable texts, probably describing the loss of the town and what had become of it. From what Carly could see, no one had ever returned since the late 1800s, the powers that be had left it alone, and no one had touched it since. The rotted buildings and silent town center were visible through the windows.

Had the people who found the empty town looked to the stars and wondered if their kinfolk were up there?

All those people... just taken away.

Carly shook her head, put the car back into drive, and got out onto the road. She was glad to put the town in her rearview mirror.

"Why did you stop?" Krissik asked.

"I don't know what I thought. I guess I just knew I had to pause and look."

Krissik nodded, but she saw him looking at her out of the corner of his eye. *Humans,* he seemed to mouth.

That's us, she thought. *Always looking for something to move us.*

She crept along the mountain, the wiper blades sloshing water away from the windshield. A bolt of lightning flashed, illuminating the side of the mountain. She drove as quickly as she dared, feeling the tires occasionally slip against the old asphalt.

"How long until they can make the jump?" she asked.

Krissik glanced at the clock on the dashboard. Three o'clock in the morning. "The jumpgate needs to build power. Rikist saw signatures when is appeared last night. They maybe keeping tabs on Mandy through human agents here, but we only came through jumpgate when power is ready."

"Signature?"

"Rikist is been tracking power surges for potential jumps," Krissik said. "Scanning every twenty-four hours should have been enough. I wonder is they timed it that way."

Smart cats.

Carly saw the turn-off for the mine and took it, further slowing her speed. The visibility was much worse now, and the rain was coming down harder and harder. Mist blurred around the road, creeping up on the truck. It was shaping up to be a nasty storm—and here she was, driving toward God knew what. She could barely see a few feet in front of the truck.

"Stop here," Krissik said.

Carly braked.

"A little further forward."

She edged the truck along the road, and then braked again—directly behind a black van. *The van that took Mandy?* She supposed it could not be a coincidence—not at this point. She shut off the engine and turned to Krissik. "How did you know?"

He grinned. "I vision is better than yours."

Of course, it was.

Carly pulled the keys from the ignition and tucked them into her pocket. "So, now what do we do, Kris?"

Krissik pressed the smaller of their two guns into her hands. It was a pistol—or at least she thought of it as a pistol.

"You say you learned to shoot? You aim, you pull the trigger."

"No safety?"

"What?"

She checked the gun. No safety. Krissik's people certainly lived life on the edge. "Never mind. But what's the *plan?*"

"One moment."

Krissik pulled out his cell and dialed in several numbers. He placed it to his ear, holding up one finger to keep Carly from saying anything. She heard Rikist's deep voice on the other end of the line, though, between the growing thunder and the rain pattering against the windshield, she could not make out what he was saying.

"We is arrived at mine," Krissik said. "We found the van." He rattled off the license plate numbers, innocuously enough—and then nodded. "Yes. Is the one."

Rikist spoke a bit longer. Carly stared at Krissik,

waiting for him to put it on speaker, but he did not. Krissik tapped his fingers against his thigh. Nervous.

"Yes," he said. "See you soon."

He hung up.

Carly looked at him expectantly. "Is he going to be here to help us?"

"He is on his way. He is tracking... tracking *us*, I suppose. He has databases he checks, and this van is listed. Is the human element of the operation."

Carly sat back. "So, he worked with the guys inside?"

"Maybe one time." Krissik sighed. "He has no schematics of what is inside, if is a base at all. Rikist thinks the humans is just *in* there, waiting. We must go in blind."

Carly listened to the rain tap against the windshield, a sudden sense of calm spreading over her body. If they pulled this off...

If? There was no if.

They would go in shooting, grab Mandy, blow the jumpgate, and flee. It was essentially a mission of destruction, and destruction of a sort had always followed Carly around. She imploded relationships, friendships, and people. Blasting an interstellar jumpgate and a team of hostile cat-people was a logical extension of that.

She reached over and took Krissik's hand. She squeezed his fingers, grasping at the warmth of his skin.

This time will be different, she told herself. *Together, we will get through this.*

Krissik nodded, his face worried. "We should wait for Rikist."

Carly nodded. "We should."

"You no want to."

"We can't."

Carly pushed the car door open and stepped outside, her heart rate surprisingly low.

We're just going into an ambush, that's all.

She held the gun tightly in her left hand. Krissik came around the side of the truck, and Carly's right threaded again through his left, almost of its own accord.

I just want to touch you. I just want to know I'm not alone.

Krissik gave her a reassuring squeeze. His thumb stroked along her skin. "You will be strong," he said. He bent and kissed her, rain dripping down his face. "I know you will be strong."

"I know," Carly said. "Because I have you with me. Now let's blow this thing to hell!"

They got out of the weather as they stepped under the mine's overhang. The cold continued to chill deep in her bones, and she heard the rainwater running through nearby tunnels. It was cool here, darker, the mine tunnel itself stretching away from them. Krissik squeezed her hand again, and led her forward, their advance taking shape in the darkness.

They crept down the tunnel. Carly's heart began to pound; she could hear it thumping in her ears, feel the blood churning in her veins. Her eyes adjusted slightly to the darkness; she could make out the walls around them, the empty sconces where lanterns had once hung. How frightened had Mandy been, when they took her here? Unable to see, probably stumbling against the walls, without a friendly presence like Krissik to hold her hand, to guide her?

Carly focused on Krissik, letting herself fall into the pool of warmth radiating from his slightly trembling hand. She knew he was scared as well; Krissik was a desk jockey, a brilliant student of architecture, not a soldier like his brother. Yet, here he was, putting himself between Carly and the threat before them to save Mandy.

Carly choked back the thickness welling in her throat. She had never loved him more.

The tunnel sloped downward, and they ventured deeper into the mountain. Krissik stopped and tilted his head to the side, listening for something Carly could not quite hear. He released her hand, then took her wrist, and pushed her hands together around her gun.

Carly understood the signal well enough: *get ready to fight*.

She nodded in the darkness. She had the gun, and she could shoot it or throw it or rush someone or...

Oh hell, what am I supposed to do?

Krissik stuffed the disk-like bomb into the back of his belt under his shirt, keeping both hands on his pistol, and set off again, one foot in front of the other. Carly saw him moving away, the bulk of him invisible to her except for traces of his stealthy movements. She kept him within her range of vision as the tunnel began to twist and turn. She knocked into the walls and had to slow her pace even more. Humans were not meant to move through such darkness. She turned a bend and froze at a junction illuminated by dim, green light.

Shit. Where was Krissik?

Carly's breath hitched in her throat. Her eyes searched the darkness, unsure which direction he had gone.

Krissik's hand reached back, found Carly, pulled her to his chest. He was warm, solid, and strong behind her. Carly breathed in his scent, holding off the edge of panic.

I am safe. I'm safe with Krissik, and we are going to do this.

"You can stay," Krissik whispered. "Stay here safe, Carly."

Carly shook her head and kissed him. "I'm not leaving you."

Krissik's lips trembled as he kissed her again. He nodded and pressed his forehead against hers before stepping back. "Brace."

Carly clutched the gun.

They edged around another corner.

Carly jerked back, briefly dazzled by the light show they had just walked into. The tunnel had fallen away, revealing a massive high-ceilinged chamber dramatically lit from hanging lights above and below. This could not be the original mine itself—this was the result of years of recent digging work and careful thought. Carly had to blink several times to make sense of it all.

Nothing moved below them. They had walked in on an empty operation.

"We're too late," she whispered.

Krissik shook his head and put a finger to his lips. Then he gestured with his gun to a crate just beyond what Carly assumed was some sort of platform. She saw two hands wrapped around the bars. Small hands.

Mandy!

Krissik considered the layout, perhaps turning over a plan in his head. Carly pointed at the hexagon-shaped platform, which had several metal rods sticking out from various points around it. By far, it was the most technical-looking thing in the vicinity, surrounded by computer consoles, fancy buttons, and switches in myriad colors.

Jumpgate? she mouthed.

Krissik nodded.

Carly's instinct was to lob the explosive at the jumpgate and rescue Mandy in the ensuing chaos, but Krissik began to edge down the narrow pathway that led to the interior of the base. Carly followed him down a single, narrow ramp that extended from the cavern's wall, running along the inside of the hollowed-out space until it reached the floor. The men could not have brought Mandy through here, Carly realized, not in a cage, anyway. They must have had another way in and out of the mine.

They reached the floor. Carly was glad to step away from the rickety walkway.

"Is been here a while," Krissik whispered. "I wonder which faction they serve."

The jumpgate platform lay directly to their right. Carly pointed at it, but Krissik shook his head again.

"No," he whispered. "If we blow it... I no know how strong blast is. We need to get Mandy outside first."

Carly started to move across the floor to reach the grate, but Krissik stopped her. He pointed overhead. "Easy pickings."

They crawled around the base of the platform. Krissik crouched on full alert, examining every hollow, staring at every circuit board. He was taking stock of their situation, Carly figured. She could identify things to hide behind, watching their backs as he worked.

They reached the cordoned-off section with the crate. Carly could see Mandy now, hands wrapped around the bars, shivering—a miniature version of Samantha weeping silent tears. Carly's hands tightened around her weapon. How anyone could do that to anyone else—a *kid*, no less—deserved nothing less than a very slow, painful demise.

Fucking bastards.

Krissik suddenly shoved Carly behind him.

The predatory footsteps came silently, barely audible. Mandy gasped and shrank away, and two alien guards came into view. Krissik looked right, then left, then lifted his pistol and fired off three shots. The first went wide, burning a hole in the pallets against the wall, the others finding their marks in the center of the men's chests.

The fell silently in crumpled piles, their skin smoking.

The green lightning that zapped out of Krissik's gun sent Carly straight back to Las Vegas. Her heart leaped into her throat, and the mining base fizzled out of sight, replaced by the dark corridor of the hotel. Uniformed men were running by, and she had lost sight of Samantha again—*don't leave me, don't leave me!*

But Samantha was gone.

She always left.

Everyone left.

"Carly!"

Krissik's claws at Carly's neck jerked her back to the real world, to the base they were trying to infiltrate. "Carly!"

Carly shook her head, blinded by tears. *No, I can't have a breakdown here of all places. I can't!*

"Krissik?"

Krissik's face flushed with relief.

"Carly?" Many cried. "Is that you?"

Mandy's soft voice brought Carly back to herself. The tears subsided, and Carly stepped out of the shadow, crossing the distance to the crate. Mandy sat up, pushing her hands across her face, disbelief written across her delicate, dark features. "I—oh my God, you're *here*. Is Samantha—"

"It's just us," Carly said. "Sorry to disappoint. Are you hurt?"

Mandy shook her head.

Krissik came forward, and Mandy's eyes widened. She scrambled back against the crate, putting as much distance between herself and the man as possible. "He's—he's one of *them!*"

Shit.

All their haphazard planning and no one had thought to consider how Mandy might react when she saw Carly working in league with one of her kidnappers.

"No, no! He's a friend. He's here to help." She turned to Krissik. "Kris, can you get her out?"

Krissik stepped around Carly and began working on the locking device that kept the crate shut. "Give a moment," he said.

Mandy shrank back further.

Well, they might as well get the awkward introductions over with.

"Mandy, I'm sorry to dump this on you. Your sister's dating a cat-man alien. So am I, for that matter. She got all caught up in some of their world's shenanigans, and you're caught in the crossfire, and we're going to get you out." Carly placed a hand on Krissik's broad shoulder, squeezing it. "This is Krissik."

Mandy sputtered a response and then fell silent.

"Mandy?" Carly's voice came surprisingly calm and authoritative. "No breakdowns until we're back at the farm, okay? You can freak out all you want then. I know I'm long overdue for a panic attack myself, but we don't have the luxury of that right now, okay?"

Damn, I'm pretty good at pep talks.

Carly was even convincing *herself* not to flip, which, she had to admit, was something her psychiatrist would have been very proud of. Mandy was nodding, edging forward, looking at Krissik now with more interest than fear.

The lock clicked, and Carly heard something inside the device powering down. The crate slid open, and Mandy, without the shadow of the bars across her face, was free.

Mandy leaped out and into Carly's arms. "I was so scared," she whispered.

"That's okay," Carly said, deciding not to acknowledge that she, too, was deep down terrified. If she gave in to fear, even just for a moment, she would just freeze up, and that would be the end of this entire rescue operation.

I need to be strong for Mandy, strong for Samantha, strong for Krissik. I need to be strong for everyone.

She rubbed Mandy's back, took the girl's face in her hands, and looked her in the eye. "I know you're scared. But we're going to get out of here, and it's going to be fine."

Mandy nodded and blinked back tears.

Carly pointed at the two men sprawled next to the crate. "How many of those were there?"

"Four... five others. Maybe six?" Mandy sniffed. "And six men in suits."

"Men," Krissik said. "Men, like humans?"

Mandy started when Krissik spoke, and her lips trembled. "Yes."

Krissik frowned. "Where did they go?"

"They were talking to someone on the radio... or whatever they have. I don't really know. They had some kind of meeting to get to, and they just left those two. I guess they weren't expecting a rescue." Mandy shivered; she was barefoot and clad only in a T-shirt and shorts—probably her pajamas.

Carly looped an arm around the girl, squeezing her close. Mandy's shivering eased only slightly.

"With Rikist away, why would they?" Krissik muttered and pointed at the jumpgate. "We still have element of sunrise."

"Surprise," Carly muttered, glancing at Mandy, "And surprises are very overrated."

"We no know how long is they gone," Krissik hissed in warning. "Is plant this and go, before they return."

They edged toward the jumpgate. Krissik reached behind his back for the disk-like bomb and began inspecting the control panel and the jumpgate itself, searching for the right place to affix the explosive.

"Usually, is are not so many humans present," Krissik said. "Something is wrong."

"Maybe they got wind of Rikist destroying the other gates?" Carly asked.

Krissik looked up at her, his glowing yellow eyes brightening as he considered that prospect. "Is possible," he said. "Something has them on edge. They no work with so many usually."

"Why?"

Krissik's hands moved almost too quickly across the control panels for Carly to follow. "Plausible deniability."

Mandy stepped closer to them, watching their interaction. "So, all that stuff I see on *Ancient Aliens*—that's *real?*"

"No," Carly said. "Well, I don't know. Maybe some of it is. Kris?"

Krissik waved them off. "I no know what this *Ancient Aliens* business is about."

Carly grinned. Was that the slightest hint of snobbery she heard in his tone? Carly could not be sure. She shook her head and pulled Mandy closer.

"They've been in contact with us for centuries," Carly said. "If that answers your question."

Mandy seemed to briefly forget to be terrified and let her mouth slip open a little bit in awe. The budding researcher in her briefly surfaced. If they survived all of this, there might well be a paper or article forthcoming.

If they survived. Carly rubbed her eyes. When. *When.*

Krissik tucked the bomb back into his waistband and fiddled with the controls on the gate. A readout in a series of unfamiliar glyphs sprang up over his head, and he scanned them quickly.

"They is priming for another departure. A large

one. An older gate is this and takes long time is build energy for such a jump. Is must be sufficient store of energy to ship back so many." He looked at the women. "They must intend bringing humans with them."

Carly spied movement in the area near the crate. At least one man was coming toward them, and by the looks of his hair, he was not fully human. "Krissik!"

Krissik snapped to attention, the pistol back in his hands. "Go," he said, pointing at the ramp near the entrance. "I hold them."

Carly reached for him. "But Kris—"

"Now!"

Carly shoved Mandy up the ramp ahead of her. The two of them hurried along, pressing to the outer wall as much as they could. She heard the shout when the men discovered the empty crate. Mandy scrambled in front of her, her bare feet slapping against the steel flooring.

Carly glanced down over the railing at the room below. No one had noticed them yet. They were too intent on Krissik.

The entire room took on a green tinge. A second later, the report of the laser pistol—followed by the ear-splitting roar of bullets. "*Sa Tskir!*" someone bellowed. The laser stopped, but the bullets did not.

Krissik. They were shooting at Krissik!

Mandy stumbled as they reached the top of the ramp leading to the entrance of the tunnels. Carly gave her a push. Why had she stopped?

Then she realized what Mandy had run into.

What—or, more reasonably, *who*.

The human in black smiled at Mandy, though there was no humor in it. "Going somewhere?" he asked.

Mandy, seemingly at a loss for words, gave him the finger.

Carly did not stop to think. She lifted her pistol, lined up his head in her sights, and pulled the trigger.

Green light flooded the tunnel as the man's body dropped, revealing more men in black, and at least one alien.

"Mandy!" Carly barked, "get down!"

Mandy dropped to the floor, and Carly squeezed the trigger again and again. The little gun spat out bolts of green light, flooding the corridor, casting everyone within it in its pale blaze. They were packed so closely that Carly could not help but take a few out; the rest broke rank, drawing their own weapons.

"I want them alive!" someone bellowed from within the tunnel. "All of them!"

So, I can be one of your slaves? Carly seethed. *I don't think so.*

She kept pulling the trigger, but her little gun fell silent. It was warm in her hands—too warm, as if it had discharged too much and overheated. Or maybe the charge had run down.

How do these fucking things work?

The remaining men filtered out of the tunnel. One picked up Mandy by the scruff of her neck, as a mother cat would pick up her kitten. Two men in black grabbed Carly's arms, quickly plucking the pistol from her grasp. She kicked one, and he batted her foot aside with enough force to drive her to her knees.

She yelped as pain seared up her leg, and her arms nearly went numb from the men's suffocating grip.

A tall, muscular alien pushed forward, nearly a head and a half taller than the human men at his side. Faded stripes cut across his angled features, accentuating the four parallel scars running down the left side of his face. He wore a heavy-looking uniform full of awards and insignias. Most of them were in the same glyph language Carly had seen above the jumpgate. She wondered if he was a captain, or a general, or something in between. How far up the chain of command had they gone to bring Rikist and Krissik back to their world?

The alien shook his head at the women, his pink tongue darting out to caress his lips. Mandy whimpered and tried to back away, but the man held her neck firmly. The scarred alien seemed to enjoy Mandy's response, and his lips pulled back in a sneer.

He reached out, rubbing his wrist against Carly's face in a bastardized version of the gentle greeting Krissik and Samantha often exchanged. Carly had longed to sample it, but now it just felt like an invasion —as if he were rubbing his scent on her, claiming her. She tried to jerk away, but the human men tightened their holds.

"You," the alien addressed Carly. "Are a thorn in my side. Look at all the trouble you have caused me."

Carly scanned the bodies in the hallway: three men down, and another dead on the platform.

Not bad for her first gunfight.

Then Carly realized that the shooting below had stopped, too.

"Kris," she whispered.

The golden cat-like eyes dilated, and the man straightened. "Oh, so it is the younger brother who has come to see us? Figures. Rikist would have put up more fight." He smiled, his sharp fangs gleaming in the overhead lights. "I think we should see how much damage your little friend has managed to cause."

"Go to hell," Carly spat.

A clawed hand pointed down the ramp, and the men holding Carly turned her around to drag her along.

"I assure you, my dear," the man said, "you're well on your way."

SEVENTEEN

The men marched Carly and Mandy down to the bottom of the base. Krissik stood there, his hands on his head, his eyes alight with fury. Carly yanked her arms away from her captors and ran to him, and Krissik wrapped his arms around her.

"I killed a few of them," she whispered.

"Good girl," he said.

Carly used the moment to assess their situation. They were down to four humans in black and two cats, including the scarred, sociopathic leader. Six on two seemed like far kinder odds than twelve on two, but these men were ready for any resistance. The element of surprise had been used and lost, and now—well, now they would have to wait and see.

The big cat in charge paced back and forth a few times, moving with the same sort of bored, languid grace Carly had seen in the caged tigers at the Central Park Zoo. Predatory danger rolled off him in nearly-visible waves, making Carly's heart pound in her throat.

He finally stopped in front of Krissik, his nose twitching in slight distaste. Burning amber eyes stared down at Krissik, the very picture of an angry schoolteacher disciplining a wayward student.

"You've been very naughty, young Krissik Sa Tskir," he said in perfect English.

Krissik frowned.

"You don't know me," the officer said. "I suppose I am not as important as your brother... though I was—*am*—important in my own right. Your brother would never have gotten very far had it not been for me."

Krissik stiffened slightly as a light bulb went on in his head. "You coordinate some jumps," he said. "Captain... Captain Shir-Kas?"

The officer bowed his head and swept out a hand in a fair approximation of a human acknowledgment. "So, you have seen me."

"Only on vids," Krissik sneered. "Rikist no speaks well of you."

Shir-Kas lifted his chin and tapped a claw against the scar on his cheek. "I don't exactly hold him in high regard, either."

Carly glanced toward Mandy, who was still held firmly between her two guards. She watched the officer with wide, glazed eyes. She gave up struggling, for now; or maybe the resistance had just oozed out of her as she realized the direness of their predicament.

The officer strolled over to Mandy and extended one clawed digit. Mandy flinched away from him, but he lifted her head up with his talon, turning it this way and that.

"This one is almost too young," Shir-Kas said, "but too pretty not to take as a mate. Perhaps I can ask the elders if I can keep her for myself."

Krissik hissed. "You will no *touch* her!"

"I do not believe you get to dictate anything, Krissik. I admit I was hoping your brother would come through; the bounty on his head is remarkably high, and you... well, you've just been forgotten about."

Shir-Kas left Mandy and returned to Krissik, a cold smile playing across his thin lips. "But as Rikist Sa Tskir's younger brother, you know what we do to the families of traitors."

Carly's skin went cold. *Holy shit, this guy's a regular Bond villain.*

"Our family is already dead," Krissik said.

Shir-Kas reached toward Carly. He took a handful of her blonde curls, then swept his palm across her face. She winced, trying not to breathe in the strange, musky smell of him. Krissik smelled so *good* to her, and Rikist smelled neutral. Yet something about him churned her stomach, made her throat threaten to retch in disgust.

"Are they?" Shir-Kas asked. He pulled Carly's lower lip down to inspect her teeth. "This one seems in fine flesh. *Very* fine flesh," he added, staring at her T-shirt and the curve of her breasts. Carly instinctively wanted to shrink back but did not want to give him the satisfaction of seeing her afraid.

Krissik uttered a single, low growl.

Shir-Kas released Carly's face. "Human women are enticing creatures, aren't they?" he asked, moving back amongst his troops. "Something about them just sets the heart alight. So spirited, so fiery. Wonderful creatures to possess."

Krissik twitched behind her. The remaining two cat officers kept their guns leveled on him, one pressing the tip of the barrel against the base of his neck.

Shir-Kas grasped Carly's arm and jerked her away from Krissik. Carly dragged her feet, but the man's strength was inescapable, and she found her struggles futile.

Shir-Kas sniffed at her, and his lips curled back into something very far from a smile. "So, you have paired with this one already," he said. "Very interesting, Krissik. Did you not like the one you brought back initially? Or did your brother like her better? Rikist always gets what he wants, doesn't he?"

Tears stung at Carly's eyes as Shir-Kas spun her around and leaned over her.

This guy's a royal grade-A asshole.

She tried to gauge the distance between her hand and his sidearm. Maybe she could grab it, pop him in the head, and cause a diversion.

"You don't like me," Shir-Kas observed. "That is all right. You will, when his scent fades." He stroked Carly's hair, smiling again as she flinched and cringed.

"Krissik, dear boy, you *did* mark her. I didn't think you had it in you. All your files talk about your mildness, your willingness to follow another's lead. I would not expect to find you here, leading such... such an expedition."

Marked me? Carly almost swung around to look at Krissik but did not dare twist away from Shir-Kas. He was the sort of person you did not take your eyes off—if you wanted to keep your eyes.

"It's a shame you did not wait a little longer before racing off to Earth, Krissik. You would have benefited from our new solution."

The captain gestured to one of the other officers, who reached into his pocket and withdrew a vial. It was shaped similarly to the vial of pheromone that Krissik and Carly used. This vial was bigger, though, and the way Shir-Kas held it was triumphant rather than seductive.

His gaze drifted back to Mandy. "One dose of this, and your resistance will crumble. We have always managed to make the women of Earth desire us on a primal level... but this will wipe all hesitation aside. They will be ours. All of them."

"All of them?" Carly asked. "Little greedy there, aren't you?"

"He no means for himself," Krissik said darkly.

"No, of course not." Shir-Kas signaled to two of his men, and they came forward to hold Carly. "As I said, Krissik, you should have waited longer. Whatever went wrong with your *original* mate could have been fixed.

One sip of this new formula my men have designed, and she would never have looked at another man." His smile twisted even more. "And you would have returned to Earth soon enough, anyway."

Shir-Kas stretched out his hand to run it through Carly's curls again. "The women will win us the war, don't you think?"

Carly tried not to pull away from him; it would only encourage his behavior.

The vial was suddenly beneath Carly's nose again, and she caught a hint of mint. Much to her horror, her body responded immediately.

Shir-Kas must have seen it, must have seen the dilation of her pupils, sensed her slight intake of breath. An evil grin spread across his face and he knelt before Carly, leaning forward until his nose was only inches from the front zipper of her pants.

Tears slipped down Carly's face. She wanted nothing more than to knee the bastard in the face and watch blood drip from a broken nose. Yet, her knees had gone weak and her skin hot with a sudden rush of electricity as silky wetness pooled between her legs.

Shir-Kas breathed in through his nose, testing the air. He nodded and then ran a hand along Carly's thigh as he stood.

"Half a bottle of this, and they will do whatever we ask of them," Shir-Kas said. "*Whatever* we ask. I will not even need an invasion force, with half of Earth's population on our side, and I will finally secure my deserved rank."

Carly started. *He wants our planet.*

"Taking the women isn't good enough for you?" she asked. "Invasion force? You want our planet, too?"

If she strung him along, got him talking, Krissik might be able to work his way free, or maybe she could think of a plan. *Just distract him. You're good at distracting men.* Granted, she usually did her distracting in a slinky dress and without a mass of dirt and sweat clumping her curls together, but she could do this.

Shir-Kas's flat, golden eyes sized her up. Carly did not like the way he looked at her: like she was a piece of meat, a fish to be batted around. It was the way she had looked at many of her boy toys, and she found she did *not* fancy the glint in his eye.

Carly's heart felt a little twinge. Had she ever looked at *Krissik* this way?

Shir-Kas extended his claws and inspected them, much like a woman would study a new manicure. Then he looked back at Carly, his fangs showing as he offered her a wide, predatory smile.

"Your kitten did not tell you the full story of our world, did he?" he asked. "He did not tell you that we are doomed. All the centuries of warfare."

"Some," Carly said.

Shir-Kas nodded. "We have destroyed our world, much as you humans are destroying your own. Our planet can no longer sustain life, to any degree. Within twenty years, our last resources will be drained. So, we will come here." He paused. "To

Earth. To save it from human hands and repurpose for our needs."

"You're just going to take it over?" Mandy asked.

Shir-Kas swept away from Carly and approached Mandy, his claws outstretched. Mandy shrank away, but he only buried his hand in her long, dark hair, jerking her face upward so he could better look at her.

"I say, Krissik, you did have excellent taste. The files of your lost Samantha show a great beauty. But her sister is even prettier." He lowered his head to her neck and sniffed—once, twice, three times—and a satisfied tremble coursed through his body. Then he smiled, showing all of his teeth. "And unmarked by any other. She's fresh. Untouched."

Krissik twitched.

"Your species will welcome us," Shir-Kas said to Mandy's neck.

He nuzzled her, rubbing his cheek against her throat, and then nosing his way down, pushing her shirt collar aside to better sniff at her. Mandy squeaked in protest, writhing away from him. The captain snuffled along her body, and then pulled back, still smiling wide.

"I must admit, I did not expect this mission to be so fruitful. I have two doses of this new serum with me, Krissik. Which lady do you think I should use it on first? This little one here... or your pretty golden girl?"

Krissik drew back his lips from his teeth and let out a harsh, high-pitched hiss. His eyes burned as the guard's gun tips pressed against his temples.

"This little one is so resistant," Shir-Kas cooed. He stroked Mandy again, much as one might stroke a housecat. "But she is not the test market, is she? We already have a formula that will make her do exactly as we please, and she will enjoy doing it. We need to test it on something *tainted*."

Tainted? Carly felt her lips pulling into a scowl.

Wait. He's talking about testing that shit on me!
Fuck.

Shir-Kas swung back to Carly, the intent in his gaze obvious.

"What if we try it on a woman already claimed?"

"I'm not claimed," she growled.

The captain's boots clicked softly on the grated floor as he approached. "Oh, but you are," he said. "You smell of Krissik... you *reek* of him, actually. Your senses have dulled over time, but anyone with a functioning olfactory capability can see—*smell*, pardon me—that you are his, and he is yours."

Carly closed her eyes and looked away, unable to look at Shir-Kas, at Krissik, at any of them.

"Well," Shir-Kas amended, "for now, at least. I am curious to see how this works on a mated woman."

His hand grabbed her face. Carly yelped in surprise, then slammed her mouth shut when she saw the vial coming toward her. Shir-Kas gripped her jaw and jerked her toward him, away from the officers holding on to her arms. "Let us see the women stand at our sides when our ships begin landing."

Shir-Kas' talons pinched Carly's face. Carly

ground her teeth, ignoring the thin rivulets of blood that ran down from her pierced flesh. Shir-Kas worked the stopper out one-handed using his teeth, and brought the vial up to Carly's lips. The scent of mint and a touch of something else, some additional chemical or reworked pheromone, washed over her, even more fragrant than the vial Krissik usually used.

Carly's body reacted. Her core ached, and she felt her pants damped as her knees gave way. Shir-Kas wrapped his arm around Carly's waist and held her upright, his face dipping to brush against her breasts.

Carly knew instantly what the reaction meant if the liquid made it past her lips: she would drink this, and Krissik would be a distant memory. He would no longer matter. Nothing would matter. She would swear allegiance to Shir-Kas, do whatever he asked, and she would be the beginning of the end.

Oh, no. I don't think so.

Carly brought her right knee up between Shir-Kas' legs. He doubled over, the vial slipping from his fingers. Pain seared Carly's left cheek as his claws slipped away, and she gasped and stumbled back. She heard his men startle, heard them moving toward her—and did not care. Shir-Kas had released her, and she balled her fists and hauled off to strike him across the face.

"Fuck you!"

It was a meager hit in the scheme of things. It probably would not even leave a bruise.

Carly heard a grunt and a squeal behind her,

followed by the discharge of an energy weapon, and she turned.

Krissik had broken loose, punched one guard, and shot another. They struggled for control of the weapons, the guns shooting off around the cavern.

Carly reached for Shir-Kas' gun, pulling it out of the holster at his hip, aimed and pulled the trigger. The energy burst hit the captain in the shoulder, sending him sprawling.

Carly sprinted away from him, toward the jumpgate, only one thought on her mind: *I have to destroy this thing.*

She pointed the gun at the console and began pulling the trigger. The gun had minimal recoil, and green lightning hissed and spat out of its muzzle, dancing across the electronics. Sparks flew, and steam began to rise.

"Die," she said through gritted teeth. "You won't have me *or* my planet—"

Thick arms wrapped around Carly, knocking the gun aside and trapping her hands to her chest. Carly tried to wrench herself free, and half-spun around, facing the irate Shir-Kas and his cold, gleaming eyes.

He held up the vial and wriggled it before her. "You will come to regret that you little bitch," he hissed.

He did not even seem to notice the damage Carly had done to the jumpgate. Maybe he did not care. Why would he? There were probably dozens of jumpgate sites around the world. This one was hidden away, mostly forgotten, and allowed for the element of surprise, but it was hardly the only thing available to them.

She struck at him.

Shir-Kas swiped at her. His claws tore across her shirt, and Carly squeaked in pain as new fire bloomed where the talons nicked her skin. Red ran down the front of her T-shirt, and Carly stumbled backward, her arms folding over herself.

So, this is it. Krissik, I am so sorry.

Shir-Kas stepped toward Carly, the vial held high. "I have not worked this hard to gain power to have some human bitch destroy my plans." He bared his fangs. "You *will* fucking want me."

Green fire crackled behind him, and Shir-Kas stopped, as if startled. He looked down at a sizzling hole in his chest, and then over his shoulder. A second and third beam of laser fire ripped through his chest and side of his throat. The smell of seared flesh billowed outward in a thin line of smoke.

Then Shir-Kas toppled forward in a heap. The vial rolled away from his limp hand, its precious fluid dribbling onto the floor.

Rikist stood panting and dripping wet above Shir-Kas's body, a charged laser pistol in his outstretched hand.

"You know," he said, "I always fucking hated that shit."

EIGHTEEN

Rikist lunged toward Carly, plucked her dropped gun from the floor, and shoved her behind one of the metal pillars that supported the ceiling of the base. Perhaps stunned into silence by Shir-Kas' fall, the others in the room regained their senses, and the shooting began anew.

"Krissik!" Carly called out.

"I'll get him," Rikist said. He pointed a clawed finger at her. "You stay here. *Do not move.*"

He left her there, clutching her weapon.

Something splattered against the floor beside her. Standard bullets—Carly realized—not the alien-issued guns. She looked up and saw two more of the black-suited human men standing there, firing on her. She lifted her gun up and fired back, too angry to worry about aiming properly.

She heard the brothers shouting to each other in their native tongue like angry lions howling. Carly stepped out slightly, still shielded by the pillar, and lined up one of the suits standing on the catwalk and fired.

Green light enveloped the man, and he tumbled toward. His partner shrank away, sticking to the relative cover of the cave they had entered through. He was picking his shots; he knew Carly was there, waiting, with her gun.

How many more are there? How big was this base?

"Carly!"

Krissik and Rikist joined her behind the pillar. Blood ran down the side of Krissik's face, his left eye bloodshot and swollen. Carly forgot all propriety for a moment, forgot about the firefight, and instead wrapped her arms around Krissik. He hugged her back and then released her when he felt the blood running down her chest.

"He hurt you."

"It's fine," Carly said. At least, she hoped it was fine. Maybe it was not fine at all, and she was going to slowly bleed to death... but at least she was of her own sound mind, and Krissik held her in his arms.

That was all that mattered anymore.

Carly looked up. "Where's Mandy?"

"They still think they're going to bring *someone* through that gate," Rikist said. "They want something to show for their trip. Though I think Carly shooting up the coordinates may have bought us some time."

He leaned around the pillar and fired several shots

in the opposite direction. The other side returned fire, and Rikist jerked back behind cover.

"What did you find out?" Krissik said.

"At least two of my previous contacts have been killed," Rikist said. "I think there was a coup back home. It's the only explanation why Captain Priss over there could come through at all."

"Priss?" Carly said.

Rikist grinned at her. "Shir-Kas is known to be... high maintenance. He coordinates many of the jumps but doesn't often come through on his own. If he's out here, there's been a change in leadership."

"The triumvirate?" Krissik asked.

"Maybe."

More fire splattered against the other side of the pillar. Carly looked at the men. "How about we discuss politics back at home. What do we do now? Wait until they run out of ammunition?"

"We don't want them sending backup," Rikist glanced overhead and spotted one of the men who had been shooting at Carly. "Right now, the problem is that jumpgate. Others may come through. We can destroy it and figure out what's going on back home afterward."

Krissik shifted his gun to his left hand, dug behind his back and pulled out the bomb. "I made this."

"Fucking genius," Rikist said. He gave his brother an approving look. "But how do we get it there?"

"We need to get Mandy," Carly said.

Rikist frowned at the mention of Samantha's sister

and then nodded. "Jumpgate first," he said. "They can't take her anywhere if that's gone."

"But they could kill her!"

Krissik's fist closed around the explosive. "Is two of us, and both better shooters than Carly. Can we give cover fire?"

"Does she even know how what to do?" Rikist asked.

"I can teach her."

"We shouldn't risk her."

"You have better ideas?"

Rikist stared his brother down, the challenge evidently not sitting well.

Carly looked between the two of them, shook her head, and said, "For God's sake! Tell me what to do, and I'll do it!"

Another few seconds, another wordless exchange between the brothers. Carly knew the aliens depended heavily on body language—a twitch could mean anything; a long stare might take the place of an entire conversation.

At last, Rikist nodded. "Tell her what to do," he said, leaning back around the pillar. "I'll cover us."

Carly and Krissik crouched down. Here, behind the pillar and close to the floor, she could almost tune out the sound of bullets and laser beams smashing around them, could almost enjoy the sweet scent of kitten fur and man that blended together in such a tantalizing fashion. Krissik reached into his pocket and retrieved the bomb and held it out before her.

"Is very simple," he said. "Place it like so, on one of generators—"

"Generators?"

A look of annoyance flashed across Krissik's face. "The... the things, is poking out."

Carly craned her neck to get a look at the platform with its jutting apparatus and nodded. "Got it."

"Place this side down... is hooks will hold it to anything solid."

Carly nodded, absorbing his instructions. "How do you set it off?"

Krissik's brows came down. "I no have time to make a trigger," he said. "You will push in both sides, like this..." He mimed squeezing the bomb. "Is will set off countdown. You have ten seconds to get away from it."

"Countdown?" Carly could only picture countdowns from the movies, usually on large nuclear devices one had no chance of outrunning. She balked at him. "It's not going to blow up the whole mountain, right?"

Krissik blinked at her. "What is you think I am capable of? Is localized and take out jumpgate. We no need to blow up entire mountain."

Of course. They did not *need* to blow up the mountain. Good of him to point that out. Carly gave him a grim smile. "Where do I put it?"

"On side of round thing, there." Krissik moved around so that he was sitting next to Carly, and he pointed at the arch situated in the center. "Just place, squeeze, and run."

Carly nodded, mentally picturing the base they were in. "Okay. I can do this."

"Is my girl." Krissik reached over to touch her face.

After Shir-Kas' lingering, slimy caresses, Krissik's gentle manner nearly made Carly weep in gratitude.

Krissik sighed, running one talon down her cheek. "He tried to mark you."

"It was awful."

"Hey," Rikist crouched down to join their circle. He grimaced and shifted his weight off his bad knee. "Can you two confess your true love for each other later? Let's blow that jumpgate, and then get the fuck out of here?"

"He's right," Carly said.

Rikist's feral eyes were downright troubling—anticipation rippled across his face as if he were looking forward to the upcoming firefight. Carly glanced at the scars lacing the backs of his hands, crisscrossing up his forearms as they laced through the fading stripes.

Scary as hell or not, at least Carly felt a little better having the big cat at their backs.

"We'll lay down cover fire," Rikist motioned with one hand. "Carly, after you plant that bomb, run straight back to the walkway out. We'll be behind you. I'll go first."

"But your leg," Krissik said. "Is only ten seconds after Carly arms—"

"It'll work."

"But can you move fast—"

"It'll *work*, Krissik." The hard-edged military persona seeped out of Rikist's pores, his fangs bared in authority. His pupils dilated and contracted in the amber irises. He placed a hand on his brother's shoulder and gave a reassuring squeeze. "Trust me."

Krissik hesitated, his face pained as he looked between Carly and Rikist, and then finally nodded.

Carly straightened up, held her pistol tightly in her left hand, and took the bomb in her right, being careful not to squeeze it too tightly. They would not want to set the thing off before she had even had time to plant it correctly.

"On three," Rikist said. "One, two..."

Krissik yelled out, "Three!" and leaped around the pillar and opened fire.

Green bolts flew around the room, and Rikist swore briefly in his native tongue before jumping out after him. The brothers advanced on the other side at a dead run, laying down a heavy amount of fire to distract their opponents from what Carly was about to do.

What I have to do.

Carly took a deep breath, hefted the bomb, and took off at a dead run for the jumpgate. She took the platform steps two at a time, skidding to a stop in front of the console, where she saw more of the glyphs and mysterious etchings. She bypassed them, moving straight to the arch, to the jumpgate itself—the business part of the device. This was how the aliens had come through, and how they might summon backup. This was where they would take Mandy if they got their way.

Carly slapped the bomb against the arch and squeezed the sides. It fused immediately, the tiny hooks embedding into the surface. A blue light beeped, indicating it had fixed itself properly.

At least, I think that's what it means.

Carly realized the sign might be telling her something was wrong, that the explosive would not go off, but she had no idea how to tell otherwise—and with ten seconds to get the hell away, she really did not give a damn.

Carly glanced over her shoulder. Rikist and Krissik had retreated behind separate pillars, each driven back and pinned down by the alien forces. The aliens and their black-suited companions had set up a defensive perimeter by the cages. They seemed snug and safe behind a wall of large boulders and sheets of steel.

Boy, are you in for an unpleasant surprise.

Carly squeezed the bomb. She felt a minute click as something engaged, and then the blue light began to blink steadily. She sprinted away from the jumpgate, her sneakers slapping on the grated floor.

"Go!" she shouted at Krissik and Rikist as she blew past them. "Go! Go! Go!"

The brothers fell in behind her, Rikist at the rear, his gun firing at the gathering of men on the other side of the base as Carly and Krissik retreated.

Five...four...three...

Carly flung herself behind one of the support pillars on the opposite end of the room. Krissik joined her, and he wrapped his body around hers as a shield.

One.

Rikist dove toward them as a flash of blue light exploded, flooding the chamber in brilliant shades of neon. Carly nearly dropped her gun in her effort to shield her eyes. Low rumbling swept through the base, and the ground shook beneath her feet. Overhead, the mountain groaned, dust particles raining down from the ceiling.

Carly looked up, trying to see between the pulses of lights in her eyes. If the whole cave collapsed, they were all going to die.

Carly watched an enormous chunk of rock ceiling give way and plummet toward the ground. The rock landed hard on the opposite end of the room atop the aliens and their makeshift perimeter. Two men—humans by the sound of it—began to scream in pain.

"We won!" Carly hollered, looking around.

"Is too strong," Krissik muttered.

Rikist stood, alarm across his face. "The entire structure is coming down!"

"*What?*" Carly gasped. Krissik had given her a tiny bomb, not something big enough to bring down an entire cave. Right?

Krissik fumbled with his gun, a hard look in his eye. "Rikist, get Carly out. I getting Mandy."

Carly's heart jumped. "Krissik!"

"Now!"

Krissik vanished around the pillar, and the moaning cave lit up with the sound of his shooting. Rikist grabbed Carly's upper arm and gave her a shove toward the ramp leading out of the cave.

The lowest section of the ramp attaching it to the cave wall began to groan, buckling beneath the cavern's rapidly-bowing interiors. The bolts against the wall snapped, and the ramp dropped. Rikist leaped forward and caught the steel ramp as it slid sideways, straining under the weight as he pressed it against the wall to hold it in place.

"Go," Rikist yelled. "Get out of here!"

Carly took a few steps onto the ramp and then stopped.

I can't just leave Krissik.

I won't.

Carly turned. She could just make out Krissik on the other side of the base, his auburn hair catching the flickering overhead lights. Their eyes locked, and the sudden tenderness she saw there briefly took her breath away.

"Hold it for us, Rikist!" Carly yelled, ducking under the handrail and past Rikist toward Krissik.

Rikist bellowed behind her in warning, but Carly tuned him out. Dust from the ceiling choked the air, and small stones hailed down.

Carly reached the barrier and came face to face with one of the men in black. She did not think twice; her gun came up, she pulled the trigger, and the man did not even have time to wince before he fell away from her. Carly squeezed between two portions of the barricade, stepped over his body, and moved into the fading light on the other side of the cave. The lamps there had shut down entirely, leaving only the emergency red lighting to guide her way.

"Mandy!" she called into the darkness. "Krissik!"

"Back here!"

Mandy's voice. Carly picked up the pace, trusting her feet to carry her over any rocks or obstacles. The corridor was still quivering, and dust particles descended faster than ever. They needed to get out—and fast.

She found Krissik and Mandy by a pile of rocks. "Cave-in," Krissik said matter-of-factly. He had Mandy in his arms. "Back other way."

Carly led them, gun at attention, searching for any sign of their enemy. The men in black had gone down, as had the cat-men; either crushed by falling rocks or shot by Krissik as he came by. They scrambled past the barricades and into the cavern proper, where larger rocks were beginning to fall from the ceiling.

"Come *on!*" Rikist roared.

Carly bounded up to the ramp, ready to sprint the final distance to freedom, when she heard Mandy shriek.

She skidded to a halt and turned, and there, holding an energy rifle, stood Shir-Kas, his uniform stained with blood and his left leg dragging behind him. Aside from that, he looked quite mobile.

God, how the hell was this guy still alive? Carly

lifted her pistol to train it on him, but Shir-Kas had his gun pointed firmly at Krissik, who still had his hands full with Mandy.

"I wouldn't, little golden girl," Shir-Kas said. "I can take off his head or hers. Which would you prefer?"

I liked you better when you were trying to seduce me. Carly did not dare look up at Rikist, still holding the ramp that was their only way out of this mess. If she pretended he was not there, perhaps Shir-Kas would not notice his presence.

Shir-Kas edged toward Krissik and Mandy. Carly began edging toward them, as well, her gun pointed at the floor now, trying not to look like too much of a threat.

"You have been very, very bad, as they say in English," Shir-Kas said. "When our leaders find out, and they will, you will be very, very sorry indeed."

What was there to do?

Nothing.

It was Krissik Shir-Kas would kill. Mandy, as a female, had automatic value; if his planet intended to take over Earth for its females, then killing Mandy would be the worst move he could make. No; he would shoot Krissik. That would leave Rikist to deal with, but Shir-Kas was obviously willing to take that chance.

Krissik saw her from the corner of his eye. "No, Carly," he said. "No."

Don't what? Don't hesitate? Don't shoot? Don't worry?

Carly kept her aim steady. Shir-Kas looked her way

and smirked, seemingly unmoved by the increasing rumbling of the cave.

What could they do, really? If they stayed here, they would all die when the cavern collapsed beneath its own weight. If Carly did nothing, Krissik would die, and Mandy would be taken captive... and then they would all die anyway.

Strange, how easy the choice was—when there was really no choice left.

She began firing, her finger holding down the trigger. The gun had little recoil, and Shir-Kas danced about as the bolts struck him. His own gun went off before flying away, clattering to the ground.

Krissik jerked as the energy bolt zipped past his head, grazing his temple. Then he snapped into action, closing the gap between himself and Carly.

"Run!" he yelled.

Krissik hurried ahead of Carly, cradling Mandy in his arms. Carly raced after them, the surprised expression on Shir-Kas' face permanently etched into her mind as falling dust nearly blurred her vision and burned her eyes.

Rikist shook under the weight of the walkway. His bad leg quivering uncontrollably. "Go," he said, I'll hold it."

Krissik tested his weight on the edge of the ramp. He grimaced as Rikist's hold wavered.

Rikist groaned. "Hurry the fuck up, Krissik!"

Krissik scrambled up the ramp and deposited

Mandy on a more secure level. He walked back to the edge and held out his hand for Carly.

"Carly, come on!"

Carly stepped onto the ramp. A sudden quake rocked the ground. Rikist cried out as his boots slipped, and the walkway came crashing down. Carly jumped back and held her breath as Rikist rolled out of the way, inches from being crushed.

"Carly!" Krissik shouted.

Rikist coughed and pushed himself to his feet. He looked up at Krissik elevated high above them. "I'm fine too, asshole. Thanks for asking."

Rikist held out his hand for Carly. "Come on."

Carly hugged her hands around her chest. "Come where? That was our only way out!"

Rikist grimaced, flashing his fangs. "I'm aware."

Carly yipped as Rikist hefted her up in his arms. "Tuck your legs in."

Carly snapped her head up. "What?"

"I'm going to throw you," he grinned. "Been wanting to for a while."

"What!" Carly screeched. "Wait, what about you?"

Rikist's grin wavered, then he shifted his stance. "Krissik, get ready!"

Carly's heart nearly stopped, and she held her breath as Rikist's strong arms tensed and knees bent. She closed her eyes and prayed.

Oh, holy Mary mother of—

Carly screamed as the wind rushed past her face as she flew through the air. She opened her eyes to see the platform rush toward her at an alarming speed. Krissik's hands were suddenly before her, and then Carly blinked, and she was in his arms on the platform.

She let out a gasp of air and blinked. "Shit!"

Krissik pushed her up the platform toward where Mandy crouched. "Get out!"

"What about Rikist?"

Carly leaned over the railing, looking down at Rikist. The ground heaved beneath Rikist's feet, sending him rocking sideways. Several more chunks of rock fell from the ceiling, and he dodged as a massive boulder crashed on the ground below.

Rikist looked up, his face covered in dirt and sweat. He panted as he looked between the edge of the platform and the fallen boulder. He took several steps back, his shoulders tensing.

"He's not going to jump, is here?" Carly asked. "There's no way he can make it. We're at least ten feet up."

"Fifteen," Krissik muttered. "Twelve if you take away boulder."

Carly gaped. "You're shitting me, he's—"

Rikist crouched, his hips wiggling like a tiger preparing to pounce on its prey, and then he dashed forward.

Krissik pushed Carly back and then dropped to his stomach and hooked one elbow around the handrail.

Rikist used the fallen boulder as a boost and leaped into the air toward the platform, his arms extended.

Carly's jaw dropped as he flew through the air toward them, slowed, and then started to fall.

The platform jerked and swayed as Krissik caught Rikist's arm. Krissik cried out as he slipped, his elbow wrenching against the steel pole. Carly dove and threw her weight against Krissik's legs as he slid forward toward the edge, and Mandy wrapped her arms around Carly's waist and braced her legs and against the wall. Krissik groaned and held on as Rikist reached up to the platform.

Rikist's sharp claws bit into the metal walkway. His head and then shoulders appeared as he dragged himself up. His chest heaved as he rolled onto the platform, his face pale.

Carly met Rikist's eyes, and she nearly laughed out loud at the wild look on his face.

OK, she thought, *at least I wasn't the only one about to shit my pants.*

Rikist grinned at her and then stood and hauled Krissik to his feet. He slapped Krissik's back and pushed him up the ramp.

"Let's get the hell out of here."

NINETEEN

They emerged into a wild, summer storm, rain whipping around the entrance to the cave.

Rikist led the way to Samantha's black SUV parked beside their old truck. He pulled Carly aside before she could reach for the door handle, his low voice.

"Look after Mandy," he said. "We're going to make sure nothing ever happens here again."

Carly nodded, though she did not quite understand. Hadn't they just destroyed the jumpgate? They were done, right?

Once inside the SUV, tucked away from the howling wind and sleet, she understood at least part of what Rikist had meant. Mandy shivered, rain and tears streaming down her face. Carly dug around in the backseat between Rikist's overnight bag and cooler, found a blanket, and wrapped it around the girl.

"It's okay," she said. "You're safe now."

Mandy's teeth chattered. Carly rubbed the blanket up and down her arms, trying to restore circulation and give her an ounce of comfort. A puddle of water spread around her on the seat.

Carly leaned into the front seat. The keys were still in the ignition, and she cranked up the engine just enough to get the heater started, and then switched the dial on that to full blast. Hot air poured out of the vents, quickly warming the car.

"Aliens," Mandy murmured, "they're *aliens*..."

"They're nice aliens," Carly said. "At least, these two are."

The passenger door abruptly yanked open. Krissik stood in the rain. "Carly, we need help."

Carly patted Mandy's knee. "Just stay here and warm up," she said. "I'll be right back."

She climbed back out into the rain. Rikist stood next to the black van, uncomfortably looking up at the sky. He started when Carly appeared and then pulled open the side door and pointed inside. Carly glanced at Krissik, and when he nodded, she poked her head in.

"Whoa."

Technical equipment lined the walls. Carly had not realized vans like this really existed—she had seen them in TV shows, of course, usually when an FBI agent was snooping on someone or other. To see one in real life, filled to the brim with sophisticated equipment, was pretty freaking amazing. She stared at the keyboards and brightly lit panels, the lettering in both English and cat-glyphs, and shook her head.

"What the hell is this? I mean, I see what it *is*, but what are they doing with it?"

"Colluding," Rikist said. "This goes high up. If there's *this* amount of equipment at an old jumpgate like this... I don't want to imagine what might be elsewhere."

Carly pulled her head out of the van and turned to stare at him. She swiped at her eyes, trying to push the rainwater away. "They said they were looking for *you*, Rikist. That they tracked Krissik to you. Is it possible this is a one-off? They brought all their gear because they were looking for you?"

Rikist seemed to mull over that idea. Krissik smiled at her and nodded, indicating approval of her line of thought. Carly smiled back.

Look at me, thinking like a military strategist.

"It's possible," Rikist said at last. "But I don't know if we can risk it. This needs to go, either way."

Carly nodded her agreement.

We can't get the car started, but we can push it over the cliff while you steer." Rikist said.

Carly could comprehend what Rikist intended to do but could not prevent a mental vision of the van—with her in it—sliding over the side of the cliff and plummeting into the abyss.

"Um," she said.

"I no let you get hurt," Krissik said. "Trust me."

Well, Carly, he hasn't let you down so far. Carly nodded and squished down her feelings of discomfort. "All right. Let's do this."

She climbed into the driver's seat, released the parking brake, and shifted the van into neutral. Rikist yelled that they were going to move, and she turned the wheel to the right. The van lurched forward, propelled by the strength of the brothers.

The van sloped downward to the right. Carly jammed her foot down onto the brake.

Holy shit, holy shit, this is a stupid way to die, holy shit!

Krissik appeared at the door, pried it open, and held out a hand. "We're done here, lass," he said in a horrible British accent.

Carly would have laughed aloud if she were not currently in a van dangling off the side of a cliff. She took his hand, and he pulled her from the van and wrapped his arms around her, his sturdy bulk shielding her from the cold and rain. Rikist gave the van a final shove, and it squeaked past them before rolling right over the cliff.

She heard the impact in the abyss below and saw a brief flare of light that was quickly obscured by the mist and rain. One less item in the hands of those who wanted to pursue them.

They turned back to the SUV. Mandy had switched on the headlights, briefly illuminating the three of them through the sleet. Carly slipped her arms around Krissik's waist, taking solace in his comforting, solid form.

"Can we go home?" she asked, her voice slightly muffled in his chest.

Krissik nodded. "Yes. We can go home."

They packed themselves into the SUV. Rikist took the keys and climbed into the driver's side; no one protested. Carly was not sure she could handle getting them back down the mountain, and Krissik—well, Krissik had had enough adventure to last all month, as far as she was concerned. He could just kick back and relax while Rikist drove.

"I'll have someone come pick up the truck tomorrow," Rikist explained.

"Someone should call Samantha," Carly said.

Krissik tossed her his phone.

THE SUV ROLLED to a stop in front of Samantha's house just before ten o'clock.

Just in time for breakfast, Carly thought.

Samantha had not said much when she called—she had mostly listened, so quietly that Carly had to confirm she was still on the line multiple times. Carly gave her the bare details: they had found Mandy, she was fine, and they were on their way home, completely intact and with one less jumpgate in the world.

Samantha had not really responded. Maybe she had not been capable.

Mandy had fallen asleep with her head in Carly's lap, and her shivering had finally stopped. The heater stayed on full blast for hours, until the men were visibly uncomfortable in the heat and Rikist had to crack a window. Even so, Mandy had continued to shake and whimper long after her clothes and hair dried.

There would be no easy fix for this. Carly thought of her own nightmares, of the lingering fears and terrors that had followed her from the Las Vegas invasion. Hers had continued even when she had reasons and understood the motives, if not the men themselves. They could not very well brainwash Mandy and tell her there had been a gas leak or some kind of mass hallucination like had happened countless times before with their government's aided abductions.

Rikist and Krissik were *here*, and they were staying, and in a few months, Mandy was going to become an aunt to some kind of hybrid.

My God, when did my life get so weird? And when did *Mandy's* life get so weird?

At least, Carly had had some time to absorb what was going on and figure out how to react to things. Mandy was getting dumped in headfirst. Krissik had been a towering pillar of strength for Carly; perhaps Carly could be there for Mandy in some similar fashion.

Yes, she would need friendship, Carly decided. Friendship, a strong shoulder, and someone willing to listen to her when things seemed unbearable.

Rikist turned off the car and sat there for a moment, listening to the ticking of the cooling engine. "We're here," he said, more to himself than to the passengers.

Krissik nodded. "Yes. We are."

The front door of the house flew open, and Samantha thundered out onto the porch, wearing the same jeans and T-shirt she had had on the day before. One look at her distraught expression and Carly wanted nothing more than to give her a hug—but she knew it was not Carly that Samantha wanted to see.

Rikist's calm demeanor all but evaporated, and his claws scrambled for the handle as he threw open the door and lurched out of the car to greet her. His big arms wrapped around her, and Samantha let out a sort of high-pitched keen, a wail that carried across the driveway and nearly stabbed Carly in the heart.

Carly watched them embrace for a moment, and then she nudged Mandy. "Hey," she said. "Your sister will want to see you."

Mandy lifted her head, blinked several times, and seemed surprised by the sunshine and the view around the car.

"The house," she said, reaching up to rub her eyes. "The house... we're back." Her eyes welled up, and she fumbled for the door, her fingers slipping off the handle. "I thought it was all a dream, that I was still with them."

"You're home now," Carly said. "You're safe, you're with us."

Mandy looked out the window and watched her sister with Rikist, and her eyes widened. "He's one of them, isn't he?" she asked. "He seems more human without the stripes, but..."

"He is. And he's one of the good ones." Carly touched her arm. "I know you'll have a ton of questions, and that's okay. Just think of them as people. Some are good, some are bad, and some probably just want to sell you something."

Mandy did not laugh at Carly's poor attempt at humor. Still, she did not dissolve into hysterical sobs, either, which was more than Carly had hoped for.

Mandy just nodded, then apparently bucked up and said, "Okay, I'm ready."

Carly reached for the door, got it open, and tried to get out—only to be jerked to a stop by her seatbelt. She unhooked the clip and slipped out, holding the door open for Mandy.

Mandy climbed out of the SUV, her bare feet touching the warm dirt. Samantha saw her, released Rikist, and rushed over, her arms wrapping around her younger sister.

Carly glanced up at the front porch and saw Rodolfo standing there, a wide-brimmed hat on his head. He touched his fingers to the brim of the hat, and she bobbed her head in response.

Samantha released Mandy and grabbed hold of Carly. "You brought her back," she whimpered into Carly's neck. "You brought her back!"

Carly realized it was probably the first time she had ever come through on a promise more substantial than bringing over coffee or a pizza. The feel of her friend's shaking arms around her was enough to know she had to this more often; Carly had to live for other people, not just for the daily pleasures of life.

Carly squeezed Samantha and then pushed away, running her hands through her friend's tangled hair.

"I'll always be here for you," she said.

Samantha smiled through her tears.

"Now go talk to your boyfriend," Carly whispered to her. "You have big news, right?" She stepped back, intending to give the two of them space.

Indecision flew across Samantha's face; she obviously had not considered how she would deliver this news, or how Rikist would receive it. Carly knew Samantha also had Mandy to consider now; Mandy, who had been there when they made the discovery, who had brought home the pregnancy tests, who now knew her sister was sleeping with some kind of alien. This had to be the weirdest introduction to a significant other *ever*.

Carly hesitated. *Should I stay here or leave them be?* Mandy leaned against the SUV's side, basking in the warmth of the sun.

Samantha made some sort of decision, grasped her sister's hands, and said, "Mandy, I guess it's time you met Rikist. Unless you guys are old friends already."

Mandy took a deep breath, nodded, and stood up straight with a smile. "No. No official introduction yet."

Samantha steered her toward Rikist, who tucked his hands behind his back and dug his toe into the dirt, a remarkably nervous move for such a large, powerfully built man.

Carly hid a smile and started to edge away, then bumped into a wall of warmth. Krissik stood behind her, and he delicately threaded his arm around her shoulders. Carly sagged against him, her exhaustion catching up with her. Her eyes felt gritty, she was sure she needed to brush her teeth, and her jeans and footwear were never going to recover from the beating they had received.

"You need to rest," Krissik said.

"You probably do, too."

Probably? Carly mentally shook her head. Krissik needed to sleep for at least a week, just like she did. She took solace in Krissik's strength, wanting nothing more than to crawl between the sheets and doze off, her head tucked into the crook of his shoulder. They could figure out everything else later.

They headed up to the front porch. Rodolfo stood waiting, his expression as unreadable as ever.

He extended his hand to Krissik. "Good work," he said. "Both of you."

Krissik shook Rodolfo's hand tentatively, as if not entirely sure what this custom entailed. He had shaken hands before, but Rodolfo had always viewed him with mild suspicion, at the very least. The old rancher was unfailingly polite, but there was an undercurrent of distrust that had lingered. Carly was glad to see that it seemed to have faded.

Rodolfo looked past him, back to the SUV. Carly turned around. Samantha was speaking earnestly to Rikist, a shaking hand pressed against her mouth half the time. Rikist's eyes grew wide, and he dropped to his knees. Then he hugged her waist and placed a tender kiss against Samantha's belly.

So, she told him.

Carly wrapped her arms around herself. "I guess he's happy."

"Oh, yes," Krissik said, his voice slightly choked. "Is all he has ever wanted. A family and a child. He had a taste with Lindsey, a hint... and was taken from him."

Rikist's shoulders tensed, and he slowly turned to face the porch. Carly felt Krissik still beside her, and she spared a glanced at his profile. Krissik's face was stoic, his eyes wary.

Rikist took a deep breath, his jaw tight as he and Krissik stared at each other. Tension crackled across the driveway in nearly visible waves.

"Krissik," Carly started reaching for his arm.

Krissik waved her away walked down the porch steps. Carly followed cautiously behind. Rikist stood still as Krissik approached, his nostrils flared, and he squared his shoulders as Krissik stepped close enough that either one of them could have clawed the other's throat out.

Samantha met Carly's eyes, and Carly saw the uncertainty, the fear.

Carly's heart raced. She knew the history between

the brothers, the friction and mistrust that had hovered over their homestead ever since Krissik's arrival. She had hoped their harrowing escape together had removed all doubts, but from Rikist's body language that massive fissure still remained.

Krissik's arms lifted, and Rikist flexed his claws. Though the younger brother moved faster and wrapped an arm around Rikist's broad shoulders.

"Congratulations," Krissik whispered, barely audible.

Rikist's eyes went round, and he blinked several times before he pulled away just enough to meet his brother's eyes. Then he smiled and returned the embrace.

"Thank you," Rikist said, "Brother."

Carly let out the breath she had not realized she had been holding and looked at Samantha's relieved face.

Rikist broke the hug, and Krissik turned to Samantha and gave her a short embrace before facing the couple.

"I really happy for you," Krissik said. "Is all you ever wanted, Rikist."

Rikist swallowed and slid his arm around Samantha. He nodded and kissed the top of her head. "Yeah."

Krissik gave them one last smile and then took Carly's hand and led her back up the porch steps.

Carly's mind raced as they approached the house. She certainly could not picture herself with another man—and did not even want to try. Before Krissik, she had gone about her life as she pleased, but now she found that she could not quite imagine a life without him in it. He was more than a fun lay or a friend to goof off with around the farm. He had become something else. Something significant.

Family.

Family. What is family?

Carly looked over her shoulder at Samantha and saw a beloved sister. Rikist could stand in as an occasionally frightening brother-in-law.

And Krissik... well, Krissik was Krissik.

"I don't want you to go anywhere," she said, pulling him to a stop. "I want you to stay with me and be with me, but I need you to know...I'm not ready to be a mother like Samantha. Not right now. And I don't know if I'll ever be."

Carly cringed to say that last part, but Krissik had to hear it. She had not been entirely truthful with him for so long, and now she *needed* him to know everything—needed him to hear the words, to know entirely what he was getting into.

"Kris, I love you," she said, the words spilling out of her mouth in a rush. "But I've been a mess for years. I'm still a mess. And I need you to be aware of that."

Krissik nodded. Perhaps sensing that he ought to distance himself from this conversation, Rodolfo retreated to the other side of the porch and sat down on the old swing.

"You love me, do you?" Krissik's smile was downright devilish.

"Mmph," Carly said. "Don't spread that around. People will think I'm getting soft."

"You is soft," he said. "You is soft and wonderful, and everything a woman needs be. And if you come with..." he searched for the word, "challenges is just makes you all much better." He grinned at her and enfolded her in his arms once again. "We need no worry about anything just now. I settle for exploring Europe."

Not this again, she started to think. *You can't...*

But couldn't he? They had just pulled off a daring rescue and defeated the government's joint forces *and* the aliens. If they could do that, then why the hell could Krissik *not* see the world and take in the architecture that he loved so much from afar? They could make something work. They had found a way to rescue Mandy, and they would find a way for Krissik to get off the farm.

They would do it. Together.

"Okay," she said.

"After we disable rest of jumpgates," Krissik allowed. "Things changed too fast in home world for us ignore. We *must* rid of them, to protect Sam and Mandy, you, to protect rest of Earth. Is could take a while."

Carly nodded again. "You said it could take years. Just traveling from place to place, shutting things down, fighting...?"

"Maybe less, if Rikist say us help."

"If? He'll have to."

"He let *me* help," Krissik asserted. "I no want you in danger."

"Kris."

"You no know how badly this things can—"

"I blew up that jumpgate on my own, didn't I?"

"But *missions*—"

"Krissik!"

He looked down at her, and all his protests melted away into a vaguely embarrassed veneer. "Sorry," he said. "I is carried away."

The love Carly saw in his eyes was almost too much for her to bear. A few months ago, she would have run away from it, would have fled the country entirely and holed up somewhere far away, where his gentle eyes and soft touch could not track her.

But here he was. And he was hers.

Carly rested her hand on top of his, trying to fully immerse herself in his warmth and scent. She was tired, so tired... but she loved him, and that was all that mattered.

"Can we save the world tomorrow? I just... I really want to sleep."

Carly felt him smile against the top of her head.

"Of course," he said. "We go inside."

They slipped into the cool dimness of the house. All looked exactly as it had when they had left the night before, and the screen door banged shut behind them. Carly paused when she looked into the kitchen:

a smorgasbord of Mexican delicacies no doubt rustled up by a nervous Rodolfo and Maria while they waited.

"Well," Carly said, eyeing a steak sandwich and a plate loaded up with carnitas, "maybe sleep can wait a little longer."

TWENTY

Carly retreated to her bedroom as soon as everyone else started feeling the effects of the food coma.

She heard Krissik coming after her and paused when she reached her bedroom. The place had been utterly torn apart; obviously, the people who took Mandy had scoured Carly's room before deciding she was not there. Carly picked up a sneaker, frowned at it, and sighed, tossing it aside. Her clothes had been torn out and strewn across the floor, and her closet door had been yanked off its hinges and tossed aside.

"Ugh," she said.

"We fix it," Krissik said.

"Later," she said.

She swiped the clothing, shoes, and books off the bed, clearing a space for both of them. Sleep. She wanted to sleep. More than that, she wanted to feel Krissik's arms around her, wanted to melt into him, nod off into the deep sort of sleep that would heal her, and chase away all the dark thoughts that licked at her mind.

Krissik grasped the bottom of her shirt and tugged at it. Carly obediently lifted her arms, and he pulled the shirt up over her head, casting it aside. "I should shower," she said, feeling his nose sniffing at her skin. "I'm so gross right now…"

"You beautiful," Krissik said, his tongue darting out and dabbling at her throat. "You taste beautiful, and you beautiful than most."

Carly quirked an eyebrow at him. "Most?"

Krissik frowned, silently mouthing the words again as if to find his grammatical error.

Carly chuckled. "I'm just screwing with you."

Krissik's arms closed around her from behind. One hand reached up to cup a breast, his fingers rolling over her left nipple. The other hand smoothed down her belly, then pried open the fly of her jeans and burrowed down beneath her lace underwear.

Carly moaned softly and leaned back against him, splaying her legs slightly to give him full access. He played with her clit a moment, massaging the bud gently. Sparks all but flew inside her, the warm heat between her legs quickly rising to an aching burn. Carly pushed her jeans down the rest of the way, shuffling out of her shoes and kicking her feet free. She rested her hands on the bed and hopped onto her knees. She leaned forward to scramble properly onto the disheveled covers.

Krissik's hands seized her hips, and he dragged her

back to the edge of the bed. He pushed her knees apart. Carly bent close to the bed, her hardened nipples brushing against the sheets.

"Krissik," she whispered. "Kris, wait…"

"No." His hot breath found her center, and his ribbed tongue slipped out, giving her one long, raspy lick. Carly's hips jerked as she spasmed, growing even wetter.

"Perfect," Krissik said.

Carly heard him unzipping his own jeans, and he stepped close to her, his cock brushing against her lifted thigh.

"Just stay this way," he said. "I can see all of you…"

Krissik slipped his wide tip between her folds, teasing her slightly. Carly whimpered, and Krissik seized her hips, thrusting all the way home. Carly buried her face in the blankets, stifling her moans as he drove into her. If he did not have his hands on her hips, he would have shoved her clear onto the bed, but he kept her pulled snugly against him, his thighs slapping against her ass as he pounded in and out.

Carly bit down on the blanket.

Krissik withdrew abruptly, leaving her empty and wanting. Before Carly could cry out in protest, though, Krissik grabbed her legs and flipped her over onto her back and knocking her legs even further apart. He climbed up on top of her, sliding his cock back home with one slippery, wonderful thrust.

Carly wrapped her legs around his hips, arching her back to drive him deeper. "Yes," she breathed, trying to keep from screaming, "Yes, harder. Please, Kris...."

Krissik's arms slipped beneath her, pressing her against his chest. He thrust frantically into her, drawing them close together—so close she could not tell where she ended and where he began. He was hers. She was his.

"I love you, Krissik."

Krissik's head snapped up, his eyes wide. He let out a single, almost unbelieving laugh, and then he kissed Carly as if her lips were the only things keeping his soul alive.

Carly's orgasm built swiftly, pressure coming to an apex between her legs and abruptly letting go with a gush of sensation and smoldering heat. She cried out as Krissik bit down on her collar bone, his teeth marking her skin.

Claiming her.

Krissik finished a moment later, releasing inside Carly with a jubilant howl.

He moved in and out of her a few more times, then stopped, sagging on top of her.

"Well," Carly said, "if our roommates didn't know what we were doing before, they sure do now."

Krissik chuckled, his fine days' worth of stubble tickling her neck. "Is all family here. I sure they forgive us."

Carly wrapped her arms more firmly around him, slicking them down his sweaty back. Carly twisted her head to plant a kiss against his rough cheek, then snuggled him closer.

"I still need a shower."

"So do I," he said. "We take one. After this next time."

Carly's eyes widened. "You want to go *again?*"

Krissik propped himself up on his elbows to grin down at her. "We just save someone," he said. "Is means we go at least twice. I want rank this next one at least ten of ten."

Carly laughed, pulled him close, and kissed him. "Eleven," she said. "Let's go for an eleven."

The End

THANK YOU FOR READING!

Thank you for supporting independent authors with your purchase!

If you enjoyed the book, please take a moment to review it online. Reviews are golden to authors and help show your support!

READ ON FOR A SNEAK PEAK OF THE REMAINING

Book Three of the Sa Tskir Brothers Chronicles
A Sci-Fi Alien Romance

By Danielle Kaheaku

THE REMAINING: BOOK THREE

"Carly, get out of there!"

Samantha hissed into the face of the two-way radio, then let go of the talk button to listen intently to the static. She stood on the back porch of her single-level Colorado ranch house as her eyes scanned the darkness. She gripped the radio tighter, eyeing the pre-dawn sky. The moon still shone brightly behind a scattering of dark clouds hinting at a razor-thin lining of sun-kissed pink. Even the crickets were still, likely terrified to move if they attracted the attention of the danger lurking in the shadows.

"Samantha?" Carly's high-pitched voice squawked through the radio. *"Can you see anything?"*

Samantha let out a sigh of relief. They had not been found.

Yet.

"Nothing," Samantha said. She stepped farther

away from the back door and the safety of the glowing porch light. The yellow glow illuminated her figure as she tiptoed along the boards, the wood creaking under her weight. She leaned against the railing, one hand cradling the swell of her growing belly. "Where are you?"

Samantha looked up at movement as Carly poked her head out behind the chicken coop and gave a small wave. She saw Krissik's arm reach out and jerk her back behind cover.

"*Krissik, what?*" Carly's voice came through the radio. "*Hey, watch your claws! That was close to my skin.*"

Samantha grimaced, realizing Carly kept holding down the talk button on her radio. She tried clicking the talk button on her own device, but as long as Carly had her radio live, Samantha could not reach her.

"*Shh,*" came Krissik's hushed voice. "*Over there, by the barn.*"

Samantha stilled and tried to follow Krissik's clue. From her angle, maybe she could get a better view of what they were up against. She knew she could not see as well in the dark as Krissik's feline-like eyes. Still, Samantha was sure she caught a glimpse of movement to the right of the barn, barely discernible in the darkness. She glanced at the sky again. Pink spread across the clouds, and the moon dimmed as dawn approached.

"Carly, get off the damn radio!" she muttered to herself.

She clicked her button again but gained no response.

Samantha watched as Krissik and Carly crouch-walked around the edge of the coop, edging closer to the house. Krissik's lean form bent toward Carly's ear, his nose pushing aside her halo of blonde curls.

"When I say run," Krissik's whisper crackled through the radio, *"get to the house. Lock the door."*

"What about you?" Carly asked.

"Do not wait for me."

"Kris."

"Carly, please."

Samantha heard shuffling over the radio and watched as Krissik gave Carly a chaste, hurried kiss.

Krissik's breathing quickened before he hissed, *"Run!"*

Carly pivoted around and darted through the darkness toward the soft glow of the back porch light where Samantha stood. Her footsteps sounded heavy and loud over her ragged breathing as she dashed toward the house.

Snarling ripped through the air on Samantha's left, and she spared a glance to see a large black figure with reflective orange eyes sprinting across the space behind the barn toward Carly at a rapid pace. Samantha's heart skipped a beat.

Carly was too far from the house.

Samantha set the radio down on the handrail and leaned forward to scream, "Run, Carly!"

Carly looked up at Samantha's cry, then back at the

approaching assailant. At the last moment, Carly dropped to the ground and rolled.

Samantha watched the figure reach for Carly, overshoot, and skid sideways.

Carly let out a strangled shriek and scrambled back to her feet. She made a rabid dash halfway to the house when strong arms wrapped around her waist and yanked her backward and into the air. Carly gasped and tried to claw at the man's mask and push him away.

"Get off me!" she screamed.

A forearm corded with muscle wrapped around Carly's neck and squeezed. Carly struggled to free herself, fear etched into the corners of her eyes as she gasped for air.

Samantha gasped and headed for the porch steps. "Carly!"

A second form launched itself out of the darkness, slamming into Carly's attacker and sending them both sprawling across the ground. Carly cried out as she fell and rolled away from the struggles. Boots scraped against the dirt as Krissik and the man roared and clawed at each other.

Carly scooted away and found her footing. "Krissik!"

Krissik snarled at the masked man, his long, canine fangs flashing in the dying moonlight. He tried to twist around to get a grip on the other's arms, but the attacker was larger, faster. The man wrapped his clawed hands into Krissik's shirt and threw him to the ground. Krissik landed with a thud, and he blinked to clear his vision. The attacker did not waver as he grabbed Krissik's arm and twisted it behind his back, his other hand locked around the nape of Krissik's neck.

Krissik cried out in pain, his lips pulling back from bared teeth. His eyes found Carly's. "Run!"

The attacker's head jerked up, glowing amber eyes searching.

Carly gasped when the eyes landed on her.

The masked man heaved Krissik over his shoulder and threw him several feet into the air then bolted toward Carly before Krissik hit the ground.

Carly ran as fast as her legs could carry her. She gasped for air as she reached the bottom step of the stairs.

"Samantha!" she screamed.

Samantha reached for Carly, one hand on the railing for support.

A calloused hand clamped over Carly's mouth and the thick arms wrapped around her shoulders, pinning her arms at her sides. Carly dropped to her knees and rolled to her back as the masked face roared in her ear.

Out of instinct, Carly brought up one knee and kicked out as hard as she could. The bottom of her heel connected in the center of the man's groin with an almost audible crunch.

The man yelped, let go of Carly, and dropped onto his side.

Carly scrambled on all fours up the remaining

three steps and slapped her hand against the back screen door. Then she spun around and jabbed a finger toward the stairs.

"Take that, bitch!"

Samantha winced in the man's direction and then crossed her arms and leaned against the railing. "Looks like you won this time, Carly."

The man at the bottom of the stairs groaned and rolled to his knees. He lifted one black-tipped clawed hand and yanked off the black mask, revealing a tousled head of reddish hair above a not-quite-human face. Pale, tiger-like stripes were barely visible in the porch light, partially hidden by a three-week growth of beard covering the square jaw and chin. Amber, cat-like eyes burned with anger under a heavy brow scrunched in pain.

"What the hell, Carly?" Rikist's gravelly voice came out as a growl. He shook his head and took in a deep, shaky breath. "That hurt."

Carly gulped much-needed air and stood, brushing off her clothes and smoothing her blonde, curly hair out of her face. "Sorry, Rikist," she panted, "I didn't plan that." She frowned. "You were getting a little rough, though."

Rikist hunched forward, grimacing. "Damn."

Krissik appeared in the circle of the porch light, blood seeping from a cracked lip. In the dim light, the horizontal tiger stripes across his cheeks and neck appeared starker than usual against his farm-tanned skin. He narrowed his golden eyes, the pupils constricted to angry feline slits. He tested the wound with his tongue and glared at his older brother.

"You did not have to throw me like that."

Rikist snorted and stood, rising a full head taller than Krissik at six-six and nearly two hundred and eighty pounds of muscle, spit, and fangs. He gritted his jaw in annoyance and rolled the thick muscles in his neck and shoulders as he flexed his claws. Despite the fading stripes on his face and neck, at the moment, he looked much more alien and feral than his younger brother.

"It has to be real or, when the attack actually happens, you won't be ready." Rikist turned and stared hard at Krissik. "You asked me to train you. So you can help protect Carly and Samantha and this ranch. This is what it's going to take."

He sniffed the air and looked over at Carly. He pressed his lips together and reached for Carly's hand, snatching her wrist before she could react. He turned her arm over to examine a shallow scrape. Blood speckles dotted the wound edges.

Rikist frowned. "Sorry," he said after a moment.

Carly pulled her hand away and nodded. She grinned. "Sorry about your baby-makers."

Rikist grunted and trudged past her up the stairs. He greeted Samantha by bumping his head against her temple and rubbing his cheek against hers, and then slipped a hand beneath her chin to tilt her face up for a kiss.

Samantha leaned into him as he kissed her, his full

lips warm and moist, and then pulled away and playfully slapped at his chest.

"Go shower, you smell like a wet cat."

Rikist made a rumbling sound deep in his chest. "You like it when I sweat on you."

"Hmm, depending on the situation," Samantha laughed. "Not so much right now."

Rikist shot Samantha a crooked smile and bent to place a quick kiss on the front of her belly before he strolled into the kitchen, slapping her backside as he passed.

Samantha grinned at him over her shoulder as waited for Carly and Krissik to ascend the steps. She held the screen door open as they approached. "That was close tonight."

Carly shrugged. "Lucky shot, I think. Literally, right in Rikist's balls." She glanced over her shoulder at Krissik. "You, my love, got your ass kicked."

Krissik frowned. "You distracted me."

"Rikist's point," Samantha cut in, "is that you'll always be distracted."

"A little fun distraction now and then wouldn't kill your boyfriend." Carly rolled her eyes. "That guy is a total hard-ass when it comes to training. I mean, the guy just got home yesterday from his mission in Arizona, right? Has he even been to bed yet?"

Krissik nodded. "He is pretty dedicated."

"Dedicated is not the word I'd use. Zealous is more like it." Carly winked at Samantha. "Tell him to lighten up a bit, yeah? We all can't be on-call for battle twenty-four-seven."

SAMANTHA LED Carly into the master bedroom as Rikist and Krissik left to shower. Since Carly was leaving in a few hours to visit her mother back east, Samantha asked Rikist to give her and her friend some time alone. Rikist had grudgingly agreed to use the guest bathroom and walked out with an armful of clothes and toiletries.

Their living conditions were the perfect set up: Samantha's inherited family ranch had become the ideal hideout for the two aliens, and the spacious ranch-style house had enough space for the two couples to have their own privacy and yet live communally as they worked together to improve the land and their prospects.

Though the little slice of heaven started out on a rough note. Their entire living situation began after Krissik initially snagged Samantha during an organized alien abduction in Las Vegas as his intended mate to help procreate their dying species. When a test showed Samantha as sterile, Rikist jumped into action to keep her from being sent to the planet's slave trade pits, where all non-productive females were sent to free eligible males up for a new mate. The daring escape-turned-pursuit by Krissik and their resulting marooning on Earth caused a significant rift between the brothers, nearly killing them both in the process.

The past few months, and the introduction of Carly into Krissik's arms, helped smooth out the tensions between the brothers and allowed the foursome to develop a friendly if not familiar existence.

Rikist's involvement in their homeworld's civil war as a rebel arms smuggler—something he continued while marooned on Earth—provided a stipend that covered a large portion of their bills and helped saved the little, failing family ranch. Krissik also proved extremely valuable; his near-genius in engineering doubled the ranch's production, setting them up in a much more comfortable position than when Samantha ran the ranch alone.

Besides, Samantha enjoyed the extra company and her little extraterrestrial self-made family. While it was temporary, Carly's short trip to visit her mother felt odd and a bit sad after several months with a full house.

Carly set the pink box down on the bed and lifted the lid. Samantha moaned and crawled onto the mattress beside the box and lifted out a large frosted cinnamon roll.

"You are amazing," Samantha said as she took a bite and closed her eyes. "Oh, my God, this is so good."

"They're from that twenty-four-hour place on the corner of Nutmeg. They have the best donuts." Carly settled on the bed beside Samantha and chuckled. "Do I need to leave you and the donut alone for a bit?"

Samantha shook her head. "No, me and the box."

Carly laughed and sipped on her coffee. "I haven't actually asked in a while... How are you feeling?"

"Hungry." Samantha took another bite. "All the time." She licked her fingers. "I don't remember Jen being so hungry all the time."

"Jen?"

"Remember the girl in our world lit class? She dropped out a week before finals?"

"She wore glasses."

"Yes."

"I don't remember. Her being pregnant, I mean. I remember who she was, but that was about it."

Samantha shoved more of the donut into her mouth. "I'm just... I was looking online at these baby sites, and I don't know if I'm matching up on their trackers."

"What do you mean?"

"I was sixteen weeks yesterday. Online, it says the baby should be about the size of a big avocado."

Carly paused with her coffee near her open lips and regarded Samantha's belly. "That's a lot of guacamole in there."

Samantha threw a pillow at her friend.

Carly laughed and hit it out of the way. "I'm just kidding!"

Samantha pointed at her midsection. "But do you agree? I almost look six months pregnant! I feel like I'm a lot bigger than I should be."

Carly frowned and raised an eyebrow. "Did you

make sure to download the my-baby's-daddy-is-an-alien app? Or are you going off the human growth chart?"

Samantha's face went blank. "I didn't think of that."

Carly sipped at her coffee. "Have you asked Rikist about it?"

Samantha shook her head. "Not yet... he's been focused lately on this last run, closing the jumpgate in Arizona and all."

"It's his baby, too. He should be involved."

"He is! He's just been gone all week and really stressed. It's not a big deal. I just didn't want to throw all my pregnancy insecurities at him the minute he walked in the door."

"At the rate your belly is expanding, I'd say it's a pretty big deal."

Samantha frowned. "You have horrible bedside manners."

Carly reached into the box and pulled out a sugar twist. "Then ask Krissik. He seems to know a little about everything."

"I'm not discussing my pregnancy with Krissik," Samantha said. "I know we're all good now, but that seems a little over the line."

Carly waved her off. "Trust me, that ship has sailed. I worried about it for a while, but it really is a non-issue." She took a bite. "Wouldn't you want to know if you're having one or a whole litter?"

Samantha nearly choked on the last bit of

cinnamon roll. She stared at Carly. "Don't joke with me like that." She rubbed at her face and then picked through the box again, lifting up a cream-filled pastry. "Seriously, not funny."

Carly smirked. Then her face went blank. "John."

Samantha furrowed her brow. "What?"

Johnathan Merrick was not a name used freely in their household. Despite John being the local veterinarian and one of Rikist's human medical contacts on Earth, he was also Samantha's ex-fiancé. That little bit of sexual history rubbed a constant sore spot with Rikist. Samantha felt the alien had calmed down enough about the past relationship over the last few months to get his job done; however, she did not care to test the theory by adding unnecessary contact.

"You did an ultrasound at the beginning, right?" Carly continued. "When it was like a pea?"

"Yeah, but not since. We don't want the doctors knowing about Rikist."

"John's a vet and treats pregnant dogs. He should have an ultrasound machine. Ask him to ultrasound you."

Samantha nodded. "That's actually a good idea."

"Of course, it is. I said it." Carly sucked sugar off one finger, pulling the digit slowly out of her mouth. She frowned when she caught Samantha staring. "What? What is that look?"

Samantha blushed. "Nothing."

Carly grinned devilishly. She licked the tip of her finger. "Is that turning you on?"

Samantha groaned and fell back against the pillows. "No. Yes?" She covered her eyes. "Everything?"

"Explain."

"Everything. Carly!" Samantha struggled and then managed to sit up. "Everything turns me on! I am so damn horny all the time."

"Oh, this rich!" Carly doubled over laughing. "You've got alien sex hormones running through your pretty veins, sis!"

"It's not funny!"

Carly straightened and wiped at her eyes. "You haven't told him, right?"

"Who, Rikist?"

"No, the mailman," Carly said flatly and shook her head. "Of course, Rikist."

"No."

"Good. Don't." Carly held up a finger. "Ever."

Samantha wrinkled her nose. "What's the big deal?"

"Because then he's going to think he'll get it for free."

"Rikist isn't like that."

Carly gave her an incredulous look. "*All* men are like that. Even aliens. Don't ever tell him."

A knock sounded on the bedroom door, and it opened without invitation. Rikist poked his head in. He looked fresh and showered, his hair slicked back from his strong brow, accentuating the hard lines of his jaw. "Tell me what?"

Samantha's face went red, and Carly giggled.

Rikist's natural resting frown deepened. "What?"

Carly cleared her throat and winked at Samantha, "Nothing big, just discussing your sympathy pounds."

Samantha covered her mouth as Rikist's face twisted into confusion.

"I don't..." he began. "What is that..."

Carly's grin spread. "Oh, don't worry. It is completely normal. Besides, the dad bod is totally in this year."

Rikist's eyes betrayed his uncertainty, and he backed out of the room as quickly as he arrived. "Krissik is looking for you, Carly," he called through the door before his footsteps disappeared down the hallway.

Both women burst into laughter. Samantha held onto her belly, gasping for air.

"Oh, that hurts!" she wiped at her eyes. "You know what you said isn't true. That man doesn't have you an ounce of fat on him."

Carly smirked and climbed off the bed. "Of course, I know that. But I had to get back at him for throwing Krissik this morning."

Samantha shook her head. "You're so bad."

"No, my little horn dog, you are."

CARLY AND SAMANTHA finished off another donut each and then carried the half-empty box into the family room. Rikist lay sprawled on his back across the couch, flipping through his phone. Krissik knelt by the front door, zipping up a suitcase.

"Hey," Krissik said and leaped to his feet, "you ready to go?"

"Yeah," Carly said with a smile.

"Did you want me to drive you?" Samantha asked. "I forgot to ask."

Carly shook her head. "I already paid for parking at the airport." She turned to Krissik. "Want to help me load the car?"

Krissik nodded, but his face looked unhappy. "I wish I was going with you."

"Kris," Carly began.

"I know." Krissik forced a smile and crossed the room to plant a firm kiss against Carly's lips. "I am going to miss you."

Rikist snorted.

Carly glared down at him on the couch. "What's your problem?"

Rikist made a face. "Nothing. You're both acting as if you're going off to war. You're going to be gone, what, three days?"

Krissik bared his fangs and then hefted the luggage without a word and left through the front door.

Carly sneered at Rikist and dropped the box of donuts on his chest. "Eat up, Daddy."

Rikist lowered his phone enough to meet Carly's eyes. "Bye."

Carly blew him a kiss and walked toward the front door. "Don't choke on those pastries."

Samantha rolled her eyes and followed Carly outside. She had gotten used to their bantering: Rikist being his grumpy-ass self and Carly's flippant bitchiness that grew to be especially protective of Krissik. Samantha knew it was mostly harmless if not tiring, though at times she wished she could knock their heads together and force them to get along.

Carly turned at the edge of the porch and gave Samantha a tight squeeze. "Keep your cat in line while I'm gone."

Samantha smiled. "Have fun."

Carly rolled her eyes. "Since when was visiting my mother fun? I can't imagine what she wants to talk about."

"At least you'll be in the big city again. There's shopping."

"There is that!" Carly's face lit up, and she turned to leave. "I'll bring you back a few things."

Samantha shook her head. "You know that's not necessary."

"And you know how totally untrue that is for me."

Samantha smiled and waved as Carly trotted down the steps into Krissik's waiting arms. They embraced and then kissed. Carly learned into Krissik as their mouths worked, his long tongue sliding back toward her throat and hands pawing at her ass.

Samantha leaned against the doorjamb, mentally agreeing with Rikist's earlier observation.

Carly finally broke for air. "Gotta go. Don't want to miss my flight."

Krissik opened the door and then shut it after Carly turned on the ignition. She blew him a kiss and waved out the window as she drove down the dirt road.

Samantha waited for several heartbeats before straightening and walking to the back door.

"Come on, Romeo," she called.

Krissik trudged up the stairs looking as if the playground bully had just popped the last balloon.

Samantha chuckled and gave him a hug. "She'll be fine, Krissik." She opened the screen door. "Want a donut?"

Krissik wrinkled his nose. "I will leave the sweets to Rikist."

Samantha stumbled over the raised threshold. Krissik caught her arm and waist and steadied her.

"Are you all right?" he asked.

Samantha leaned against Krissik's arm for a moment, letting the dizzy spell pass. She swallowed down a wave of nausea and then gave Krissik a smile. "That was weird."

Krissik's gold eyes narrowed in concern. "Maybe you should sit down." He paused. "I have been reading…"

Samantha patted Krissik's striped cheek in a sisterly fashion and continued into the kitchen. "I'm fine. Probably lightheaded from all the sugar."

Rikist was not in the family room when they stepped back into the house. Krissik stayed at Samantha's back as she filled a glass of water from the sink. Samantha eyed him over the edge of the rim and held up one finger.

Krissik's English skills had improved tremendously over the last two months. While Samantha was ecstatic at his progress, she knew it meant the walking dictionary now had a hard time shutting up once someone opened the door to a new conversation.

She smiled as she drank, watching Krissik shift his weight from foot to foot as his patience wore thin. Samantha's stomach ached, full, but she forced herself to finish the drink to delay the inevitable.

Finally, she lowered the glass and licked her lips. She smiled at Krissik. "You were saying?"

Krissik's face beamed. "So, I am reading about human pregnancies, and I do not think it is far different from ours. Though maybe the timing is different."

"Did Carly say something to you?" she frowned.

Krissik at least had the decency to look sheepish.

Samantha eyed him. "How much different?"

"Is hard," Krissik grimaced, "because time here is months, and we measure seasons. But, maybe around two months?"

Samantha's eyes bugged at the idea of a nearly year-long gestation period. "Longer?"

Krissik shook his head. "Shorter."

Samantha tilted her head to one side, relieved. "Well, that probably explains why I'm bigger than I think I should be. And fewer weeks of potentially walking around like a stuffed sausage isn't necessarily a bad thing."

Krissik did not seem to understand the visual. He smiled. "I am excited. I have never seen a real-life child before."

Samantha gave him a sad dip of her head, noting the hint of regret in his voice. Starting a family had been a goal for both brothers, something seemingly out of reach back home with the lack of females and even fewer viable pregnancies leading to the decline of their species and the subsequent need to search for mates.

For Krissik, Samantha knew the dream might not ever come to fruition as Carly did not seem interested in having their own children. Krissik appeared to accept the terms of their relationship, though he always seemed to be hopeful.

Samantha's pregnancy was a dream come true for both brothers, not just for Rikist as the father but also for Krissik. The idea of helping raise the baby—a non-existent concept on their planet—had the soon-to-be-uncle reading expecting magazines and honing his woodworking skills to craft furniture for the nursery.

Samantha smiled at him. "Thanks for the info, bro."

She lifted her free arm, and Krissik bent to circle her shoulders in a hug. He kissed her cheek as he straightened and peered down at her with eagerness.

"When do we know if it is male or female?"

Samantha wrinkled her nose. "We won't, Krissik."

His smile faded. "But, the sites say…"

"That's for normal, human pregnancies. I'm not doing regular prenatal care, remember? Otherwise, the doctors would notice..."

Krissik frowned. "I had forgotten." He smiled, though the disappointment did not leave his eyes. "That is OK, we like surprises, yes?"

"To a degree," Samantha laughed. "But yes, it will be a wonderful surprise for all of us."

ALSO BY DANIELLE KAHEAKU

The Sa Tskir Brothers Chronicles

The Scouting

The Abduction

The Keeping

The Remaining

The Recruit (2026)

The Daemon Progeny Trilogy

Artificial Selection

Cells of Time (2026)

The Dark Clone (2027)

Standalone Novels

He Rode a Dark Horse

Anthologies

In Love with an Alien

Alien Embrace

California Screamin'

Abaculus

Abaculus II

Abaculus III

The Axels and Allies Trilogy As Dani Kane

Wormholes: Book One

FOLLOW THE AUTHOR

Follow her online at:
https://www.Kaheaku.com

Instagram:
https://www.instagram.com/daniellekaheaku

Facebook:
https://www.facebook.com/daniellekaheaku

www.ingramcontent.com/pod-product-compliance
Lightning Source LLC
LaVergne TN
LVHW041620060526
838200LV00040B/1356